MATT NIX

The Bad Beat

TOD GOLDBERG

OBSIDIAN

OBSIDIAN

$7.99 U.S.
$8.99 CAN.

ISBN 978-0-451-23409-4

9 780451 234094

5 0 7 9 9

S EAN

**Praise for the Novels and Stories of
Tod Goldberg
Finalist for the *Los Angeles Times* Book Prize**

"Well plotted and deftly written. . . . Goldberg serves up heaps of Miami's lush lifes and low lifes while exposing its drug and arms underworld."
—The Huffington Post

"A keen voice, profound insight . . . devilishly entertaining."
—*Los Angeles Times*

"Goldberg's prose is deceptively smooth, like a vanilla milk shake spiked with grain alcohol."
—*Chicago Tribune*

"[A] creepy, strangely sardonic, definitely disturbing version of Middle America . . . and that, of course, is where the fun begins."
—*LA Weekly*

"Perfect . . . with all the sleaze and glamour of the old paperbacks of fifty years ago."
—*Kirkus Reviews*

"Striking and affecting. . . . Goldberg is a gifted writer, poetic and rigorous . . . a fiction tour de force . . . a haunting book."
—January Magazine

continued . . .

The *Burn Notice* Series

The Reformed
The Giveaway
The End Game
The Fix

burn notice
The Bad Beat

TOD GOLDBERG

Based on the USA Network Television Series
Created by Matt Nix

AN OBSIDIAN MYSTERY

OBSIDIAN
Published by New American Library, a division of
Penguin Group (USA) Inc., 375 Hudson Street,
New York, New York 10014, USA
Penguin Group (Canada), 90 Eglinton Avenue East, Suite 700, Toronto,
Ontario M4P 2Y3, Canada (a division of Pearson Penguin Canada Inc.)
Penguin Books Ltd., 80 Strand, London WC2R 0RL, England
Penguin Ireland, 25 St. Stephen's Green, Dublin 2,
Ireland (a division of Penguin Books Ltd.)
Penguin Group (Australia), 250 Camberwell Road, Camberwell, Victoria 3124,
Australia (a division of Pearson Australia Group Pty. Ltd.)
Penguin Books India Pvt. Ltd., 11 Community Centre, Panchsheel Park,
New Delhi - 110 017, India
Penguin Group (NZ), 67 Apollo Drive, Rosedale, Auckland 0632,
New Zealand (a division of Pearson New Zealand Ltd.)
Penguin Books (South Africa) (Pty.) Ltd., 24 Sturdee Avenue,
Rosebank, Johannesburg 2196, South Africa

Penguin Books Ltd., Registered Offices:
80 Strand, London WC2R 0RL, England

First published by Obsidian, an imprint of New American Library,
a division of Penguin Group (USA) Inc.

First Printing, July 2011
10 9 8 7 6 5 4 3 2 1

For Wendy

ACKNOWLEDGMENTS

I am, as ever, indebted to Matt Nix for allowing me to bring Michael Westen to the page. I have enjoyed working with Matt over the course of these five books and have always appreciated his willingness to let me interpret his characters as I see fit. A better freedom a writer could not ask for. Thanks also to my brother Lee Goldberg for his sage advice, my agent Jennie Dunham, and my editor Sandy Harding for shepherding these books so well. And, as usual, I'd like to remind readers not to attempt to build any incendiary devices based on what you've read here, nor should you attempt any covert (or overt) operations using the tactics outlined herein. You'll blow up.

1

When you're a spy, repetition becomes second nature. Spend ten days in a cave in Afghanistan staring at the same tent waiting for something, *anything*, to happen and you either learn how to avoid the perils of boredom or you risk blowing your mission or, worse, getting yourself killed. So you learn how to play games with your mind. You catalog. You assess. You occasionally see if you can remember every song you learned at Silver Spur camp that one summer you and your brother were sent there for "accidentally" blowing up your neighbor's Fiat. And then, when your shot comes, you take it, get out and move on to the next repetitive exercise in some other foreign land. Because when you're a spy, you live for the five seconds of adrenaline that result from weeks of paper preparation and solitary scouting.

Which is why, against my better judgment, I agreed to go with my friend Sam Axe on an errand. It was the kind of errand that required me to bring a MAC-10 with me, which was fine. It's always better to be overprepared than underprepared in these situations.

We pulled up across the street from an office park

on Northeast Fifth Street, just a few miles from my loft. It was one of those 1970s-era one-story bungalow-style office parks where businesses could actually hang a sporty shingle advertising their notary services, just as Grayson Notary & Associates had done. It was quaint, in a way that was being eradicated from Miami one Coconut-Grove-mauve-colored-open-air-shopping-district at a time.

I'd agreed to go with Sam on his errand primarily because he'd shown up at my loft looking more vexed than usual, as if maybe he hadn't had his proper number of mojitos yet, which, for a Saturday, was troubling. More troubling, however, was that he asked me if there was an extra MAC-10 around that he could borrow for the afternoon. And also that he was dressed in a navy blue suit.

"An extra?"

"Yeah," he said. "I let Fiona borrow my favorite one a couple weeks ago when we shot it out with those bikers."

"Which bikers?"

"You know, the murderous ones. Not the vengeful ones. Or the ones who kidnapped that kid. You remember. The bloodthirsty, evil, murderous bikers bent on killing."

"Ah, yes," I said.

"Anyway," he said, "I've got a little thing I gotta do today that would be helped along with a MAC-10."

"Why don't I come with you?" I said, figuring, naturally, that if I came there was less of a chance that Sam would actually use the MAC-10.

"Oh, Mikey, this isn't anything you need to be mixed

up in. It's just a favor for a buddy of mine. Some free-lance intimidation of a bad guy."

"You don't need to pay me, Sam," I said.

"That's great news, Mikey," Sam said, "because I'm actually a little short right now."

"Really," I said. I'd known Sam Axe for the better part of the last twenty years and during that time he'd almost always been a little short. But since I returned to Miami a few years ago (minus my cover, my spy credentials burned, my life thrown into regular tumult as I looked first for the people who burned me and then, later, for a way out of their net of deception), Sam has been in a slightly better financial situation. As a former Navy SEAL, he has skills, along with those of my ex-girlfriend (and occasional gunrunner) Fiona, that have allowed the three of us to earn a better-than-government salary helping people solve rather *delicate* problems. "I'm happy to help, Sam. Makes me feel needed."

"Thing is, Mikey," Sam said, "it's just one of those jobs that really feels beneath your time. You've got bigger fish to fry. This fish, it's like a rainbow trout, and I feel like you're out there fighting a barracuda on the line. One of those boys with big old snapper teeth."

"Sam," I said, "whatever it is you're attempting to avoid telling me? It's not making me want to help you. And that means I don't want to lend you my MAC-10, either."

"See," Sam said, "the point of that last bit? I was hoping you'd just give me the gun and then later on, when things got bad, I'd call you and ask for help and then you couldn't ask me any more questions, because it would be too late. It's how we do business, Mikey, and it works. This is messing up my whole plan."

"Fine," I said. I left Sam in my kitchen, went upstairs and then came back with a duffel bag filled with guns. "Here," I said and handed the bag to Sam.

He opened it up and peeked in. "You old dog, you gave me the Steyr TMP, too."

"I'd hate for you to be alone with only one fully automatic pistol at your fish fry," I said.

"Well," Sam said, "I mean, if you want to come with me, I wouldn't say no. I'm a man who likes company. You just can't ask me anything until we get to the spot."

"That's fine, Sam," I said.

"Really?"

"What time were you going to pick up Fiona?" I asked.

"It really depended on how this went," he said. "She said she was busy dusting her knives today, so I didn't want to bother her."

Fiona loved intimidating bad guys, so if she couldn't be bothered with Sam's errand, that was a good sign. Or what amounted to one in my life.

"Then pretty please, Sam," I said, "can I come with you?"

"No questions until we get there."

"Fine," I said.

"And Mikey," he said, "could you put on a conservative suit? Something that says low-level government operative and not gallivanting spy?"

I agreed, even to the suit, because now I had to know

what Sam was embroiled in. To get Sam Axe to put on a shirt and tie, one normally needed to first promise him either untold riches or a single woman with untold riches, or at least one with a decent alimony settlement. We pulled up across the street from the office park and Sam cut the engine and for a good three minutes I kept my promise and stayed quiet. It was a Saturday, so the parking lot was nearly empty, save for a red Camaro.

"Sam," I said, "why does that car look familiar?"

"I dunno, Mikey," Sam said. "It's a popular American automobile. And that counts as your one question."

"We had no predetermined number of questions I could ask," I said. "And just so I know what the operation is, should I be keeping an eye on that car? Because it both looks familiar and reminds me of several previous bad experiences."

"That car could belong to anyone," Sam said.

"Sam," I said.

"The thing is," Sam said, "people tend to remember cars emotionally. So my thought is that you probably had an experience with a red Camaro sometime in your childhood and now, well, now it's just a harbinger of bad things."

"That's Sugar's car," I said.

"Sugar?"

"The drug dealer who used to live next door to me," I said. "The drug dealer who took five bullets the last time he engaged us to help him. The drug dealer who let another drug dealer and his thugs smack you around. Sugar."

"Oh," Sam said. "Sugar. Right. That is his car. I'll be."

"You hate Sugar," I said.

"I do hate Sugar," Sam said.

"Tell me you're not working for him."

"We're not," Sam said.

"I never said 'we.'"

"He called me up a couple of days ago and said a buddy of his, a notary, was getting hassled by some Russians who wanted him to pay a weekly tribute."

"How much do the Russians think they're going to get out of a notary?" I said.

"Well, seems they thought notaries worked for the government," Sam said. "So, they probably thought he was their conduit into the deep, deep pockets of the U.S. government's lucrative notarization coffers."

"Not exactly the KGB anymore," I said.

"Right," Sam said. "Which is why I told Sugar I'd be happy to show up looking like a federal agent to scare them off in the event they were not scared off by the sheer amount of self-tanner he uses."

"What time are the bad guys due?"

"Sugar said they usually came by around four," Sam said. "So right about now."

"What's Sugar's big plan?"

"He was going to be waiting inside the office instead of having his buddy there. Then he was going to let them know his buddy the notary was already paying him off. The old switcheroo. And then I was going to come in and bust them both up."

"How were you going to do that?"

"The full faith and credit of Charles Finley," Sam said.

"That sounds like a great way for Sugar to get murdered," I said.

"Mikey, I trust that if these guys were really fearsome, Sugar would be smart enough not to engage them. He said they were just a bunch of lightweights in track suits."

I didn't say anything. I just let Sam's words swirl around inside the car for a few moments to see if they might land somewhere near his common sense.

Sam drummed his fingers on the steering wheel. He adjusted the rearview mirror. He opened the glove box and looked for a Kleenex. And then, finally, it hit him.

"Oh. Oh. Oh, no," Sam said.

"Yeah."

"Oh, this isn't good."

"You have Sugar's cell?"

"Here," Sam said and handed me his phone.

"Watch for the arrival of the lightweights," I said and then called Sugar.

"Go," Sugar said.

"Go?" I said.

"Who is this?"

"Michael Westen," I said.

"Uh-oh, someone called in the big gun. We ridin' again! How you doin', brother?"

"I'm fine, Sugar," I said.

"You down to help me with the rope-a-dope?"

"Trouble, Mikey," Sam said.

Three Denalis, each with blacked-out windows and, it appeared, bulletproof frames, pulled into the parking lot and surrounded Sugar's Camaro. Ten men stepped out of the trucks. They all wore track suits. It wasn't clear if they were Russian, but judging by the fact that they each had a nine casually shoved down the front of their pants, it seemed clear enough that they weren't there to get anything notarized.

"Yeah, about that rope-a-dope," I said. "Is there a back door where you are, Sugar?"

"Yeah, yeah. Is that where you guys are gonna bust in when I give the word?"

"No," I said, "it's where you need to run out. Right now."

"I don't run from anything," he said.

"Sugar, can you see out the window?"

"No, I got the blinds drawn."

"That's good," I said, "because that way the ten armed men standing twenty feet from you won't know you were waiting to ambush them."

"Ten?"

"Make that seven," I said. "It looks like the three drivers are sticking with the cars."

"This ain't what my boy told me was the situation," Sugar said.

"Your boy might not have known," I said, though that didn't sound plausible. "But if you'd like to elucidate your disappointment to your friend from this world versus the next, I'd get out of the building, Sugar. We'll pick you up on Third Street in ten minutes. Just start walking."

"What about my ride?"

"You'll have to come back for it."

"When?"

"When there's not ten guys strapped with nines peering into it," I said.

"Peace," Sugar said and was gone.

I gave Sam his phone back and waited for him to apologize.

"How do you want to handle this?" Sam said.

"Which part?"

"Well, there's the bad guys and then there's your awkward silence."

"The bad guys are going to attack an empty notary office," I said. "If the owner of the shop is smart, he has an alarm and insurance, so he'll end up coming up on the right side of this."

"That's a great point, Mike," Sam said.

"But maybe write those license plates down," I said. "And the awkward silence will end once you apologize for getting us into business with Sugar."

"Technically," Sam said, "I told him I'd do this one on trade. He's got a buddy with an in with the Dolphins. Fifty-yard-line seats and a full concession package free of charge, baby."

An hour later, Sugar stood in the middle of my loft swearing at his cell phone. It was just the two of us since I'd sent Sam on an errand of my own, to track down the identity of the lightweights in the $100,000 armored SUVs.

"Man, there never was good reception in this neighborhood," Sugar said. "I'm happy I moved up out of here."

I decided not to remind Sugar that I'd forced him

out of the neighborhood. He was having a bad day, after all.

"Maybe it would help if you didn't use stolen cell phones," I said.

"Like you're all legit now? You rolling AT&T?"

"I have certain technological skills that you don't," I said. I went into my kitchen and pulled out two yogurts and set them on the counter. "You should eat something."

Sugar picked up the yogurt, examined it and then put it back down. "You got anything with a cream filling?"

"Yogurt is all cream," I said.

"Well, whatever," Sugar said. "My boy Brent, he's probably thinking all this shit is done with now, and here I am holed up like a mouse."

"I'm sure if your boy knows you well," I said, "he knows that maybe there were complications."

"Maybe, maybe," Sugar said. He walked over to the window that looks out over the canal on the other side of my building and actually appeared contemplative. That he was no longer looking at me also made me think maybe he felt just slightly ashamed—two emotions that I wasn't previously aware Sugar possessed. It's hard to look emotional when you have peroxide white hair, wear wife-beaters and sweatpants and walk around like you're looking for a fight, even after it's been proven you aren't much of a fighter. "Thing is, man, I might have implied to him that Sammy was playing a bigger role in this than I was. You know how it is."

"How much did he pay you, Sugar?"

"No, no, not like that," Sugar said.

"Then what is it like?"

"I just wanted him to feel . . . safe."

"What didn't you tell Sam?"

"You know, you got a pretty sweet view from up here," he said. "You can see all the little boats and shit. It's very pleasant."

"Sugar," I said, "you're a guest in my home and I'm happy to have you here, but I will throw you out that window if you don't turn around and look at me." Sugar did as he was told. "Tell me about your friend," I said.

Sugar stepped away from the window and sat down on the steps leading upstairs. "I met Brent professionally a couple years ago," he said.

"So he's an addict?"

"Naw," Sugar said, "he used to buy a little weed every now and then. And then one day I had a legal problem and needed some shit notarized and he helped me out."

"How old is this guy?"

"Eighteen, nineteen. He's still coming up in the game."

"The notary game?"

"Naw, naw," Sugar said. "That was his dad's game."

"So, wait," I said. "Were you helping out your friend or his dad?"

"Both, I guess," Sugar said. "Brent's dad? He plays the numbers, you know, horses, football, baseball, whatever's in season, and I guess he came up on some bad beats lately and just straight boned out."

"Sugar," I said, "in English."

"He owes a bunch of money to some bookies."

"So the Russian Mob wasn't trying to shake down your friend for tribute?"

"No."

"Why did you think you could handle these guys?"

"Man, I got five bullets in me," Sugar said. He stood up and pounded on his chest. "I'm hard to kill. You think I was scared of some guys who play fantasy football?"

"Six," I said.

"Six?"

"Bullets," I said. "I shot you once, too."

"See? I survived Michael Westen, boy."

"Sugar," I said, "those guys who showed up today were not just guys who run a book for giggles. They would have killed you. And if your friend is smart, he and his father will go to the police. This is not any kind of 'game' he wants to be involved in."

"That's the thing," Sugar said. "His dad boned out, like I said. Brent doesn't know where he is, but these guys want their money. I thought I could explain to them, businessman to businessman, that Brent didn't have nothing to do with his daddy's debt. But I guess they weren't gonna hear that, if I get you right."

"You get me right," I said.

Sugar thought for a moment. "You said they surrounded my car?"

"I'm sure it was just a coincidence," I said. "It was the only car in the lot."

"You think I could be in danger?"

"No more than usual, Sugar," I said. "You are hard to kill, after all."

"And now I can't get my boy on the phone," Sugar said. "You think maybe they got to him?"

"I don't know," I said. "Do they know where he lives?"

"They might have hit his dad's house," Sugar said. "But Brent lives in a secure facility, you could say."

"He's in prison?"

"Naw," Sugar said. "The dorms."

"In English," I said again.

"That was English. Homey lives on campus at the U. You can't get into the dorms without, like, CIA clearance."

My cell rang then. It was Sam. "What do you have?" I said.

"You're not gonna believe this," Sam said.

"Let me guess," I said. "Those Denalis aren't registered to members of the Russian Mafia."

"No," Sam said, "that's exactly who they're registered to. All three come up as being owned by a guy named Yuri Drubich. He's a Ukrainian businessman. Ex-KGB. Now works in the import and export business."

"Heroin?"

"Technology," Sam said. "He's legit in America, or at least his shell company is. They move technology from America into Russia and the former Soviet states. Microprocessors. Cell phone tech. Russians are about three years behind on most of this stuff, so he's bringing in the latest tech and probably selling it at a ten thousand percent markup."

"Wouldn't it be cheaper to just move it out of China?" I said.

"Probably," Sam said, "but then you gotta deal with the Chinese Mafia, too. In America, he's just buying from geeks. Not quite as dangerous. He's probably also moving product to Iraq, Libya, wherever."

"What does he import?"

"Women, arms, whatever makes money," Sam said.

This didn't make sense. I told Sam what Sugar had told me about his friend Ben's problems. It just didn't line up. Yuri Drubich wasn't in the numbers business, that was certain. It was too small fry for a guy like him. If they were hitting him, it was for something much larger.

"What does a guy like Drubich need with a notary?" I said.

"Maybe he had a legit business reason. Every couple years, don't you need something notarized?"

"Sure," I said, "but I rarely bring ten armed men with me."

"Man probably can't be too careful," Sam said.

"Do me a favor," I said. "Drive back by the office park and see what kind of damage they did." I looked over at Sugar. He was back at the window, staring pensively outside. "And check on Sugar's car."

"Where are you going to be?" Sam said.

"I'm going to go meet our client," I said.

2

When attempting to infiltrate a secure government facility, you have to assume that smart people have created the devices meant to keep you out. These smart people are usually a lot like you. They've been trained by the best minds the government has access to. They've been given state-of-the-art machinery to play with. If given the choice between spending one dollar and one billion dollars, the smart people will spend the one billion dollars. They will overprepare. They will train for the one day they get to fight you.

If these people are exceptionally smart, they will arm the most vital entry point with the world's best tactical weapon: a person with a clipboard. If you have a clipboard, you don't need a gun. You don't need to know five different martial arts. All you need is the ability to look down at your clipboard, examine the names on it, and say a single word: no. "No" is a difficult word to get beyond, even for a spy, since it is both an answer and a threat. *No*, it says, *you are not allowed in*. But it also says, *No, you are not allowed in and if you attempt to get in, proper authorities will be called, since this clipboard tells me that's the next step*. When you don't have a gun, the authority you possess is the conviction of your beliefs.

So when I saw two twentysomething University of Miami students—a young woman and a young man, each with a clipboard, and each with so many Greek letters on their clothing you'd think they were guarding the Parthenon—sitting behind a small desk in front of the doors to one of the two Hecht Residential College towers, a Soviet-looking dorm complex consisting of two 12-story towers (except that the Soviets were never big on adorning their buildings' green space with lush palm trees, deer grass and well-maintained topiary), I knew I had my work cut out for me if I wanted to go up to see Sugar's friend Brent Grayson.

They were the first line of defense, but the building also looked to have a key-card system in place and it was surrounded by security cameras. This was good. If anyone came here with the intent to hurt Brent, it would be easy to identify them and it would also be at least somewhat difficult for them to get inside to do the hurting.

"Try calling your friend again," I said to Sugar. We were only twenty yards or so from the tower and I could see that the sentries were doing their job fairly well, steadily turning away visitors at a nice clip. They both looked awfully perky. It's hard to deal with perky people. They don't take offense as easily as muscle-bound bouncer types do, which means there's less opportunity to punch them in the mouth or break their wrists.

Sugar pulled out his phone and dialed, but after about a minute he clicked it off. "Still nothing, bro," he said. "What if he's on a dirt nap?"

"It's unlikely," I said. "He's not worth anything dead to the bookies. And I can't imagine the Russian Mob would need to kill him for any reason, can you?"

"Man, people kill one another every day for no reason, you know?"

I guess I did. "Okay," I said. "Just follow my moves here and don't say a word, all right?"

"Cool," Sugar said.

"I mean it. Don't speak."

"I get it. Silent and deadly."

"No," I said, "just silent."

We walked up to the desk and waited patiently behind a kid named Zach while he tried to convince both the young man and the young woman that he needed to get up to the computer lab, even though he didn't live in the building. He had a skateboard under one arm and with his other free hand he kept nervously pulling at his long goatee.

"Zach," the woman said, "if I let you in, I could lose my job. So it's not about doing you a favor. I need the priority registration if I'm going to graduate on time."

"I totally appreciate that," Zach said, "but I'd just run up and run right back down. If she's up there, cool. If she's not, I know she's lying to me. And that's not cool. I should know that, don't you think? Ben?"

The young man, apparently named Ben, shook his head. "I feel you, dog. But Tiff is on point here. You've got to respect our position on this. You call and get someone to sign you in, bingo, you're in. Otherwise, dog, it's just not going to happen. No disrespect."

Zach took this news poorly. He pounded his fist on the desk, hard enough to make both Ben's and Tiff's clipboards jump up. "Hey, hey," Ben said. He stood up and I saw that though he was festooned in Greek letters, he was also covered in muscle. He reached out and grabbed Zach by the shoulder, but not in an aggressive way. He conveyed strength without conveying asshole. If I were still actively employed, I'd give the kid a card, see if he might want to consider a life in the spy arts after college. "Dude, that's not cool. You have to get ahold of yourself. You can't just be hitting our desk, okay? The desk didn't do anything to you, okay? Just be cool."

"I'm sorry," Zach said. From behind, I could see that the kid's shoulders were shaking. The poor guy was crying. "I'm just so, well, you know."

Ben gave Zach's shoulder a squeeze. "You need to get ahold of yourself," he repeated. Zach nodded once and sulked away. It was impressive work on Ben's part.

All four of us—even Sugar—watched Zach for a few moments as he attempted to ride his skateboard and cry simultaneously. It was more difficult than one might expect.

"Poor guy," I said.

"He's sweet," Tiff said, "but he's a little on the stalker side."

"He's gotta nut up," Sugar said.

I glared at Sugar. A wonderful development: Five seconds in and he was already speaking. I wondered if maybe he had a touch of ADD. Or maybe he just didn't know how to follow directions. Tiff and Ben didn't seem to notice or care that Sugar was speaking, but both were looking at him with something near recognition. Another not great development.

"I'm sorry," I said. "My cousin sometimes says things when he shouldn't."

"It's true, though," Sugar said. He smiled at Tiff. "No means no, right, baby doll?"

"Right," she said. She stared at Sugar and then smiled. "How do I know you?"

"I don't think you do," Sugar said. "Yet."

"How do I know you?" Ben said. There was just a hint of menace in his voice. I liked Ben already.

"I don't think you do, either," Sugar said. He shifted his weight a little bit and then stared at his feet, which was good because I was drilling holes in the side of his head with my eyes.

"What year are you?" Ben asked.

"I don't go here," Sugar mumbled.

"You play ball? High school maybe?"

"No, no," Sugar said. "I pretty much just stay home and keep to myself. Like to read and shit. You know."

Sugar's answer was met with silence. Of all the people who looked like they stayed home and kept to themselves, much less read . . . and shit . . . Sugar was among the least likely.

"He sells drugs," I said. I let that sink in for a second or two and then laughed and clapped Sugar on the back as hard as I possibly could without actually putting him on the ground. He might have been hard to kill, but he wasn't hard to beat up and at that moment I regretted not leaving him in the car or, better yet, the notary office. "Oh, my, my," I said. "I can't take him anywhere without people thinking they know him. Usually they think he's Eminem. I personally don't see it, do you?"

"Little bit," Ben said.

"Totally," Tiff said.

"I usually think he should just button up his shirt and stop dyeing his hair," I said, "but then I'm old-fashioned."

"OG," Sugar said, which earned him another glare from me.

"Anyway," I said, "we're here to check up on my nephew. Brent Grayson."

"That's mine," Ben said. "I'm A through L." He flipped through his clipboard and then ran his finger down a page until he landed on Brent's name. I could see that he had no names listed and also that he was in room 804. "Brent doesn't have any approved guests listed, so unless he called a pass down for you, I can't let you in."

"I understand that, of course, of course," I said. "It's Ben, right?"

"Yes," he said.

"And you're Tiffany?" I said.

"Tiff," she said. " 'Tiffany' makes me sound like I'm a thousand years old."

"Well, Ben and Tiff," I said, "here's the problem. Can I expect a level of confidentiality here?"

"Of course," Ben said. Tiff didn't look so sure, but she nodded in agreement.

"My nephew, he lives on the eighth floor, correct?"

"That's correct, sir," Ben said.

Sir. That was nice. I looked up the side of the building. "That's a pretty long fall, isn't it?"

"Remember there was a girl on the sixth floor who

jumped last fall?" Tiff said to Ben. "It was the saddest thing. She got her first B and that was it. Splat."

"So you understand the situation here," I said.

"Oh," Ben said. "Gosh. Brent, really?"

"He's had a rough go of it lately," I said. "And now we haven't been able to get him on the phone for the last two days, so, as you can imagine, there's some concern."

"I could go up and knock on his door," Ben said.

"Yes, you could," I said, "and under normal circumstances, I think that would be more than enough. But in this case, I'm afraid he'd know that, well, we broke his confidence. How well do you know Brent?"

"I see him around the building," Ben said.

"I don't even know him," Tiff said. "Do I, Ben?"

"He's the—pardon the expression, sir—he's the squirrely one."

"Oh, no, really?" Tiff said.

"Really," I said and then I tried to look hurt by Ben's description. *Squirrely.* What was wrong with kids today? Couldn't more of them be like young Mr. Ben?

"I'm really sorry," Ben said to me. "We give everyone nicknames. You know, long hours out front and we get a little nutty."

"I understand," I said, "and I hope you understand how sensitive this is for all of us."

Ben bit down on his bottom lip and concentrated on his clipboard for a few seconds. He ran a finger up and down his list and then stopped, looked down and said, "Did you say your name was Kurt Riebe?"

"Yes," I said.

He ran his finger up and down again, stopped, looked and said to Sugar, "And you're Delmert Boggs?"

"Naw, man," Sugar said. "Something cooler than . . ."

I put my hand over Sugar's mouth. "Yes, he's Delmert Boggs." Ben made out two guest passes for us and then handed us both lanyards to wear.

"I appreciate this," I said. "Brent will, too, I hope."

"He's very sweet," Tiff said.

"Just make sure Delmert doesn't sell any drugs inside," Ben said. "And it would be good if Delmert didn't show back up at some later date to try to sell drugs. Like at any of the frat houses."

Sugar looked over his shoulder, as if someone was calling his name, and mumbled something unintelligible.

"I'm sure that won't be a problem," I said.

Ben got up and opened the door into the tower with his key card and waved us in. Sugar started to talk just as soon as we were in the lobby but I hushed him until we were in the elevator.

"How'd you do that Jedi shit?" he asked.

"I don't look like a drug dealer," I said.

"That shit was wrong," Sugar said. "That was some profiling shit right there."

"Maybe don't sell any drugs around here for a few months," I said.

"You know what the market is out here? I could make my full nut each month just on Adderall and HGH, but I respect that this is an educational facility," Sugar said. "Kids learning and shit. So maybe I drop a little weed in the area now and then, but it's not like I got kids on the black tar, man."

"Well, that's a relief," I said.

"You know what the kids really want, though?"

"A better life?"

"Ambien. They want that crazy Tiger Woods Ambien sex now. That's my number one growth industry. Stupid cuz you can go to the doctor, tell them you're not sleeping and Mom and Dad's health insurance will pick it up for four bucks a bottle. So I get a huge mark-up."

The problem with talking to Sugar about anything related to his business was that it constantly reminded me of why I didn't like him in the first place. He'd come to me not long ago when he was in a jam and I'd gone to him not long ago when I was in a jam, but this new relationship where he was the middleman to a client just opened up my antipathy for him. The sooner I was done with him and could help his friend, the less likely it was that Sugar got bullet number seven.

When you're a spy, you often enter into business propositions with people not good enough to spit on. Dictators. Presidents. Warlords. And the occasional peroxide blond drug dealer.

The elevator doors opened onto the eighth floor and the first thing I noticed was the smell. It wasn't death or decay or the coppery smell of blood. Instead it was a just-as-nauseating mixture of patchouli, the oversweet-smelling body lotion favored by strippers and sorority girls alike, the indiscriminate odor of young men (usually a combination of unwashed socks and unwashed hair with a couple dashes of sadness and desperation sprinkled in for flavor) and macaroni and cheese.

Students milled about the hallway in between open apartment doors from which loud rap music and the static hum of televisions bleated out. None of the students appeared to be over twenty and none of them appeared to be in a hurry to get anywhere—they all walked with a nonchalance that bordered on liquidity; it was as if they didn't have spines like normal humans, particularly with the way their heads lolled back and forth without any seeming purpose.

A few looked at me with passing disregard, but I thought I saw at least two or three of the kids nod at Sugar.

"When was the last time you were up here?" I said.

"Couple days ago."

"Just to see Brent?"

"Yeah, yeah," Sugar said.

"Why don't I believe you?"

"Man, I don't know. Maybe cuz you're all covert and shit?"

Maybe. But probably not.

On the walls, posters and flyers for various campus events were stapled haphazardly onto corkboards. Apparently Tuesday was Taco Tuesday at a local bar. Apparently Wednesday was Wicked Wednesday, also at a local bar. Thursdays, according to all of the flyers, were Thirsty Thursdays. There were also notices about opportunities to study abroad, to teach English in Korea and, oddly, to join the Marines. Looking around, I didn't see a whole lot of candidates who'd be getting Semper Fi tattoos in the near future.

There were security cameras over the elevators, above the two vending machines and at either end of the hall-

way. Each moved a slow 180 degrees, essentially cap-
turing every inch of space in the common areas. I didn't
know where this information was fed, but I suspected
it went to the campus police. It wouldn't be the sort of
thing that was monitored unless a crime was committed, which meant I wanted to avoid committing any
crimes . . . or allowing Sugar to commit any.

"Brent's room is down that way," Sugar said, point-
ing. "Third one on the right." There were six rooms
visible and five of them had wide-open doors, so it was
obvious which room was Brent's.

"The door normally closed?" I said.

"Naw, he's a pretty open dude, usually," Sugar said.

"How many times have you been here?"

"Half dozen? Usually real quick. Just pop in, trade
product and I'm out."

"So none of these people know you?"

"I keep to mine," he said.

"Sugar, this is important."

He looked both ways down the hall and then
shrugged. "Not personally, you know? But a few times,
I maybe hooked some people up on this floor. A head
nod here or there, you know. But I'm not going to the
big dance or anything. Not my scene, bro."

"Wait here," I said.

"You gonna go down there and kick his door in? He
don't know you."

"Sugar," I said, "if there's something bad to see—
like a body—you don't want to be anywhere near it,
okay? You also don't need to be seen on camera."

Sugar thought about this. "I'll hang back," he said.

I walked down the hall and peered into the other

rooms as I went. In the first room, two young men sat motionless on beanbag chairs playing a video game, their jaws opened just enough to allow airflow. In the second, a young woman wearing only a bathing suit top and cut-off shorts walked in circles talking on her cell phone about someone named Lyle being an asshole, and in the final room before I got to 804, a young man and a young woman sat quietly—amid thumping rap music—reading. None of them bothered to even look my way as I walked by. No one is naturally as uninquisitive as someone who is twenty years old and likely drunk eighty-five percent of the time. All of the dorm rooms looked to have the same layout—a small living room and kitchenette with a bedroom and bathroom off to either the left or the right. It was, in fact, more Soviet on the inside than on the outside.

I got to Brent's door and knocked loudly. There was no response. I knocked again, this time harder, and said, "Brent? Brent? It's me. I'm here with Sugar." Still nothing. I couldn't hear any movement behind the door, but that was most likely due to the fact that it was a fairly high-grade fireproof door: stainless-steel hinge; frame made of zinc-coated steel sheeting; the door itself silicate aluminum, likely over a honeycomb board, which also made it nearly impossible to kick in.

He probably didn't know it, but Brent Grayson was living in the perfect place to avoid getting murdered by gangsters and bookies.

I tried the door handle. Locked.

Normally, this would be a situation where I'd pick the lock and be in the room in just under ten seconds, but with the cameras and the sensitive nature of whatever might be behind the door, I figured acting like a normal person might serve me better.

I peered down the hall and saw that there was another open door on the other side of Brent's room. There wasn't any music coming from the door and I hadn't seen anyone going in or out, so I decided to press my luck and look in. There was a young man sitting on a blue sofa tinkering around on the computer. He wore all black, including a black turtleneck, which seemed excessive in the heat of the Miami spring, but not as excessive as the white pancake makeup, black eyeliner and black nail polish he wore. Above the front door was a sign that said, WARNING: YOU ARE NOW ENTERING THE VAMPIRE LAIR, KING THOMAS PRESIDING.

If there was one person on the floor who might have an extra key, it would be the self-proclaimed vampire. Goth kids are always more responsible than the hard-drinking frat boy types, since they're usually content to stay home listening to sad music and reading Camus. Brent seemed like a reasonable enough person, or at least smart enough to give his extra key to a person who never left his room.

"Excuse me," I said.

"What?" the young man said without looking up.

"King Thomas, I presume?"

"You presume correct," he said, eyes still fixed on the computer screen.

"I'm here to see my nephew Brent," I said. "But his door is locked. You wouldn't happen to have an extra key, would you? I'm supposed to leave him some money."

King Thomas' eyes flickered in my direction and then

back to the computer. "You could leave the money with me," he said.

"I could," I said. "But I'm not going to."

King Thomas sighed, as if the conversation we were having was such an existential weight on him that it hurt his soul, and then stood up and disappeared into another room. He reappeared moments later with a ring holding at least twenty-five keys. "Everyone always asks me to keep their extra keys," he said.

"You seem very responsible," I said.

"I'm not," he said. He fumbled through the keys silently and then landed the one he wanted. "I slept through three classes this week. That's not very responsible, is it?"

"Were you in prison?"

"No, I just couldn't get up. You ever have days like that?"

"Yes," I said.

"What do you do?"

"I get up."

"I guess there's no lecture notes in real life," he said.

"Not that I've found," I said.

King Thomas removed the key from the key ring and then seemed to ponder what his next move was going to be. "I haven't seen Brent leave, so he might just be asleep."

"I tried knocking on the door."

"He takes that Ambien stuff," King Thomas said. "Every Saturday. And I'm the vampire?" King Thomas stepped into the hall and looked down at Sugar. "Hey, Sugar."

"What up, T-Dawg?" Sugar said. "How you been?"

"Chilling," King Thomas said.

"You know each other?" I said to King Thomas.

"Yeah," King Thomas said. "Are you with him?"

"Kind of," I said.

"So you're not really Brent's uncle?"

"No, not really," I said. "But I'm not here to hurt him. I'm here to help him. And, just to be clear, I don't work with Sugar. He happens to be someone I know."

"Don't worry," King Thomas said. "No one would make you for a drug dealer."

"What do I look like?"

"I don't know," he said. "Maybe a hit man?"

"Close enough," I said.

King Thomas put his key in the lock and the door opened with a *whoosh*. I put a hand on King Thomas' chest and held him back while I looked in. The living space was empty—just the same sofa, chair and nondescript coffee table as all the other rooms had—save for a few books and papers left on the floor and kitchen table. There was no blood anywhere, which is always a good thing.

I stepped into the room and listened. Nothing but the electrical undertones you'd expect. "Wait here," I said to King Thomas.

"Whatever," he said.

The door to the bedroom was open. On the floor were stacks of clothes and newspapers and Big Gulp cups and socks and dirty dishes and, finally, at least two dozen baseball caps. But the surprising thing was the number of computers in the room—five laptops and one desktop—all of which were on and linked together. It was enough computer power to run SETI, or maybe a portable NORAD installation, but certainly more than your average college student might need, even one who was a computer science major.

In the bed was a body.

Or, well, the body of a sleeping college student, which can (and often does) resemble the dead. It wasn't until a stifled snore came out of the body that I realized with certainty that it was a sleeping human and not a dead one. The smell in the room didn't help.

I stepped over the heaps of clothes, made my way around the dirty dishes and sidestepped the innumerable computer cables until I was standing above Brent Grayson's sleeping form. I tapped him on the shoulder.

Nothing.

I tapped him on the side of the face.

Nothing.

"Brent," I said. "Wake up."

Nothing again.

I looked at his bedside table and saw that he had a prescription bottle for Ambien, just as King Thomas had suggested, but the label said it was for someone named Irene Rosenblatt.

I walked back out into the hallway and saw that Sugar was deep in conversation with the vampire king and another boy, this one with dreadlocks that looked like they were matted with pet fur. "Sugar," I said, "what did I tell you?"

"Sorry, boss. I know these cats," he said.

I held up the bottle. "You know Irene Rosenblatt, too?"

"Oh, man, you know," he said.

I just shook my head and went back inside the dorm

room. I sat down on the sofa and called Sam. "We've got a body here," I told him.

"Is it messy?" he asked.

"No," I said, "it's asleep. On Ambien."

"You can have crazy sex on that stuff," he said.

"So I hear," I said. "Listen, I'm going to bring this kid home with me and I'm going to leave Sugar somewhere where he can't hurt himself or anyone else. Like Guantánamo Bay, maybe."

"Yeah, about that," Sam said. "His car is gone."

"Towed away?"

"No, I mean gone. Like blown up. Along with the entire notary office. Looks like a pro job, Mikey. These guys are legit that came out there today. This isn't someone looking to collect on a gambling debt, just like you thought."

"Well, this kid has about $20K worth of computer equipment in his dorm room, the kind of computers no college freshman would ever need. Something is going on here beyond Sugar's comprehension, that's for sure. So meet me at my place in about an hour. See if Fiona is available. I have a feeling Brent Grayson might respond to a pretty face more than to guys like us."

"Will do," Sam said and hung up.

I walked back out into the hall and Sugar was leaning against the wall chatting up a young woman. Great. I went back into the vampire's lair and saw that the exalted King Thomas was back on his computer, as if nothing had gone on outside the norm whatsoever.

"King Thomas," I said, "mind if we have a word?"

"You can just call me Tom," he said. "That's mostly a joke."

"Do you know what Brent's major is?"

"He does some stuff with video game design," he said.

"How many computers do you need for that sort of thing?"

King Thomas shrugged. "I don't know. I'm in graphic arts, so it's all crayons for me."

"Six computers seem excessive to you?"

"He downloads a lot of music, I guess," he said.

"Listen, Tom," I said. "I'm going to take Brent out of here now. If anyone comes looking for him, I want you to call me, do you understand?"

I wrote my number down on a piece of scrap paper and handed it to King Thomas. He eyed it suspiciously. "How do I know you're not a bad guy?"

"You don't," I said.

"Okay," he said. "I'll call you. Should I be expecting something bad to happen?"

"Maybe," I said. "At the very least, if Sugar should show up? Call me then, too."

"Got it," he said.

I left the king to his lair and went back into Brent's room. He was still fast asleep. I shook him as hard as I could without breaking his ribs, or neck, and his eyes fluttered open.

"Who are you?" he said.

"The person who is going to save your life," I said.

"Are you friends with Sugar?"

"No," I said. "I'm the person who saved Sugar's life, too."

"Are you Sam?"

"No," I said. "I'm Michael Westen."

"The spy?"

Nice that Sugar had been discreet in all of his dealings. I wondered if Brent had my burned dossier, too.

"Yes," I said, "the spy."

"So he brought the wolf. Cool."

"The wolf?"

"From *Pulp Fiction*. The fixer. Badass." Brent sat up and rubbed his eyes. "What time is it?"

"After three."

"Did Sugar take care of, uh . . ." Brent trailed off. "Is he dead?"

"No," I said. "And no. He's out in the hall. Now grab your stuff and however many computers you think you need and come with me."

"Where are we going?"

"A place where if ten Russian gangsters show up, your friends and classmates won't end up murdered. That sound like a good plan?"

"Oh," he said, which I took to mean he understood that the playing field had changed, that dangerous things were afoot, that he needed to listen to me and, finally, that he needed to get moving. But then he threw the covers over his head and moaned.

"Brent," I said, "you need to come out from under the covers."

"Does this mean something bad happened today?"

"It does," I said.

"Oh, oh," he said and this time—well, this time he actually got up out of bed and got busy getting the hell out of his dorm.

3

If you want to learn how to fight, don't take a course in self-defense. The best thing a self-defense course will teach you is how to lose with dignity. They are designed for those being attacked, not for those who are about to go on the offensive. The result is that the fighting skills most people possess are reactionary: What do you do when someone hits you in the face? What do you do if someone grabs you from behind? How do you fend off someone who is trying to abduct you?

Learn a martial art as a kid and it will be drilled into your head that you should use your skill only when you're being attacked. This is done for a simple reason: Children aren't smart enough *not* to go around jump-kicking everyone who angers them and thus they must be wired for passivity. The result is a generation of Americans who curl up in a ball and let bullies steal their lunch.

Americans like Brent Grayson, who, after arriving at my loft, immediately lay facedown on my bed and began his moaning again. I'd had a feeling he'd be like this—that he'd opted to sleep through Sugar's confrontation that afternoon told me he wasn't going to be a real take-charge kind of kid—which is why I made sure Fiona was at my loft by the time we arrived. I had Sam drive Sugar home so he could break the news to him about his car. I figured Sam got himself into this mess, he could be the one in charge of listening to Sugar cry. Meanwhile, Sugar's problem kept emitting this low wail that reminded me of a wounded bear. It also made me want to put him out of his misery.

"What is his issue?" Fiona asked. We were in the kitchen, which is only a few feet from my bed, but with the amount of moaning and woe-is-me-ing Brent was doing, we both felt fairly comfortable speaking in our normal voices.

"I don't know," I said.

"Have you asked him?"

"No."

"Why not?"

"Fi," I said, "he's curled up on my bed like a five-year-old. You know I have a hard time talking to kids."

"What about in the car ride over?"

"It was enough for me to keep Sugar from speaking," I said. "I might have killed them both."

"So, what, you want me to coo him into telling you why the big mean bad guys blew up his daddy's office?"

"Yes."

"And then what? We both read him a story and put him to bed?"

"Fi," I said, "he just needs a sweet voice in his ear right now. I'm afraid I might shake him to death if he continues to whine."

"Fine," she said. She walked over and sat down on

the foot of the bed. "Brent, honey," she said, "turn over. Let's talk."

"Oh," he said, but didn't move.

Fiona leaned over and rested her hand gently on the back of his neck. "Sweetheart," she said, "we're here to help you. Do you want our help?" She stroked his neck lightly. I know it was wise to bring her over.

"I guess," he said.

"Then either turn over and stop babbling," she said—and then I saw her squeeze his neck with a bit more force than a cougar does its young—"or I will break your neck. Okay, sweetie?"

Brent flipped over and stopped making noise.

"There," Fiona said to me. "He's all yours."

"Thanks, Fiona," I said. Sometimes I forget that Fiona isn't really like other women, particularly as it relates to the care and concern of wounded animals and such.

I pulled a chair next to the bed and looked at Brent. He had brown hair that hung loosely over his eyes, a complexion that could use a bit of exfoliation but was otherwise fine and teeth that had benefited from what was probably very expensive orthodonture. His clothes were brand name and he didn't have any obvious track marks on his arms and wasn't constantly wiping the cocaine from his nose. So how was it he was mixed up with such bad people?

"Can I get you something to eat?" I asked.

"No, I'm fine. I ate, like, last night."

"Can I get you something to drink?"

"I wouldn't mind a Yoo-hoo. Do you have any Yoo-hoo?"

"I'm afraid I don't," I said. "How about water?"

"Water would be fine."

"Fiona," I said, "would you kindly get our young guest a glass of water?"

"I'd be happy to," she said and got up.

"Is she going to hurt me anymore?" Brent asked.

"Probably not," I said.

Fiona came back with a bottle of water, which Brent drank down quickly. He looked back and forth at me and Fi as if trying to determine who was in charge. He settled on me. "I guess things got bad today."

"That would be correct," I said. "Your father's office was blown up."

"Like with dynamite?"

"More likely with C-4," I said. "But the result was the same."

"What if Sugar had still been there?" he said.

"That's a good question, Brent," I said. "It's why you're now in my loft and not in your cozy bed on campus. Would you care to explain why you've got the Russian Mafia blowing up your father's place of business?"

"How do I know I can trust you?" he asked.

"You don't," Fiona said.

This didn't seem to reassure Brent much. "But you're not, like, criminals, right?"

"I'm not, no," I said.

He looked at Fiona, who said nothing.

"Why do you want to help me?" he asked.

"Because you're in over your head," I said. "If you didn't know that before, you should now. And Sugar can't help you. Trust me on that. He's a good friend, but you don't need friends right now. You need tactical support." I let Brent process that bit of information for a moment. "Sugar told me that your father has a gambling problem and has disappeared. Is that correct?"

"Yes," Brent said.

"But those guys today—" I said. "That wasn't about that, was it?"

"No," he said. "No, that's my problem." Brent flopped back onto the bed and covered his face with a pillow. "I'm, like, so stupid."

"No argument from me," Fiona said.

"Not helping," I said to her. I pulled the pillow off of Brent's face. "Listen to me, Brent. You need to start at the beginning, don't skip any details and try not to say the word 'like' in the process. And you need to do all of this while sitting upright or I'm afraid I won't be able to stop Fiona from squeezing your neck again."

Brent rubbed his forearm across his eyes, sniffled once and then ran his hands through his hair. My entire life I've tried to avoid crying in all its forms— crying women, crying children, crying animals—and now I had a teenage boy in my loft who couldn't complete a sentence without spilling tears onto my comforter.

"So, okay," Brent began. "I had this class project, okay? We were supposed to design realistic Web sites to go along with our game projects—like fully integrated sites that look like actual companies, you know?"

I told him I did. It was something the U.S. government had been doing for years. If you're a covert operative working under a second identity in a foreign land as, say, the president of a tissue paper company, you need to have the same online corporate presence as any other tissue company might. The CIA was also especially fond of selecting people just like Brent Grayson to design them.

"My game, it's pretty cool; it's this world-building game where you're basically trying to become the ultimate capitalist, but, like, do good things, too, so, you know, there's like evil companies and stuff that want to exploit you. It's pretty cool."

Brent was excited, even if he wasn't saying much of anything and even though the world was crumbling around him and he was now in a spy's loft telling him his life story . . . or at least the story of his last few weeks.

"What is this game called?" Fiona asked.

"*Lifescape.*"

"Sounds like a birth control pill," Fiona said.

"Yeah," he said. "I never liked it, either. No one did. In workshop? They said it was too much like a self-improvement seminar or whatever."

"Fascinating," I said. "How do the Russians come into play?" Brent looked like he wanted to do that whole pillow-on-the-face thing again, so I took hold of his shoulder to let him know he had our support and that, if need be, I could grab him, too. "You need to keep it together."

He bit into his bottom lip and soldiered forward. "I make this killer Web site for InterMacron, this super badass tech company that has developed new ways for delivering bandwidth, because like that's the growth industry of the next twenty years, right? I mean, I do it up, because it was going to be thirty-three percent of my grade for the quarter and I'd really slacked off because of this girl who totally got into my head. It was crazy."

Brent got a wistful look on his face and I couldn't tell if he was feeling that way about the girl, the easier time or if that's just how he looked because he hadn't yet learned the joys of paying taxes and other adult activities.

"So InterMacron, the reason it's so badass is that it's come up with this way to increase bandwidth loads at a really low cost—fiber-optics, all that stuff? It's like really expensive, so InterMacron has this device they are developing called the WieldXron, which will allow wireless use to expand using Kineoptic Transference."

I looked at Fiona to see if she understood a single thing Brent said. Her mouth was agape and her eyes were a bit on the heavy-lidded side, which made me think she was about to curl up next to Brent to take a nap. I felt about the same way.

"What is Kineoptic Transference?" I said.

"It's nothing," he said. "It doesn't exist. It's just this theoretical way of using the electricity found in wind to move data. It could probably only work on Mars."

"Where did you learn of it?" I asked.

"I made it up," he said.

I had a bad feeling about this, because what he said about bandwidth was absolutely true. Twenty-five years ago, it didn't even exist, but today, with the world constantly wired (or, more accurately, wireless) and every day seeing an increased demand and a withering amount of supply. In America, it was managed by the conglomerates—the AT&Ts, the Verizons, the Sprints of the world—which means it is a managed resource and an untapped wealth because of the monopolization by the large telecommunications companies. If you want bandwidth, you need to deal with those who have created the infrastructure.

In a country like Russia, where the outlying former Soviet regions are still years behind the curve, so far back that the curve is still just a straight line, that demand for bandwidth is a gold rush for those with money to build—or influence the building of—the infrastructure. And the people with the most money in Russia often have ties to or are directly involved with organized crime.

Which was not a good thing if it meant what I feared.

I got up and grabbed one of Brent's laptops. "Pull up your site," I said.

He tapped it in and handed the laptop back to me. There, in vivid color, and including video, photos and graphs, I leaned all about the burgeoning field of Kineoptic Transference. I learned that the company was founded by Dr. Chester Palmetto, who, with a large grant from the Pinnacle Institute (which also had a linked Web site touting its desire to fund "the 22nd century in the 21st"), had embarked on a prototype of the Kineoptic Transference device to "high success" and that mass production was possible within the next five years, provided further research-and-development funds were secured.

There was a photo of Dr. Palmetto standing in front of an array of wind turbines in the California desert and the caption beneath it said: "Dr. Palmetto expects the deserts of the world, both the arid and the frozen, with their potential for wind harvestation and lack of architectural impediment to be ground zero for a new technological boom." Other photos showed Dr. Palmetto in Paris, Dubai, New York and what appeared to be Antarctica.

There were other photos of scientists, various vice presidents and CFOs, men and women working diligently in front of computer screens and outdoors.

"Who are all of these people in the pictures?" I asked.

"Just photos I found online of people," he said. "I doctored them up to suit my needs. I'm pretty much a master at Photoshop."

"What about Dr. Palmetto?" Fiona asked. "You have dozens of photos of him."

"Oh, no," Brent said. "That's my grandfather. He's dead, so I figured he wouldn't mind. Plus, he always wore a lab coat on account of being a pharmacist, so it was easy to make him look right. Pretty cool, huh? What do you think of the name—pretty cool, too, huh?"

"Chester Palmetto?" Fiona said. "Sounds like an English cigarette."

"It's the name of my dog and the street I grew up on," Brent said proudly. "If you combine the two, it's supposed to be a badass name for porn. I think it makes for a cool-sounding scientist, too."

Fiona regarded Brent with something near disdain. "When do you study?" she asked.

"You know, it's not about studying. You can totally game a lot of the classes if you're smart."

"And you're smart?" she said.

He shrugged. It was his default body motion. A series of shrugs that stood for hundreds of emotions. "I got into the U. And I'm a pretty good game designer. You ever play any games?"

"No," Fiona said.

"Not even like first-person shooter games?"

"Not for sport, no," she said.

I kept clicking through the Web site until I got to the contact page. Each of the main players in the company had an e-mail address and there was a general phone number, too. "These e-mail and phone numbers actually work?" I asked.

Brent nodded. "That was part of the assignment. It's what got me in trouble," he said. "I used to get e-mail from people all the time asking for more information, or for scientific data, or for a quote—people doing stories on bandwidth for magazines and newspapers would contact the press agent e-mail at least twice a month. And sometimes I'd get e-mail or phone calls from people interested in investing, which I thought was crazy, because I just made up all the science on here. I just thought 'kineoptic' was a cool word, you know, like combining 'kinetic' and 'optic,' so, like, there it was."

"This phone number," I said. "Where does it ring?"

"Nowhere," he said. "It's an Internet number. It just records voice mail online."

"Smart," I said.

"Yeah?" he said.

"You survive the next two weeks of your life," I said, "you should look into whether or not Langley is hiring."

"I'm pretty much a pacifist," he said.

"Well," I said, "too bad. So people would contact you and you'd do what?"

"I used to just say stuff like, you know, 'A major announcement will be made next year in Zurich and we'll be able to provide you with more information at that time.' But then I kept getting messages from this Russian technology import-export company that was very persistent in their desire to help fund my venture. I mean, I did my Googling, so I knew they were legit. I went through and looked at the coding on their Web site and all that. Even had a friend of mine who reads Russian read all the foreign stuff on them and, like, it sounded like some big faceless company, you know? Like some big asshole company that would screw the little guy. I mean. Yeah. That's what I thought, you know?"

"Even though you built a Web site just like theirs, but probably even more sophisticated, in your dorm room?" Fi said.

"Well," he said, "yeah, but, you know, I'm an American, so, yeah. And for a long time, like, it was a big joke with my classmates. If someone needed rent money or couldn't make their car payment or whatever, they'd be like, 'Call the Russians!' So when my dad disappeared and the bookies started leaning on me, that's what I did."

"When did your dad go missing?" I said.

"Two months ago," Brent said.

"You have any idea where he might be?"

"No," he said. "He's left before, like when I was a kid, but then it was only for like a week. He'd go get money somewhere and come back. He'd hook up with a bookie in some other city who didn't know him and then he'd show back up when he could pay off his debt. Stupid."

"How much does he owe?" I asked.

"I've already paid off sixty-five thousand bucks," Brent said, as if it was nothing. I didn't say anything. "But he's got big tabs with guys all over town. Every week, a new guy shows up asking for his money. I'm supposed to meet a guy named Big Lumpy tomorrow to pay off part of a debt my dad has to him for fifteen large."

"*Fifteen large*. Really."

"That's how they talk," Brent said. "That's how my dad talks. I'm just telling you everything."

"How do you know you're not getting shaken down?" Fiona asked. "I don't want to be morbid, but your father could already be dead."

"He's not," Brent said. "Because I know he's still betting. He took money out of a shared account of ours a week ago. It's this old Christmas club account my mom gave me when I was born. He drained it."

The problem with degenerate gamblers is that it's never about winning or losing; it's about the rush of playing. It blinds your ability to make good decisions. It ends up putting everything you have in jeopardy . . . like your son's life.

"Okay," I said. "So these guys come and demand money or they're going to kill you, am I correct?"

"Me," he said, "and everyone in my family. They gave me MapQuest directions to my aunt Jill's house in Austin, my cousin Matthew in San Francisco and they even showed me a picture of my mother's grave.

They said they'd dig her up and kill her again. And when they find my dad, they said they'd kill him, too, but they'd do it slowly."

"Here's the thing, Brent," I said. "If they kill you, they won't get any more money. Do you understand that?"

"Yeah. So, great, I'm paralyzed or something instead. I'd rather be dead."

"Why didn't you just go to the police in the first place, Brent?" I said.

He got up off of the bed and began to pace my loft, much like Sugar had, much like half a dozen other clients had when faced with the one question that should be the easiest to answer. It portended extenuating situations, which I presumed would lead to the Russians.

"They told me not to," he said.

"Right. Of course," I said. "But was this before or after you contacted the Russians and took their money for a device that doesn't exist?"

"How did you know?" Brent asked.

"Because I'm a spy," I said. "And because you're smart and did the only thing you could to save your father's life. And I don't know any other way you'd be able to get your hands on sixty-five thousand bucks. That nugget of information didn't elude me, Brent."

"Thanks. For the smart part, I mean."

"But being smart is also the one thing that could likely get you killed," I said. "How much did they send you?"

"Which time?"

"*Which time?* How many times have there been?"

"Well, they asked to invest in the project and so at

first I kept shining them on, just like all the others, until this all happened and I said, okay, they could get in on the Angel level for seventy-five thousand."

"And what happened next?" I asked.

"They asked where they could wire the money," Brent said.

That got Fiona interested. Money does that to her. Especially money garnered as an ill-gotten gain. "How long," she asked, "would it take you to build me a Web site like this one of yours?"

"Fi," I said. "Still not helping."

"Michael, if Russian gangsters are giving away their money, why shouldn't we profit from it? We could clearly cover our tracks much better than a dumb college kid. No offense, Brent."

"Some taken," he said. "And anyway, I didn't know they were gangsters, like I said. I thought I was dealing with an accountant somewhere in the Ural Mountains."

"What did you do with that money?" I asked.

"I paid the bookies and I paid my tuition, or else I was going to get kicked out of school. Dad didn't pay any of my school stuff for the last six months, which I didn't realize, of course, until he was gone. They were going to lock me out of the dorms and everything."

"Okay," I said. "How much do you have left?"

"Nothing," he said. "Or, well, nothing from the first payment. I had them send me another seventy-five thousand two weeks ago, which was supposed to facilitate delivery of the initial specs for the project, which, you know, don't exist."

I was silent for a moment while I tried to figure

out all of the mistakes Brent Grayson had made, all of the terrible choices he was forced to make by his father, Henry, and then the likelihood that I could be killed while trying to help him out of this barbed-wire corner.

"When did the Russians figure out that there was no InterMacron?" I asked.

"A couple of days ago, I guess," he said. "After I didn't deliver the specs, I guess they started to investigate things a little further and that's when they said they would be at my dad's office to either get their money or get their information and that's when I called Sugar. He's the baddest guy I know, so, you know, I thought he could help me with this."

"Except you lied to him," Fiona said.

"You know Sugar," Brent said. "I didn't want him knowing all that stuff."

The kid had a valid point.

"What time are you supposed to meet Big Lumpy?" I asked.

"Noon," he said. "At someplace called the Hair of the Dog. I've never been there, because I'm not twenty-one."

"You defraud Russian gangsters but you've never been to a bar?" Fiona said.

"This is the first time I've broken the law," Brent said. "I mean, other than buying stuff from Sugar. But that's just because I have a hard time sleeping."

It was no wonder.

"Tomorrow I'll go meet with Big Lumpy. I'll explain the situation to him and I'm sure he'll understand," I said. "And then we'll get to work on the Russians."

"What about my father?"

"We'll find him, too," I said.

"I can pay you with whatever is left after you pay off Big Lumpy," he said.

"I'm not going to pay Big Lumpy. And you're not going to touch the money in that account. Got it?"

Brent didn't say anything. Not good.

"How much have you spent, Brent?"

"I lent a girl I know some money," he said. "She wanted a boob job and her parents wouldn't pay for it."

"Noble," Fiona said.

"How much?" I said.

"Five grand," he said. "And I bought a scooter. To get around campus."

"How much?"

"Another five grand."

"Anything else?"

"I had a small party," he said. "And I bought another computer."

"Why don't you tell me how much of that $75K is left?"

"$45K."

"Must have been some party," I said.

"It was off the chain," he said. "So, yeah, I can pay you with whatever is left."

"You're not going to pay me," I said. "Don't lose any sleep over it. What I need from you is every single piece of information that went back and forth between you and the Russians. Do you have that?"

"It's all on my computers," he said.

"Good," I said. "All right. Why don't you try to take another nap while Fiona and I step outside. Okay?"

There was a sweetness in my voice that I found nauseating. I made a note to myself never to have children. Or at least not helpless children.

"I'm not tired."

"Then just sit here quietly," I said.

Fiona and I got up to walk outside but Brent stopped us. "Look, out of all of this? I just want to find my dad and know he's okay. He's made a lot of mistakes in his life, but he's still my father and I love him. I did this all for him."

"I know," I said. "And I'll find him. I promise."

We left Brent and walked down the stairs and out onto the street in front of my building. It was almost five o'clock and I was still alive. Not bad.

"What do you make of it, Michael?" Fiona asked.

"I don't see Yuri Drubich coming after him that big for $150K," I said. "That's a lot of money, but not enough to send ten guys with explosives to Miami."

"You think he's lying?"

"No," I said. "I think Drubich probably resold the information he had and now he's in a serious pinch. I wouldn't be surprised if he tried to kidnap Brent so that Brent could stand in front of some very angry men to explain his deception."

"And then what?" Fiona said.

"And then they'd kill him."

"Do you believe his father is still alive?"

"I don't know," I said. "It's a classic shakedown the bookies are doing on him. If they got access to the bank accounts to make Brent think his father is still alive, well, that's pretty smart. But I just don't see these guys going after a kid. Most bookies, they've got a code. A terrible, stupid, dangerous code, but a code no less. Brent's not in the game, so I can't see them doing this to him if his dad was dead."

"Maybe they'll tire of him," Fi said.

"Maybe when the money runs out."

"Or when he runs out of blood," she said. It was just a matter-of-fact statement, which made it all the more chilling. "Personally, Michael, I find these Russians far more dangerous. They blew up a building in the middle of a Saturday afternoon. What's stopping them from blowing up your loft tomorrow if they find out Brent is here?"

"You," I said.

"I was hoping you'd say that," she said. "Please tell me I get to play dress-up."

"You get to play dress-up."

"And do I get to indiscriminately shoot people and devastate entire city blocks?"

"Probably not," I said.

I took out my cell and called Sam. "You get rid of Sugar?" I asked after he answered.

"Yeah. Boy, Mikey, he's pretty torn up. He said his best quality was his car."

"He was right," I said.

"What did you get from the kid?"

I told Sam what I knew and what I didn't.

"So what's our first move?" he asked.

"Well, your first move is to find out all you can about Brent's father, Henry Grayson, and then tomorrow, why don't you join me to meet with Big Lumpy. I have a feeling that might be a challenging conversation."

4

Tracking down someone who has disappeared of their own accord is never an easy process. In fact, if it was up to him, Sam Axe would prefer to look for someone who'd been abducted. Abductors tend to leave evidence, because if you're in the business of abductions, you're probably not very bright, or you're acting on impulse, or you're acting on someone else's impulse, which means you're strictly doing work for hire and people doing work for hire don't always pay really close attention to detail.

Which is maybe why, Sam realized, he hadn't exactly prepared with his usual monastic dedication when Sugar initially called him for help. He was blinded by those Dolphins tickets. Well, he wouldn't dwell on that. Or, well, he couldn't if he wanted to, since Sugar had admitted he didn't really have the tickets and was hoping Sam wouldn't really ask for payment after all.

But anyway: Someone grabs you, there's likely going to be some spilled blood, some broken glass, maybe even a witness. You disappear yourself, you've got time to clean up, to plan, to leave false trails. Maybe you even kiss your kid good-bye.

Not that Sam thought Henry Grayson was smart enough to do all of that, exactly, but that he left his son to deal with these bookies just made Sam angry. What kind of father does that to a son? Thing was, if Henry was really lucky—which he clearly wasn't in light of his predicament—he might look upon leaving his son to deal with all of this as the ultimate good luck: The firebomb that destroyed his office had, as Michael had told him, insurance windfall written all over it. Plus, the guy was a notary and notaries were responsible people, right? Sam thought if you couldn't depend on a notary, the very people put on this earth by God to make sure things got . . . notarized . . . well, who could you depend on? Not just everyone gets to use a fancy seal every day.

So Sam drove back over to Henry's burnt-out husk of a business to do some poking around. When he'd been there earlier in the afternoon, all he saw was fire trucks and hoses and gawking neighborhood onlookers, all of which was to be expected. It wasn't every day that an entire side of an office park was bombed. A little slice of Fallujah right in the middle of lovely Miami.

Now, however, the street was packed with late-model American sedans: Chryslers. Oldsmobiles. Mercurys. Sam even spied a couple Chevrolets, not an occurrence one usually witnessed in nature. This meant one of two things: insurance companies or federal employees. Homeland Security usually rolled up in SUVs, but lower-level CIA and FBI operatives typically got assigned Impalas and the like. If they were lucky, maybe they got a Chrysler Sebring with a moon roof. Not even spies got Aston Martins.

Judging by the clusters of men drinking coffee out of Styrofoam cups, Sam decided that most of the assembled were insurance adjustors. In Sam's experience, if something big was destroyed in some dramatic fashion, it was only a matter of time before the insurance companies showed up and began to set up their own coffee station. It was good public relations, Sam supposed, and made for good photo opportunities: "The Men of State Farm Pause with a Warm Cup of State Farm Coffee While Inspecting the Total Destruction of Hurricane Katrina." Plus, insurance guys preferred short-sleeved shirts with ties, whereas government types tended toward blue suits and Sam counted at least a dozen men with excessively pale forearms poking out of lightly starched white shirts. It was as if they all shopped at the same Marshalls.

Sam pulled up to one of the clusters and rolled down his window.

"Pardon me, boys," he said, "but I'm looking for the agent in charge."

The cluster looked at one another in confusion. It was very strange. It was as if once they all got together they couldn't manage a single thought or action on their own. Maybe that's what being in the caution business did to you. Finally, one of the men—the only one wearing a Windbreaker, Sam noted—stepped forward. "I guess that would be me," he said.

"No," Sam said. "Federal agent."

"Oh, I don't think anyone like that is here," Windbreaker said. "We've been working the scene here for the last couple of hours and it's just been fire and police."

"Dammit," Sam said.

This was perfect. He made an exaggerated motion of slamming his car into PARK, even letting it roll a couple of inches in NEUTRAL first, so that the car made a noticeable lurch. He thought about jumping out of the open car window, but decided that might be a touch over the top for the situation and he also wasn't entirely sure he could get through the window in light of the three-beer lunch he'd had. He fished around in his center console, found the perfect sunglasses among the half dozen pairs he kept there—mirrored aviators— and put them on before he opened his car door and bounded out onto the pavement like he was leading a charge up an enemy beach. Patton could have used mirrored aviators. "All right, all right," Sam said. "Then I need some answers and I need them fast. Which one of you candy asses was first on the scene?"

Windbreaker took a noticeable step back into the crowd. A born leader knows to let someone else take the fall. It's what made Nixon so good for so long. And really helped Dick Cheney out. Surrounding yourself with idiots also helped.

"That would be me," one of the nebulous short-sleeve men said.

"What's your name, son?" Sam said. The man looked to be about Sam's age, but Sam always thought calling people "son" immediately gave the air of imperial authority and opened the door for spankings if need be.

"Peter," he said.

Sam took a pen out of his pocket and wrote the name PETER on the back of his hand. Every man Sam had ever met who was willing to take notes on his flesh was a man who meant business. "Peter what?"

"Handel," he said. "Like the composer." Peter had a mop of gray-flecked brown hair and a goatee that was about twenty years too late for his face. Sam thought he sort of looked like Ringo Starr if Ringo Starr had thrown it all away for an exciting career in the insurance field. Sam did admire a guy who had an interesting enough—or, depending upon how one looked at it, boring enough—name that he needed to tell you someone else who had it. Sam wrote HANDEL on his palm.

"Well, Peter Handel, I'm Chuck Finley and I'm like nothing you've ever seen," Sam said. "Give me the stats."

"Uh," Peter said, "I'm sorry, but I'm not sure I know what you're looking for."

"Peter Handel, let me *compose* something for you, okay, son? This is the tenth bombing I've seen like this in the last month. Des Moines. Five dead. Cupertino. Three dead. Lake Charles. No human deaths, just two very crispy Dobermans. You seeing where this is headed, son?"

"I'm sorry," Peter said again, "but where did you say you were from?"

Used to be people in the insurance business respected authority but now that they *were* the authority half the time, well, they were getting a bit on the cocky side. Sam preferred the old world where you could go to whatever doctor you wanted, any repair shop you wanted, and they'd both take a bullet out of your backside without a question. Now, it was all guys like Peter Handel. Mr. Question Man. Sam gave an exasperated sigh that was meant to convey all of that to Windbreaker, since clearly he was a man who would agree with Sam since not just anybody can wear a Windbreaker without irony.

Problem was, Sam couldn't find Windbreaker. In fact, in the short time they'd been speaking, most of the sewing circle of insurance men had stepped away. They were like stealth bombers. Sam would have to deal with Peter Handel-like-the-composer.

"Where am I from?" Sam said. "I'm from a little town in Virginia called Langley. You heard of it? Or do I need to spell it out for you? Would it help if I called in a black helicopter?"

"Uh, no, no, sir," Peter said. "I'm sorry. I just—you understand, protocol is that we don't provide confidential information to third parties, and as I wasn't sure who you were, I . . . well, you understand, right? Sir?"

Sam took out his pen again. "What's your Social Security number, Handel?"

"I'm sorry?"

"Your Social. Give it to me right now." Peter rattled off nine numbers that Sam made a big show of carving into his palm. "Good. Good. Well. I'll check you out. If you've got no priors, haven't visited Pakistan in the last month, I'm sure everything will be fine. In the meantime, I need all of the information you've gathered here today if you value living in a free society. You value that, don't you, Peter?"

"Yes, yes, of course," Peter said. There was a fine sheen of sweat covering the poor guy's face and for a moment Sam felt sorry for him. He was just doing his job and, actually, doing it according to rule. Well, Sam thought, at least now he'd have a story to tell about the time he worked with the CIA. "I need to get my clipboard from my car. Is that all right?"

"Which car?" Sam asked.

"The gray Taurus," Peter said. He pointed down the street where there were maybe five gray Tauruses parked.

"Okay," Sam said, "but make it fast. Every minute you take is another minute we're closer to a terrorist action, you understand?"

"Yes, sir," he said and scampered off.

Sam walked over to the parking lot where Sugar's car still smoldered. It was unlikely that Sugar's name was associated in any way with the car, since Sam had a hard time imagining Sugar either going to a dealership to purchase the car or executing the actual act of mailing off a check each month for the payments. And there was no way Sugar was mentally capable of keeping up with his registration and insurance. He was sure the car had those things in the glove box and he was just as sure they were forgeries.

A young detective stood next to the car and wrote notes down on his notepad. Sam couldn't figure out what it was about young detectives that made him edgy, particularly since they were both fighting the same war, at least metaphorically speaking. Sure, maybe Sam blew things up in the middle of the city periodically, and, sure, maybe he'd done some work over the course of the last couple years that straddled the line between legal and illegal, but it was all for the greater good. Anyway, it was probably that this batch of new detectives dressed like they were in a commercial for self-tanners and polo shirts.

"Help you with something?" the detective said.

"Finley," Sam said and extended his hand toward the detective, who in turn just stared at it.

"You a reporter? If so, we've got no comment, okay?"

"Not a reporter, son," Sam said. "I'm in from Langley." He let that sink in for a moment but when the detective didn't seem to show any recognition, he added, quietly, because these CIA guys tended to be all monosyllabic and quiet, "Langley, Virginia. Where the CIA lives? Maybe you're familiar with it?"

The detective straightened up a bit but still didn't seem to be a hundred percent invested in believing Sam. "You got some ID?"

"Yeah," Sam said. "The Department of Homeland Security just hands out badges that say TERRORIST LIQUIDATION OFFICER on them. Listen, son, I've got about five minutes of time here and either you're going to help your country or you're going to hurt it. Which is it going to be?"

The detective looked over his shoulder at the smoldering building. "This terror-related?"

"That's what I'm trying to determine. This car stolen?"

"Yes, sir," the detective said.

"And the office, it was the notary?"

"Yes, sir."

"That makes fifteen," Sam said.

"Fifteen what?"

"Classified," Sam said. He took out his pen again

and this time wrote "15" on his forearm. "This place owned by Henry Grayson?"

"That's right," the detective said.

"Find him?"

"No, not yet."

"Good. Good. How many men you got on him?"

"None as yet. We've been calling his known numbers and getting disconnects. The insurance guys say he's behind on payments, which they're thrilled about."

"Fucking carrion," Sam said. "Pardon my Greek." He stepped around the detective and looked into Sugar's car. There wasn't anything inside it now that could ever be tied to anyone—it was just ash and melted leather inside a metal frame. "Stolen, right?"

"VIN is for a Chevy van stolen in Orlando three months ago," he said.

"Same guy, then," Sam said. The insurance agent had made his way back and was waiting patiently a few yards away. He had a fancy clipboard, one of those that was encased in metal and had a flip top. Impressive. "Here's what I need from you, Detective, and I don't have time to wait around for an official report, you understand? For America?"

"I do," he said. He stood up a little straighter. No matter the situation, in Sam's experience at least, you ask cops to do something for America and they have an atavistic response that requires them to be completely honest and to improve their posture by at least twenty-five percent "What'd they use to blow up the building? C-4?"

"Shoulder-mounted rocket launcher. Don't know the make yet. But looks like maybe an M90."

Shoulder-mounted rocket. Jesus. "Expected," Sam said. "Same with the car?"

"Yes, sir."

"All right," Sam said. "What's your name, Detective?"

"James Kochel."

"You ever think about working in something that is actually challenging?"

"Yes, sir, I have."

"Good," Sam said. "We'll be in touch." He stepped away and then did a quick pivot, added a touch of military flair to his persona (while, he noted, tweaking something in his calf) and addressed the detective again. "This Grayson fellow. You got anything on him with organized crime?"

The detective licked his lips in a way that reminded Sam of the guys he played high school football with but who, clearly, were never going to be as important later in life as they were then. Guys like that always licked their lips before something exciting. It freaked Sam out in high school and it freaked him out now. "Fact is," the detective said, "I probably shouldn't even be saying anything, but we're all on the same team, right?"

"America's team," Sam said. "Like the Dallas Cowboys. Just one big interdepartmental huddle, Jimmy."

The detective liked that. He leaned in toward Sam and then lowered his voice. "A year ago we had this place under surveillance. Thought he was running a high-stakes book out of it. Never got him on anything, but he had shady guys coming in and out at all hours."

"Any Al-Qaeda?" Local cops loved to feel like they

were just inches away from finding Bin Laden sitting inside the local Dairy Queen.

"No, no. Local talent."

Sam looked at his hand and then licked his lips, too. Let him know they both had the same tic, make him think he'd fit in over in Langley. Though his godforsaken Dockers never would. "The name Big Lumpy mean anything to you?"

"It does."

"The word 'Hamas' mean anything to you?"

"It does."

"Good. Keep away from Big Lumpy for the near future—you got it?"

"I wouldn't have guessed that," Kochel said.

"Sleeper cells all over the place."

"But didn't he go to MIT?"

MIT? Sam tried not to show any surprise. He couldn't imagine anyone presently called Big Lumpy ever attending MIT, but clearly Kochel knew something he didn't.

"You tell me, hotshot," Sam said. The beauty of ignorance mixed with authority (real or imagined, in this case), Sam believed, was that people tended to feel like they needed to impress you with their own importance. It's what makes criminals think they can talk their way out of jail or convince a jury of their innocence on the power of personality alone. In the wrong hands, well, it's clinical narcissism. In the right hands, it's essentially been American foreign policy since Vietnam.

"When ATF was out here last year, that's what they told me, anyway," he said. "That's how he got the nickname Big Lumpy, because he's actually very skinny, right? But his brain, it's big and lumpy, right? I heard he had an MRI when he was in college or something and it just stuck. But that could all be myth, right?"

Big Lumpy was the nickname of his *brain*? Oh, Sam thought, this is just getting more and more weird.

"That's right," Sam said. "Now, how many guys you think are in Hamas who have a degree from MIT and who can get hold of the kind of money he has access to? Starting to make sense?"

"Wow," Kochel said. "Wow. Yeah. Wow."

The problem with local cops wasn't that they were ineffective, because Sam was sure they must be pretty good at solving something, though certainly they'd never put the pieces together on any of the cases he and Michael had worked on, which made them perhaps blind and deaf, particularly since half the time they helped someone, Sam ended up blowing up half a city block. No, Sam thought, the problem with local cops everywhere was the same: They wished they were doing something more exciting. So all anyone really had to do to get them to spill what meager information they might have was to, well, ask them. Cops were the very worst confidential sources on the planet.

"Keep that information on the down low now, okay? It's national security level. You'll notice I confirmed nothing. And I was never here, got it?"

"Yes, sir." Sam could tell Kochel had something eating away at his conscience. His voice had gone all timid. These guys always thought guys like Sam—or, well, guys like who Sam was pretending to be—had all the answers. "Can I ask you a shop question?" Kochel asked.

"Sure, hotshot, but make it quick."

"Maybe you don't know this, but I have to ask . . ."

Sam waved the detective off in midsentence. "It was Oswald. He acted alone. The guy on the grassy knoll was one of our guys."

Before Detective Kochel could respond, Sam thanked him and then made his way back to Peter Handel and his metal clipboard. No sense prolonging the experience or answering anything about Area 51. "What do you have?" Sam asked Handel once he reached him.

"Bare bones? Guy hasn't made his last payment, so on the record, this isn't on us to pay out on the hazard insurance or fire or anything. Now, off the record, he's been a client for ten years, so maybe he sues and says, Okay, I've made enough payments that if I'm forty-five days late, you're not going to honor my account? Take it to mediation, we'd probably settle, but we'd make him sweat it. It would be a bad beat, but we'd take it."

"You're a prince," Sam said.

"It's the business," Peter said.

"What else?"

"Well, again, off the record, he actually took out a life insurance policy three weeks ago. Pays out two million five to his son in the case of his death. Paid the premiums on that two years in advance."

Two years. Savvy, Sam thought. He also began to rethink how awful he considered Henry to be. He'd left his son to deal with this shit but also left him set up for the rest of his life.

"He just sent in a check?"

"No, paid by credit card over the phone."

Smart again, Sam thought.

"Off the record?"

"You're talking to a federal agent, Handel. None of this is off the record."

"Right. Right. I just . . . guess . . . Well, I guess here's the weird thing. He paid for the premiums using a VISA gift card. It's basically the same as cash, but he puts close to six grand on it and buys life insurance. It was very unusual."

And very smart, Sam realized. He could have purchased the gift card at any time and loaded the money on it over the course of a very long time, which would essentially render it traceless in the event he needed to use it to disappear. No usable trail of the money transfer if he did it early, no usable trail of the credit card purchase if he did it early, either. And if he's smart, he called using Skype and thus no way to triangulate his location until long after he was gone, not that the insurance company would have been looking to do that. But if you're angry enough, Sam knew, any information could be bought. And it seemed like these bookies were angry.

"Tell me something, Concerto-boy, before this month, was Grayson regular on his payments?"

"He'd usually pay a year in advance. Sometimes in cash. Come by our office on Grand Street and hand over an envelope. We don't encourage that, but some people in Miami are . . . eccentric."

"What's his full loss payout?"

Handel flipped through his pages. "Not a lot," he said. "Just the base minimums. A notary, all he really needs is his satchel of stamps, plus the books he has to keep for the state; that's why most of them are mobile now. No sense keeping an office unless you got something else going on. Most of our clients in this business are pretty lucrative, really, because they've got PO boxes or UPS operating out of the shop, or maybe they're also a greeting card place or, we've got this one in Doral that's a soft-serve joint, really strange."

Handel went on then, at length, about other odd notary businesses, which was fine. It gave Sam a moment to gather his thoughts. First, he decided that if he ever had the choice between going into the insurance industry or being eaten alive by fire ants, he'd look long into the fire ant angle. Second, he saw how odd it was that *all* Grayson did was run a notarizing service out of his office. Rents were high in the neighborhood and Sam had a hard time believing the notarization business could sustain the roof, even with his gambling. No, Sam thought, there was probably something more. Something Henry Grayson's son, Brent, didn't, and probably shouldn't, know about.

"That's all fascinating, Handel," Sam said.

"See a lot of crazy things in this business," he said.

"One last thing," Sam said. "Was there anything on his policy that was unusual?"

"Here? No. But on his home policy, yeah."

"You cover his house, too?"

"Yeah, didn't I mention that?"

"No," Sam said. "Anything else you're holding out on me? Or should I just call the IRS right now and have them start your audit while we chat?"

Mention the IRS to anyone, even the guy in charge of the IRS, and immediately people get that look on their face like someone just unscrewed something in their bowels.

"He had an unusual amount of televisions in his house," Handel said.

"What's unusual?"

"Ten."

That was unusual and it dovetailed into what the detective had said about Grayson possibly, at least at one point, running his own book. It didn't make him any easier to find, but it gave Sam a few ideas about what his next step might be after he and Michael met with Big Lumpy.

"All right, Handel," Sam said. "I'm going to do some checking into things on my end, both on Mr. Grayson and on you. I like what I see, I lose your Social Security number. I have concerns, you'll be hearing from someone. You understand?"

Handel looked grave, so Sam gave him a wink . . . which was probably hard for Handel to see since Sam still had on his sunglasses, but karmically Sam felt closer to even.

5

Taking on a disguise is not about changing the way you look. It's about changing the way you think. Someone who has never met you before and doesn't have access to DNA technology is going to have a difficult time identifying you as anyone other than who you say you are, so when you take on a new identity, you have to make sure you know all the possible angles of inquiry. If, for instance, you say you're from the South, you should have more than a passing knowledge of grits, college football and sweet tea and you should probably still have a strong opinion about the Civil War . . . or the War of Northern Aggression, as it were.

You also need to be aware of the knowledge base of the person you're hoping to deceive. If he's also a spy, your cover needs to be more than rock solid—you need a fake mother, a fake sister, a fake wife and two fake dogs, one dead, one still alive. Fiona was going to get as close to Drubich's local operation as possible using whatever cover she deemed best. Being an attractive woman often requires only that a very short skirt be utilized in the building of a backstory, so she had it easier than I did, though I assumed dealing with someone named Big Lumpy wouldn't require much in the way of world building, either.

Or at least I assumed that until Sam got to my loft that next morning.

First, he filled me in on everything that he'd learned about Brent's father—most of which was a surprise to Brent, particularly the $2.5 million he stood to earn upon his father's death—and the more upsetting news that the Russians hadn't just casually destroyed his office but had actually brought a rocket launcher with them. Not exactly the kind of thing you pack as an afterthought.

"Brent," I said, "did these guys give you any indication that they'd be coming to see you with weapons of mass destruction?"

"No," he said. He was curled up on the floor in front of one of his laptops downloading all of the information I'd asked for from him: the voice mail and e-mail from Drubich's people, Brent's correspondence, a trail of every dollar he'd spent (I had a feeling this would be difficult, but I wanted to make sure he wasn't omitting anything that might cause all of us trouble down the line) and the text of all of his Web pages. "They just said either they'd get what they paid for or they'd kill me."

"And so you thought Sugar could fix that?" I said.

"Sugar and Sam," he said. "But I didn't think they were serious. I mean, you know, we're businessmen."

"Really?" I said.

"Well, sort of."

"Neither you nor the Russians are businessmen. You're both fakes. You just happened to piss off a fake named Yuri Drubich who typically does business with Chechnyans and the odd Afghan warlord moving poppy seeds."

"Cool," Brent said.

"No," I said. "Not cool. Not cool at all."

"I didn't mean it was cool literally. I just, I guess, think it's kinda crazy that I'm involved with people like that. It was just a Web site."

It was just a Web site, true, but it was also a fantastic idea for a new way to move information, even if it was one born out of total fantasy. That someone like Drubich found it and wanted a piece of it said a lot about Brent's idea and about his actual smarts. Even if his smarts didn't exactly pop up on display in casual conversation.

It occurred to me that I'd failed to ask him perhaps the most important question. "How did Drubich know to send his men to your father's office?"

Brent stopped typing for a moment, but didn't look up from his computer. "I made another mistake," he said quietly.

"Let's just settle on the fact that this is all one huge mistake and be honest with each other, okay?" I said. "I need you to be a man, Brent. And that means owning up to your mistakes. Don't be your father."

I couldn't believe the words coming out of my mouth. I sounded . . . parental. And certainly nothing like my own father.

"All right," he said.

I walked over and closed his laptop. "Now," I said, "look me in the eye and speak."

"One of the last times I e-mailed them back," he said, "I did it from the wrong e-mail address. I used the one I have through my dad's business, so when all of this fell apart, they sent me a message saying they'd be there yesterday at three and I'd better have their money or the specs for the Kineoptic Transference devices, because they were beginning to think they'd been had. I assured them they weren't and then, you know, I called Sugar."

"And he called me," Sam said. "He ever talk to you about any Dolphins tickets, Brent?"

"No," Brent said.

"Mikey," Sam said, "remind me to never do any favors for Sugar ever again. Did you know he even promised me parking? Who promises parking and doesn't even really have tickets?"

"A liar," I said.

Sam didn't like that answer. He went into my kitchen and opened the fridge, pulled out three beers and set them on the counter. "You got any limes?" he asked.

"All out from the last time you got disappointed by life," I said. "Tell me about this Big Lumpy."

"Yeah," Sam said, "about that. I was under the impression that maybe he was some New York wise guy slumming in Miami. You know, one of those guys who gives himself a nice, threatening nickname but is mostly a businessman now?"

"And he's not that?" I said.

"No," Sam said. "You want to know how he got his nickname? His professors at MIT gave it to him. He apparently has one of the largest brains in history. So, you know, they got cute and called him Big Lumpy."

"MIT?"

"Yeeeeeah," Sam said. He opened his first beer and

drained it in a few swallows. "About *that*. Turns out Big Lumpy is actually a guy named Mark McGregor. That name mean anything to you?"

"Should it?" I said.

"No," Sam said. "No. That would be easy. Mark McGregor graduated at age nineteen, top of his class, from MIT in 1989. Worked for seven years in the NSA, then left to gamble professionally. Took down most of Las Vegas. This ringing any bells?"

"Only alarms," I said. "What did he do in NSA?"

"Computer security, intelligence analysis, game theory as warfare, that sort of thing," Sam said. "His IQ is supposed to be two hundred. That's even higher than that 'Ask Marilyn' lady in *Parade*."

"And now he's a bookie?" I said.

"He's been banned from every casino in the world," Sam said. "Might as well make his own odds, I guess."

"So he sounds like someone we can reason with," I said.

"Hmm, no," Sam said. "I made a few calls last night to some local lowlifes I happen to know? And it turns out he's known for his unusual brutality."

"Who'd you call?"

Sam coughed, opened the second bottle, drained it and then kept talking. "So, yeah, he's known to cut off important parts of people. Fingers. Toes. Eyelids. Brutal guy. Not a nice person at all. To be avoided at all costs if you happen to, you know, stiff him for cash like our young friend's father did."

"Sam," I said, "who'd you call?"

"Mikey, understand that when I say 'lowlife,' I mean that as a term of endearment, truly."

"Sam," I said, "tell me you didn't call my brother, Nate."

"I didn't call Nate."

That was a relief. . . .

"I texted him," Sam said. "I thought it was too early to call, but it turns out that when you don't go out until three a.m., nine a.m. is dinnertime."

My brother, Nate, lived in Las Vegas with his, uh, *lovely wife*, Ruth, but had spent the previous three-plus decades in Miami. He wasn't a spy. He wasn't even gainfully employed on a regular basis. He was the kind of guy who could get you a suit for a good price, because he'd found it in the back of an open truck somewhere and decided that "finders keepers" was an actual law. When he still lived in Miami he helped me out on a number of occasions, usually by mucking situations up and occasionally by shooting someone at just the right time.

He also had a bit of a reputation for, well, being a lowlife. Not a mean lowlife, just a person leading a life of slightly lower moral standards than most.

I walked over to the kitchen and took Sam's third beer, opened it and poured it down the sink. "I don't want him involved in our business, Sam. He's finally safe in Las Vegas."

"Safe in Las Vegas?" Sam said.

"My point is, you ask him for advice and then he starts feeling like he's out solving crimes and that causes bigger problems down the line. Last thing I need is for my mom to call and tell me Nate's in trouble three thousand miles away and I'm stuck here."

"I hear you, Mikey," Sam said, "I do. Problem was, I

couldn't find anyone else to talk to. I mentioned Big Lumpy to all of my normal dirtbags and most of them hung up on me. Apparently he's considered some mad genius. A buddy of mine? A guy named Sal? He told me he was pretty sure Big Lumpy was a telepath."

"I highly doubt that," I said.

"He did work NSA," Sam said. "Did you know they have a whole division of psychics?"

"Sam."

"It's true. I met one once. We were in Chile. She had a body like a rocket, Mikey, and she knew all of my moves before I even tried them. Spooky stuff, Mikey. Spooky stuff."

"You don't exactly cloak your thoughts, Sam," I said.

"Well, be that as it may, she was pretty much a Ouija board in a skirt. Could be Big Lumpy is one of those, too. Minus the skirt."

The more likely scenario was that Big Lumpy was probably just much more intelligent than the people who decided to bet with him. And if he was setting the odds, it was a good bet that he was setting them in his favor.

"If he's such a bad guy," I said, "why would anyone bet with him?"

"They don't know they are most of the time," Sam said. "Nate said the guy franchises. So you think you're betting with Frankie Four Fingers, but he's actually kicking upstairs to Big Lumpy. And the only time you find out is when you're really late and then, you know, you're probably not in a position to complain too loudly."

Which meant that Nate had been really late at some point, since I couldn't imagine he'd learned any of this information through dogged investigation. It also meant that a good many of the people Brent had already paid off could be working under Big Lumpy, too. If Henry Grayson was dumb enough to bet directly with Big Lumpy, it was likely a choice of last resort.

"Savvy," I said. And it really was. "Well, then, we'll just have to appeal to his good side."

"I don't think he has a good side," Sam said.

"Well," I said, "he hasn't met us yet."

"That's my concern," Sam said. "If he's NSA, what are the odds he still does some contract work with them? The guy is an expert on game theory warfare and has no moral center. That seems to me like two traits the NSA likes to have near for special projects. Mikey, there's a good chance he already knows you."

"Which is why I have the perfect covers for us," I said. "You're going to be an ex–Navy SEAL named Sam Axe and I'm going to be a spy named Michael Westen."

"Play it straight?"

"Yep," I said.

"I don't know if I know how to play it straight," Sam said.

"Have another beer," I said.

"What about me?" Brent said. I'd nearly forgotten he was in the room. Once he'd stopped making whining noises, he was actually very quiet.

"You're going to stay here," I said. "Fiona will be back in a couple of hours." Provided she hasn't had to shoot a bunch of members of the Russian Mafia on your behalf, I thought, though I decided not to mention that detail out loud.

"You don't have any food here," he said. "And you don't have cable, either. And Fiona is mean."

"The kid's got a point there, Mike," Sam said. "Fiona is mean."

"I haven't eaten in like forever," Brent said. "You're basically starving me to death here. You know, yogurt isn't even considered food? It's not. It's a culture."

While Brent droned on about the toil of his life, I did the one thing I really didn't want to do: I called my mother, Madeline.

"Ma," I said, "you have any plans this afternoon?"

"Are you in some kind of trouble?" my mother asked.

"Of course not," I said.

"Because I got a call from your brother a few minutes ago and he sounded very worried," she said. "He didn't say you were in trouble, but I felt like he was holding that back from me."

"You didn't agree to send him any money, did you?"

"I told him I would," she said. "He has no blood family out there, Michael. I told him I'd send him money to get a new shirt. He still needs his mother, unlike some people."

"I do need you, Ma," I said. "That's why I'm calling." Brent had now engaged Sam in a conversation that, as best as I could tell, involved other food groups that were not, technically, foods. They'd moved on to the legitimacy of salads. "I have a young man I'm . . . *mentoring* . . . and I was wondering if I might drop him off at your place for a few hours."

"Mentoring?"

"Yeah," I said. "Like a big brother–type thing."

"Really, Michael?"

"No," I said. It was just easier to be honest. "I'm actually protecting him from some Russian gangsters, every bookie in the city and Fiona."

"Oh, I see," she said.

"And he hasn't had a home-cooked meal since his mother died," I added.

"When did that happen?"

"Years ago," I said.

"Oh, I see," she said. "You're not just saying that, are you, Michael?"

"Not this time, Ma, no," I said.

"Do you think he likes tuna casserole?"

My mother's tuna casserole was notorious for having a consistency somewhere between plaster and the substance that BP used to stop the oil leak in the Gulf.

"I'm sure he does."

"Then bring him by," she said.

"Thanks, Ma. I really appreciate it," I said.

"And, Michael," she said, "will you pick me up some more shells for my shotgun?"

6

No spy likes to go into a meeting with an unknown adversary—if you don't have an idea how a person will react in a given situation, it's difficult to plan your own diversionary tactics. The nice part about working for a huge government agency is that there is always someone you can call in the middle of the night who can provide you with key bits of information. When meeting with an Afghan warlord, for instance, it's nice to know ahead of time if he has a child you can threaten, or maybe a relative living in the United States that you can abduct beforehand and accuse of being a terrorist, or even if the warlord happens to have a particular unseemly fetish you can exploit. No matter who you are, when someone presents your fetishes to you, it's more than a little embarrassing.

But when you're working alone, without all of the resources of spy planes and moles and years and years of surveillance, and are relying only on secondary information from an unreliable source—in this case, my brother, Nate—you need to work on instinct, which is what Sam and I had to do.

"They don't make dive bars like they used to," Sam

said. We'd arrived early to the meet-up at the Hair of the Dog Saloon in hopes of catching a glimpse of Big Lumpy, but instead had spent the better part of thirty minutes watching young women drinking coffee.

The Hair of the Dog Saloon sounds like one of those places decent people avoid unless they're looking for someone to hire for a contract killing. But like all things these days, nothing is as it seems.

Instead of being a dark bar located in the shadow of that old abandoned warehouse or just across from the decrepit docks that were left to rot away when the new docks were built a few miles south, or whatever other cliché might apply, the Hair of the Dog was actually tucked into the sun-dappled center of a new outdoor shopping center near the Miracle Mile in Coral Gables called the Shoppes at Mariposa Circle.

On one side of the Hair of the Dog was, of course, a Starbucks. On the other side was a Panera. There was also a clothing store called Blonde across the palazzo from the Hair of the Dog which featured clothing that could fit only on mannequins and that only mannequins would dare wear. Palm trees with overgrown fronds, presumably for shade and not for the Norwegian roof rats who liked to live among them, were placed decoratively every few feet along the inlaid-brick walkways surrounding the other shops, while young women, apparently in the midst of a nudity competition, sat on dark wood benches chatting on their cell phones and practicing looks of general disinterest. Other shops— or, as the shopping center thought of them, shoppes— extended outward from the center cluster in spokes of shaded walkways. Logistically, it was a perfect place to meet someone you might want to abduct or kill, since there were ten different offshoots from the center island, thus making surveillance a nightmare.

The Hair of the Dog had a large outdoor seating area, where patrons sat drinking beer and watching one another or one of the fifteen flat-screen televisions running ESPN. A banner stretched across the front of the bar read SHOTS AND BEER. RED MEAT. THAT'S IT. Charming.

"Most dive bars don't open up with the intent of being a dive," I said. "I think that's the difference."

Sam picked up the binoculars from between us and trained them on something in the distance. "What I like about this place," he said, "is that it's not trying too hard. Tough guys like to go to a place with a lot of flat-screen televisions. Known fact."

"And the smell of freshly baked bread wafting over from Panera is probably nice, too," I said.

"Cuts down on that meth rank," Sam said. "What I don't get, Mikey, is how the girls on the patio don't all get chest colds."

"It's ninety degrees outside, Sam."

"Still," he said. "Whooping cough is going around. I should warn each of them personally."

"You looking at the girls, Sam, or do you have something else of interest on the other side of the binoculars?"

"Both," he said. "I think I've got our guy." He handed me the binoculars. "Look at two o'clock. Just to the right of the Apple Store. Down the second spoke. White shirt. Big floppy white hat."

I looked where Sam told me and saw a man wearing a white shirt and a big floppy white hat sitting on a bench . . . staring back at me through binoculars, too. "I think we're made," I said. I waved and White Shirt waved back.

"Think so?"

"You said he was an expert in game theory warfare," I said. "You weren't kidding."

"He probably thought the kid would bring cops," Sam said. "Statistically speaking, the odds favored him bringing someone, right?"

"Let's go tell him we're someone, then," I said. "Ease his mind."

We got out of my Charger and walked across the parking lot toward Big Lumpy, but he didn't bother to get up and meet us. Either he had guys getting ready to grab us and throw us into the back of a van or he was just rude.

My bet was that he didn't care much for etiquette. NSA guys tend to think the world revolves around them, perhaps because they tell themselves that every day at work as they issue warnings and edicts about national security. But it was always men like me who ended up doing the dirty work.

When we reached the Hair of the Dog, Big Lumpy finally got up from the bench and made his way over. Sandy blond hair poked out of the bottom of his white hat and I could see that although he'd graduated from college at a young age, the years hadn't been a friend to him—he had deep lines around his eyes and mouth and red splotches on his nose and cheeks. But as he got closer to me, I realized that those lines and splotches weren't the weight of time: He had skin cancer. Or was healing from it. For a guy who was supposedly the meanest, most violent man alive, he didn't look like much.

"You're early," Big Lumpy said as a way of introduction. "Where's the kid? A safe house in Phoenix or something?"

"Something," I said.

A hostess wearing a name tag that said SANDY! on it greeted us and asked us where we'd like to sit. Another new invention: a dive bar with a perky hostess. "Outside is fine," Big Lumpy said. "I already have cancer, after all. What's the worst that could happen?" When the hostess didn't respond, because she probably hadn't been prepped for that sort of response in her extensive job training, Big Lumpy turned to me and said, "Unless you two plan to have me shot. You don't plan to have me shot, do you?"

"Not in broad daylight," I said.

"Then I'll be sure we're out of here by sundown," he said.

Sandy! showed us to a table on the patio and explained that although the sign said shots and beers only, they did have a few wines to choose from and that a selection of artisan pizzas, as well as chicken sandwiches, was available for lunch alongside the regular menu of red meat. When Sandy! finally left us alone, Big Lumpy let out an exasperated grunt. "She's not right for this place," he said.

"She seems too happy," Sam said. "And not enough tattoos."

"I'm not as involved as I should be in the day-today operations, clearly," Big Lumpy said. "Her name tag is ridiculous. That will be addressed."

"You own this place?" I asked.

"Yes," he said. "And the land beneath your feet, too."

"The bookie business must be very lucrative," Sam said.

"Let's not be foolish," Big Lumpy said. "I wouldn't dare try to launder my illegal money in property. It's much easier to buy things with my legitimate earnings. That way no sneaky government agency will try to seize it on an ill-founded whim."

"I know something about that," I said.

A waiter came and dropped off waters then and Big Lumpy ordered a bucket of beer for the table to share, along with a dozen limes. Just three buddies having a Sunday afternoon man date at a faux dive bar. Maybe later, we'd go to a strip club and tell each other Chuck Norris jokes. As it was, we'd been sitting with one another for ten minutes and Big Lumpy still hadn't bothered to ask who we were, which troubled me. It meant either he wasn't concerned or he already knew. Or both.

"Now, then," Big Lumpy said, perfectly gracious. "Where's my money?"

"You're not getting any more money," I said.

"No?" he said.

"Not from Brent Grayson, no," I said. "Besides, what's fifteen thousand dollars to a man like you?"

"Same as it is to any businessman who has outstanding debts from his clients. I'm sure you can understand that."

"It's not his debt," I said.

"Do you really think the boy doesn't know where

his father is? He's been paying off his debts all over the city. You tell me how a college student has the capital to do that."

"You know of Yuri Drubich?" I asked.

Big Lumpy raised his eyebrows in actual surprise. As best as I could tell, it was his first uncalculated move of the day. He took off his white hat and set it down on the table. His blond hair was thin and nearly translucent and I noticed for the first time that he had only mere wisps for eyebrows. I thought he was either still in chemo or was only a month or so out of it.

"That's deep water," he said.

"Deeper than he can swim in, I assure you," I said.

"I read in the paper this morning that someone blew up Henry Grayson's office," he said. "That sounded a bit more extreme than the usual loan sharking and debt collection that goes on in this town."

"They used a laser-guided shoulder-mounted rocket launcher," Sam said.

"Really," Big Lumpy said. "Overkill, don't you think?"

"I dunno," Sam said. "I heard about a gentleman in town who cuts off people's eyelids when they don't pay their gambling losses."

Big Lumpy tried to hide a smile, but then just let go and began to laugh. He said, "Don't believe everything you hear." Our waiter brought us the bucket of beer, though Big Lumpy didn't take one. "Please, help yourselves," he said, and when Sam reached in and grabbed a Corona, he said, "Mr. Axe, don't be shy. Take two."

Sam did as he was told. Might as well. It wasn't like Big Lumpy didn't know who he was at that point.

"You don't drink?" I asked.

"No," he said. "I can't afford to lose any more brain cells."

"I heard you had a two hundred IQ," I said. "What's a brain cell when you're in the top one percent of the entirety of the human race?"

"I'm dying," he said matter-of-factly. "So the chemicals inside me and my disease have already taken me down to at least one ninety-eight. I'd like to keep the rest of my wits about me."

"Skin cancer?" I said.

"Yes, but that's just an unlucky occurrence," he said. "Let's just say my entire body has gone on strike and now my skin has finally gotten on board with the rest of the union."

"How long do you have?" I asked.

"Doctors say maybe a year," he said. "But they didn't know I was having lunch today with an assassin."

"Which one of us would that be?" I said.

"Don't be coy, Mr. Westen," he said. "You can call yourself a spy, but that's just a fancy name, isn't it? A spy is a part-time errand boy and a part-time killer. Pretending otherwise does a disservice to the fine psychopaths who've held your job since 1776."

Well, that solved that.

"So, no disrespect, Mr. Lumpy, but in light of your condition, why bother with Henry Grayson at all?" Sam said. "And his son—that seems like bad form, you ask me."

"Principle," he said. "Mr. Axe, if your SEAL unit got called tomorrow by the Joint Chiefs of Staff to go into some despotic foreign land to take out an evil dictator along with maybe an entire village of his supporters, as a Navy SEAL, wouldn't you agree to do that just on the mere principle of your position? On the principle of your team?"

"It's my job," Sam said. "I chose it. And I'm not dying."

"Precisely," Big Lumpy said. "And this is my job. And I chose it. And you are dying, Mr. Axe. You could walk out of this poor excuse for a bar and be run over by a bus, or you could go home and drown on the mojito you're sipping or I could have a sniper shoot you between the eyes right where you're sitting. Or, or, maybe you stub your toe and an embolism travels to your heart and kills you before you even realize you're sick."

Sam put down his beer, got up and changed seats so that he was sitting directly next to Big Lumpy instead of across from him. Harder to shoot a man when he's practically sitting in your boss' lap. I was still in the wide open but at least Sam was safe.

"You know what I just did?" Sam said.

"Made an impulsive decision?" Big Lumpy said.

"No," he said. "I improved my odds for survival."

"Clearly," Big Lumpy said, "you know nothing about odds. But really, as it relates to Mr. Grayson and his son, it just comes down to this: Don't make bets if you can't pay up. Simple as that. Henry Grayson was never very good at that idea. Always in trouble. Always one step ahead of some violent numbers man, never smart enough to move to Las Vegas and bet legally. That's the wonder of it all, really."

"You're not curious about how Yuri Drubich is involved in this?" I said.

"Oh, I am," he said. "I can't see Henry Grayson contacting him for anything. And I can't see Yuri Drubich ever needing a man like Henry. All I can think of is that Henry must have won the Bad Luck Lottery. Do they offer that one in Florida?"

"Not yet," I said.

"Do you know that Henry always bets the favorite? Are you aware of that?"

"No," I said.

"He's a mark, Mr. Westen," Big Lumpy said. "He takes bad beats because he never plays the underdog, never plays the numbers, always just goes with the favorites. It's stupid and how frat boys bet, not grown men. So I have to assume that somewhere along the line he made a bet with Yuri Drubich and lost."

"You're wrong," I said.

"I'm never wrong. I'm just not right yet." Big Lumpy took a sip of water and then reached across the table for a lime, squeezed it into the water and took another sip. "The water tastes septic," he said. "All of this treatment has destroyed my taste buds." He put his hat back on, leaned back in his chair and closed his eyes. "Now let me spend a moment on this, if you don't mind."

"Please," I said. "I can't wait to see how a man named Mark McGregor earns a name like Big Lumpy."

For the next five minutes, Big Lumpy sat nearly motionless save for the slow tapping of his fingers on both thighs. It was as if he was typing. He was, certainly, one of the most unusual men I'd ever met. The information Sam had on him was slim enough that we had only a vague idea of what we might be dealing with, which wasn't surprising. If he was ex-NSA (or, as Sam rightly noted, likely still working for them as a consultant, since very few great minds ever really leave the covert side of the government unless, of course, they get burned), he probably controlled his outward persona meticulously. Maybe he wasn't the violent psychopath. Maybe he just employed violent psychopaths. Maybe none of that was true.

What was becoming increasingly apparent to me was that there was a way I could get Big Lumpy to help Brent solve his problem with the Russians. I had a good sense that Big Lumpy would like the chance to tangle with someone like Yuri Drubich.

Finally, Big Lumpy opened his eyes and sat forward in his seat again.

"I thought we'd lost you," Sam said.

"It's hard to concentrate completely when you know that at any moment the person sitting next to you might be shot in the head," he said. "Are you ready, Mr. Westen, to know how Henry Grayson and his adorable son got involved with Yuri Drubich?"

"Impress me," I said.

"You're already impressed by me," he said.

"Then show me you're more than just a sideshow," I said.

"You know what I like about you, Mr. Westen? You're not scared of me."

"You're a dying man dressed like a piece of taffy," I said. "What's there to be scared of?"

A thin smile worked its way across Big Lumpy's face. "Fair enough." He began to arrange the items on the table into two distinct quadrants. There were three forks, three beers and three lime wedges in front of Big Lumpy and three napkins, three sugar packets and three glasses of water in front of me. "So, imagine this as a Revolutionary War killing field or, if it's easier, a chessboard. Your side of the board represents Henry Grayson. My side of the board represents Yuri Drubich. Now, in a chess game, it would be reasonable to assume that the more skilled and ruthless player would have a real advantage over someone who, say, has played only checkers before. We can agree on that?"

"We can," I said.

"And we can agree that in an actual war, the superior armed force usually wins, discounting, of course, every war fought in Afghanistan."

"We can," I said. I wasn't sure where this was going, but at least he had my attention.

Big Lumpy began moving the items on the table in rapid succession, his pieces quickly and efficiently destroying mine: He carved up my napkins with his fork, poured beer over my packets of sugar and squeezed his limes into my water. "A superior chess player, he'll have a rank novice in checkmate in three moves. In war, maybe it's a few more steps. But if you apply just a tiny bit of game theory, you can predict well within reason what your enemy will do. I kill your napkin, you decide to flood my army with your glass of water . . . but I've already poisoned your water, so you're most likely dead. It's all about understanding provocation and the reaction to provocation."

"Okay," I said. "So what's your conclusion?"

Big Lumpy shrugged. "In order for a man like Yuri Drubich to come after Henry Grayson and his son with rockets, they would have needed to provoke him in such a way that that was the only possible result, because it is so extreme, it is so public and stupid, that it would need to be the last message, not the first. If you blow up a building, you're asking for government involvement. You shoot the son of a degenerate gambler, the police will be interested, but not for long. Scum killing scum. It makes life easier for the police. So, it's impossible. Mathematically impossible, humanly impossible—there's no possible nexus where these parties would ever meet—and theoretically impossible. I can only conclude you've been lied to."

"So you think Brent Grayson happened across a rocket launcher and blew his own father's business up?" Sam said. "The kid doesn't even wake up before noon."

Big Lumpy turned to Sam and patted him once on the shoulder. "You don't think your friend Fiona could get him a fairly good-sized rocket launcher? If she could get one, any serious black market arms dealer could get him one, too."

Logical enough. But I had an idea.

"You're a smart man," I said.

"I know," he said. "So where's my money?"

"You're a smart man," I said. "Wouldn't it stand to reason that a person like me wouldn't be helping a college kid? What gain do I have?"

"Michael," he said, "you'd help Idi Amin get his cat

down from a tree if you found out he had a bad child-hood."

"And if I haven't been lied to? What will you do for me if I can prove that it's all true? That all of your min-ions have been taking Yuri Drubich's money, which means when Brent can't pay, Drubich's eventually go-ing to come find you?"

Big Lumpy closed his eyes again. "Let me think," he said.

"How long are you going into your trance?" Sam said. "In case I need to visit the little boys' room. Or fly across the country."

Big Lumpy ignored Sam. "Shall we put odds on it?" he asked after about thirty seconds, his eyes still closed.

"No, straight up. I convince you of the truth, you stay away from Brent Grayson and you call off your stray collection dogs, too."

"His father is not in this equation," Big Lumpy said. "He came by his debts honestly."

"Fine," I said.

"And if I'm not convinced, what then?"

"You're at war with me," I said.

"Hmm, yes, I figured. You're not a difficult army to theorize against. So convince me, Michael Westen, that your client has somehow engaged Yuri Drubich."

I told him the story, even had Sam pull out a Black-Berry and show him the Web site for InterMacron.

When I finished, Big Lumpy sat quietly for a solid minute. Then he reached across the table and plucked one of the beers from the bucket, popped the cap and took a long drink. "So if I'm to understand," he said, "a college boy conned one of the biggest black market import/export men in all of Russia?"

"That's right," I said.

"This technology, what did you call it?"

"Kineoptic Transference."

"Nice name," he said.

"I thought so, too," I said.

He took another sip from the beer. "I never liked the way this tasted."

"Beer?" Sam said.

"Failure," Big Lumpy said and I knew I had him. "Do you know why Drubich so willingly put his money on the table for this? Other than greed, of course."

"I feel like you're about to tell me," I said.

"Because we've been trying to develop this technology for over twenty years. It's the next level, except no one can even find a stepladder to get there. It's all theoretical."

"When you say 'we,'" Sam said, "who are you talking about exactly?"

"The government," Big Lumpy said. "Any sort of alphabet agency that employs scientists. I wouldn't be surprised if there's a team on the Arctic Circle at this very moment trying to figure out new equations."

"I looked it up online," Sam said, "and there was nothing. Nothing but Brent's Web site, anyway."

"That's correct," he said. "That it's not been scrubbed already just means that there's a Democrat in office, that's all. A couple of years ago, Brent Grayson would be in a prison underneath a mountain, getting waterboarded for information. I promise you that."

Big Lumpy was excited. We hadn't appealed to his

good side, we'd appealed to the scientist and the gambler. It wasn't my initial plan, but now I had to set the hook.

"Clearly," I said, "there's much more money to be made from Drubich if someone happens to be enterprising enough to string him along further. Maybe a scientist smart enough to provide actual specs. Far more than fifteen thousand bucks, anyway."

"It's a big gamble," he said. "It would take me a great deal of time to come up with a convincing schematic to deliver. And what can I expect my return would be?"

"He's already paid Brent close to $150K and that's just based on what he saw on the Web site," Sam said. "You show up in a fancy suit holding your diploma from MIT in your hand and then talk in big words, you'd probably get ten times that much money."

"It would still be a challenge," he said. "He already suspects he's been duped."

"Isn't that what you want?" I said. "Isn't that what this is all about for you? This whole charade of being the most evil bookie in town? Isn't it all about intellectual challenges? Now more than ever?"

"Don't play the dying card," Big Lumpy said.

"You played it first," I said.

Big Lumpy stood up and waved his hand once above his head. A few seconds later, a white Cadillac Escalade pulled up in front of the Hair of the Dog and idled there. "I must be going," Big Lumpy said. "It was a pleasure getting to know the two most dangerous men in Miami."

"What's with all the white?" Sam asked.

"Makes me look mysterious," Big Lumpy said. "It's good for the public relations. No one expects a terrible person to always be wearing white, now do they?"

"I guess not," Sam said.

"So," I said, "do we have a deal?"

Big Lumpy stared intently at me for a few moments, as if he was trying to determine what the result might be if he reneged on our bet. He sighed once and then put out his hand to shake. His grip was light, his skin thin and feathery. "I'll need backup," he said.

"You'll have it," I said.

"And I'll need Henry Grayson," he said. "He owes."

"We're working on it," I said. "You'll have to trust me."

"I do," he said. "I'll be in touch tomorrow."

Big Lumpy walked to the Escalade and his driver— a tiny Asian man also wearing all white, including a white baseball cap and white shoes—met him on the passenger side with a portable oxygen unit, which Big Lumpy immediately hooked himself up to before getting into the SUV. He didn't close the door, he just sat there in the passenger seat inhaling. After a few minutes, he pulled his mask off and motioned for us to come over.

"Aren't you going to ask me how I knew you'd be here?" he said.

"It hadn't occurred to me," I said.

"Of course not," he said. "You're an American spy. Well, you can thank your friend Sugar."

"He bets with you, too?" Sam asked.

"No," Big Lumpy said. "I had him kidnapped last

night. I'll keep him until you deliver Henry Grayson, if you don't mind." He closed his door then and the Escalade drove off, leaving Sam and me just as he'd hoped: dumbfounded.

"Well," Sam said eventually, "that was a surprise."

"I take it you didn't leave Sugar in a safe location?" I said.

"I just took him home," Sam said. "You didn't want him in your house, did you?"

"No," I said.

"So it looks like we're in business with Big Lumpy," Sam said.

"Strange," I said.

"You believe a word he said?"

"Hard not to," I said.

"Me, too," Sam said. "Say what you want about him, but that psychopath plays it straight."

"I think he just took the right odds with us," I said, "just as we'd done with him."

"What are we going to do about Sugar?"

"Find Henry Grayson, I suppose," I said.

"You're just going to hand him over to Big Lumpy?" Sam said. "That doesn't sound like a wise plan."

"No," I said. "But if his debt is honest, which I suspect it is, then he should pay it. I just don't think he should pay with his life."

My cell rang. It was Fiona. "Where are you?" I asked.

"I just had tea with Yuri Drubich," she said. "Lovely man."

"Tea? Is that a euphemism for kneecapping him?"

"Michael," she said, "I'm not a savage. We had a nice conversation and came to some very strong conclusions about Brent's future."

"Really?" I said.

"Yes," she said. "He intends to end any possibility of it."

"Tell me some good news," I said.

"I was able to convince them to go into business with us," she said.

"That's ironic," I said, "since we just got Big Lumpy on the team, too."

"And I can assure you Yuri will keep at least one of his hands clean," she said and then went on to tell me about her pleasant cup of tea.

7

Fiona tried not to give too much thought to her transformation from top-notch criminal to top-notch-criminal-who-now-helped-the-poor-and-less-fortunate. It certainly wasn't something she could have predicted; nor was it something she'd always wanted to do, as her normal inclination was to shoot first and ask probing questions later, if at all. But being involved with Michael had secondary issues alongside the normal relationship stuff. He just didn't like to leave a trail of bodies in his wake anymore and Fiona had to respect that. At least a little. Most of the time. Half of the time. Some of the time, anyway.

So when Michael told her to go look into Yuri Drubich's local operation, she knew that she couldn't very well go in and execute every last person she encountered, as appealing as that sounded. Michael wanted information, and information meant talking. She'd do her best and if things turned bad, she'd see about hurting only those who deserved it the most, which, in these cases, was usually most of them.

But when Fiona pulled up in front of a cache of 1920s-era bungalows that had been converted into hip

Coral Gables office space and cute shops with names like Peas and Pods, apparently some kind of maternity clothing store, and Re-Treats, which offered "All of the candies you loved as a kid," she knew she could probably leave her gun in the car. She'd keep one in her purse, but that was just for normal safety. And really, since the address for Yuri Drubich's import/export company corresponded to a lovely Russian tearoom called Odessa, Fiona had the sense that she'd need to play this investigation just a tad differently than most. Alas, she thought, she probably wouldn't get to make anyone bleed today. But like that movie said, tomorrow is another day. . . .

And anyway, Fiona didn't actually see any nefarious-looking men mingling about the tea shop, only women with babies in strollers, and then one waitress who looked like she was one bad Sylvia Plath poem away from ending it all. Fiona never understood women who wore horn-rimmed glasses and clogs. It was as if they just decided to extinguish sex from their lives forever. Fiona thought that at worst, she'd end up with a nice cup of tea and at best, maybe the girl in the glasses could provide her with at least a tiny bit of information.

Once she was inside, Fiona saw that the tearoom occupied a bungalow that hadn't been renovated as much as the other shops had—the kitchen was still being used as the kitchen, but walls had been moved, clearly, and what must have been the living room now housed a small shop and a few tables. Charming, really. Most of the sitting area was out front on a sun-dappled patio that wrapped around to the bungalow's original side yard. The shop and the indoor part of the sitting area smelled like cinnamon and jasmine and, low in the background, music played. It was a female singer doing a number about being sad and lonely (or at least that's what Fiona surmised—she couldn't actually hear all of the lyrics, apart from the constant refrain of "I'm sad and lonely"). None of it felt very Russian at all. Rather, it was more like a Starbucks that had been denuded of all corporate pretension and coffee.

Fiona spent a few minutes looking at the various knickknacks—mostly different devices for storing or making tea, a field of retail that she assumed was small but apparently infinite. There were also small pieces of art—pictures on tiny easels, tea bags photographed in black and white and then matted, paintings of teacups in open fields, that sort of thing—that Fiona assumed were purchased only by people who had run out of space for cats in their home.

"Can I help you?"

Fiona turned around to find the smiling face of the Sylvia Plath girl. Surprisingly, she detected just a hint of a Russian accent. Interesting. And helpful.

"Yes. Yes, you can," Fiona said. She decided to try on one of those plain American accents she always heard inside Target when she went to buy dish soap. An accent that conveyed just enough education to be presumptuous and just enough lack of worldliness to still hold Russians in real suspicion. Or, in other words, your average government worker. "Is Mr. Drubich here?"

"No," Sylvia Plath said, her accent thicker now, her demeanor immediately defensive. Maybe she wasn't a

Sylvia Plath kind. Maybe she was more of a Natasha Fatale in a bad dress. But Natasha would never wear those glasses. Russian women always did have a certain brio about them.

"When do you expect him back?" Fiona asked.

"He doesn't work here," Sylvia Plath said.

"But you're aware he owns this establishment, correct?"

"Who am I speaking to?" Sylvia Plath asked. Her accent was so pronounced now that Fiona was actually surprised by it. This woman wasn't exactly keeping deep cover. Or else she was just your average waitress who didn't want to scare off the ladies who drink tea by sounding like the enemies they remember from childhood.

Fiona reached into her purse and took out a pen and a small pad that she usually used to write down ideas for different explosives that came to mind when she was out shopping or driving in traffic. She flipped to the middle of the notebook. "What's *your* name?" Fiona asked.

"Am I under arrest for something?"

"I don't know," Fiona said. "Have you done something wrong?"

"I asked you who you were first," Sylvia Plath said.

"This isn't two kids in a sandbox, young lady," Fiona said, and then she realized that the voice she was channeling was actually Sam's and that got her very frightened. How had it happened that a man she used to hate was now her go-to dumb American voice? Well, thank God for small linguistic favors. "Those rules of decorum don't apply, unless you steal my shovel."

Sylvia Plath glared at Fiona. Odd, Fiona thought. Why isn't this woman frightened? Her defiance told Fiona that either Sylvia Plath had been prepared for this moment or she wasn't taking Fiona seriously. Maybe it was the pumps Fiona had chosen to wear. They didn't exactly scream government worker, but even going undercover required a strict adherence to fashion trends. Plus, Fiona knew she could whip off her shoe and stab someone with its heel in one swift move. She'd done it once before to . . . who was it? She'd beaten up so many people in the last few years, it all tended to blur.

A group of women walked into the shop then and Sylvia Plath greeted them warmly, her glare dissipating immediately. Must be regulars. And truth be known, Fiona rather liked the tea selection here and, under different circumstances, could see herself popping in every now and then. Getting a decent cup of tea anywhere in Miami was impossible. She could live without the constant strain of female singer-songwriters complaining over twangy guitars about how their man did them wrong, but, well, if she were one of these ladies with babies having afternoon tea, perhaps she'd feel differently.

"If you could wait just one moment," Sylvia Plath said. Or, really, she rather hissed her words. "I'll be right back."

"Take your time," Fiona said. Fiona circled the shop and began really looking at the items for sale, picking them up and examining them, and each time she came away with another tidbit of information. A set of bone-white teacups from India. An electric teakettle from Dubai. An assortment of herbal teas from Pakistan.

Nothing, it seemed, was from America. It helps to have plenty of shipments from countries like Pakistan to ease fears that you're bringing in, say, guns or drugs. Bring in ten boats every year filled with herbal teas and people might just begin to think you're nonthreatening and not examine your load too closely.

Sylvia Plath returned to the shop holding a teakettle in one hand and a tray of plates in the other. Fiona thought that it must have been quite a cumbersome task carrying all of that while also fostering the burden of guilt for . . . well, whatever. She'd probably done something, right?

"Pardon me," Sylvia said, "I just need to set this down and then we can talk."

"No problem," Fiona said.

And then Sylvia Plath smacked Fiona upside the back of her head with the teakettle; Fiona's only thought before she slipped into blackness was that she was pretty sure the girl didn't actually read poetry.

When Fiona came to—it couldn't have been more than just a few minutes, since the same singer-songwriter woman was still going on about rainbows and her man over the speaker system—she was sitting on a folding chair somewhere in the back of the house. It looked to Fiona like a break room perhaps—a small table, three chairs, the wall decorated with papers detailing side work and the employee schedule for the next week.

Fiona wasn't tied up and there was a glass of water and a Ziploc bag filled with ice on the table in front of her. Fi took the bag and placed it against the back of her head, which throbbed with her pulse. She reached back, touched her scalp, felt the raspberry that was bulging through her hair and also a good-sized cut that slowly leaked blood, and determined that someone today was going to get some payback. It was just that simple.

Her neck was also sore and her right ankle looked a bit swollen. You get hit in the back of the head with a teakettle, it's expected you'll be feeling a touch out of it. Mostly, Fiona was angry that she'd been knocked out by a woman wearing a peasant dress and horn-rimmed glasses. Element of surprise, that's all.

She stood up and tried the door but found it, un-surprisingly, locked. She could pick it in an instant, but then she'd likely walk into the path of men with guns. . . . Speaking of guns . . . Fi's purse was nowhere to be found, which wasn't good.

It was unlikely that someone would come in and shoot her in the face considering she was still in the tearoom, so she sat back down, took a sip of water, pressed the ice pack to her head and waited patiently for whatever was to come.

She didn't have to wait long. The door opened and a man of about fifty walked in, followed by Sylvia Plath. The man sat down across from Fiona while Sylvia set out two cups, a plate of cookies and two small metal kettles along with an assortment of teas.

"Thank you, Gina," the man said.

"Shall I stay?" she asked.

"No, if there is a problem, I think I can take care of it," he said.

"Very well," she said. She looked at Fiona and shook her head slightly. "I'm sorry I had to hit you. You left me no choice."

Gina. Her name was Gina! She didn't look like a Gina to Fiona. She looked more like someone who, at some point later in life, would have her throat in Fiona's hands. That thought made Fiona very happy, so much so that when the girl left Fiona and the man alone, Fiona actually felt rather giddy.

"You smile," the man said. "This is a fun day?" His accent was off-the-boat thick, but everything else about him looked Western. He wore a white dress shirt opened at the collar, a tan sport coat, expensive jeans, black leather loafers, a Rolex.

"I'm having a lovely day," Fiona said. "No reason not to smile."

"Do you know me?" the man asked.

"Yuri Drubich, I presume," she said.

"You are correct," he said. "We have some business together?"

"Not yet," Fiona said.

Yuri picked through the teas, found one he liked and then dropped it into his kettle to steep. "Please," he said, "I bring in very fine tea."

Fiona found a bag of Adam's Peak White Tea in the box, which was really quite a find, placed the tea in her cup and poured the hot water over it. It wasn't the best way to make a cup of expensive tea, but it was a decent enough weapon in a pinch.

"Your employee hit me," Fiona said. "Is that how you treat all of your customers?"

"Only those who come in asking about me," Yuri

said. "Do you know how many people know that I own this shop?"

"Why don't you just tell me? That way we can get to drinking our tea in peace."

Yuri reached across the table for a cookie and then handed the plate to Fiona. It held an assortment of butter cookies, some covered in chocolate, others in fruit compote, others plain. Fiona opted for the chocolate and then watched while Yuri thoughtfully nibbled on his cookie. He didn't seem terribly happy or terribly upset at the moment. It was a studied ambivalence.

"Yes, well," Yuri said, "let me say this—they are all either dead or FBI. Which are you?"

"I'm from Ireland," Fiona said, "so I can't be FBI. And here I sit, drinking tea, so I must be alive."

"Before, you spoke with an American accent. Yes?"

"That was before."

"And who were you then?"

"I don't quite know," Fiona said. "Being hit in the head has left a blank space. Do you hit all FBI agents in the back of the head?"

"If you'd been FBI," he said, "you'd not be sitting here with me. Plus your car, that Hyundai? No FBI drives Japanese."

"Maybe it's my car from home. I really can't remember now. Amnesia from being struck."

"Hmm, yes, that can happen. But you do remember that whoever you were, you carried a Sig Sauer, yes?"

"I do remember that, yes."

"And you carry no identification?"

"I like to keep it simple," Fiona said. "Just a gun and a hairbrush. Maybe a touch of lipstick and some powder, but otherwise I'm a very simple girl, Yuri." She didn't just say his name. She purred it. Fiona found that men of all stripes responded to hearing their names purred. It opened up some atavistic response that turned them into fourteen-year-olds.

"I'm sorry," Yuri said. "You must think I am an idiot. I find you, how do you say, *alluring,* but I don't like my women bloody. And I don't like them spying on me." He paused. Fiona presumed he wanted to let that sink in, which it did, and then he said, "How is your tea?"

"Lovely," Fiona said. Because it was.

"You have a choice now," he said. "You tell me who you are and why you're here and we finish our tea pleasantly or I bring Gina back in to remove your fingernails."

"You think she'd be able to do that?" Thinking, *Yeah, please send her in. I'd like another shot at her.*

"She'd have someone hold you down, so, yes," he said. "I've seen her do it before. She is very meticulous. Never moves too quickly."

"And if I tell you who I am and you don't like it, then what?"

"Then we just kill you," he said. "No torture. You look like you have good, healthy organs. Fetch a good price on the market. Your hair, too."

He reached across the table as if to touch her hair, but Fiona grabbed his wrist and bent it backward. Hard. Not hard enough to break it, but that was just a matter of degree. When he tried to grab at her other hand, she grabbed that one, too. "You don't want to touch me," she said. No purring. Just a simple declarative sentence.

"You think you can hurt me?"

"I can break your wrists to start with," she said. "Compound fractures tend to cause shock. If I sever an artery, well, that will be messy. But you wouldn't really feel it."

"You wouldn't get out of the building alive," he said.

"And neither would you," she said. She applied a bit more pressure and Yuri began to sweat, feeling the pain.

"We are at an impasse," he said, his voice strained now.

"Then let me explain my position," Fiona said. She had to think fast, since the truth was that she had not expected to be in this position. Michael would understand. "Yesterday, you blew up a building we use as a front for our corporation, InterMacron. You are familiar with it?"

"There is no such thing," he said. "It is a scam. Some dumb boy. I want my money and he will bring it to me."

"Really?" she said. "Some dumb boy? Then what am I, a figment of your imagination?"

Yuri was in obvious pain, but Fiona noticed that his expression had changed slightly. Clearly, she was not some dumb boy. "I am listening," he said.

"We use several people to ferret out serious investors." Fiona thought for a moment about her situation and decided to go forward with what she figured were both knowns and unknowns, just to see how Yuri might respond. "The Graysons are one level. Our associate Big Lumpy is another," she said. He knew well enough who the players were in Miami, certainly, and that hearing Big Lumpy's name didn't cause him to giggle at its stupidity was a sign itself. "What we are doing with the wind technology and bandwidth, it is not, strictly speaking, legal yet."

Yuri's expression changed again. Now he seemed actually invested. Well, invested and in terrible pain. "Go on," he said.

"The technology, we have acquired it before the government," she said. "They call it a national security threat. So if you invest in it, if you agree to sell it for us outside our borders, we must know it will not fall into hands that might have problems with the United States."

"That is everyone," Yuri said. "And what do you care? You are Irish?"

"I love America," Fiona said. "Much better weather here."

"Where is my money? Where did that go?"

"The boy's father," she said, searching now, opting for truth over more fantasy. "He's a gambler. He ran off with the money. So the boy and his father, they are under our, you could say, *watch* now."

"And Big Lumpy?"

"He helps with our investments," Fiona said.

"Your organization," Yuri said, "what is your role?"

"I break wrists," Fiona said, "and solve problems. Hitting people with teakettles is amateur."

Yuri liked that answer. Fiona actually felt his arms

relax a bit. It was smart for him to do that, since she was certain the circulation to his hands was pretty well staunched by now and being tense only exacerbated the situation.

"We have parties who have already expressed a financial interest in your company's product," Yuri said. "Your boy has caused me much stress with his lies. And I now am facing outside pressure to provide a product."

Michael had correctly assumed Yuri's problem. That was too bad. Fiona was hoping it was a new twist that she could impress him with. "My partners will need to know who you are selling to," Fiona said. "Russians, we don't mind. Your government is probably working on this, too. But we are capitalists like you, Yuri, and we believe in a free market, within reason."

"A friend of mine from Dubai has made an inquiry," he said.

"Does he live there or is he hiding there?"

"I don't ask," he said. Fiona applied some pressure. "He lives normally in Chad. Much wind there."

Chad. The most corrupt country on the planet. At least Yuri was well connected.

"I will need to speak to my partners," Fiona said. "But the cost will be far more than what you've paid. That was you being conned. You will need to add several zeros to your checks."

"We make deal," he said, seemingly unaffected by the change in cost. "We make another deal."

Fiona had known this was coming. "You want the boy or the man?"

"Both," Yuri said. "I answer to people, too."

"Fair enough," Fiona said. She let go of his right wrist—it seemed prudent since that hand was turning an odd shade of purple—but kept a firm grasp on his left. "I'm happy to go now, so please call to your friend Gina and let her know I'll be leaving."

Yuri called out in Russian and the door was unlocked and opened by Gina. He said something to her in Russian that might have meant "she's free to go" or it might have meant "feed her to the dogs," so Fiona said, "In English, so I know that I don't have to kill anyone."

"I told her to get your purse and let you go," Yuri said. "You don't mind, I'll hold your gun for now. You have others, yes?"

"Yes," Fiona said, though she did like the Sig. But she understood. An armed person might act inappropriately after being hit in the head with a teakettle and threatened with torture.

Gina left and came back a few seconds later with Fiona's purse and set it on the table. "I hope you don't mind," Gina said, "but I borrowed your lipstick. I liked the shade and didn't think you'd be needing it." Gina smacked her lips together. "My apologies."

"No problem," Fiona said. "I'll see myself out." She bolted up from her seat and cleanly snapped Yuri's left wrist before Gina could even react. Not a compound fracture, but he'd need a cast. She dropped his arm, grabbed both teakettles and smacked Gina on either side of her head, aiming for the ears but content to make contact anywhere. If she hit her ears, Gina would be dizzy for a month.

Judging by the way Gina fell into a heap on the

floor, and judging from the blood seeping from her ears, Fiona was pretty confident she'd found her target.

Yuri was curled on the ground and moaning in Russian. His hand was pointed in the wrong direction, which seemed to cause him some consternation, so Fiona picked up the bag of ice she'd been using and dropped it beside him on the floor.

"The ice will help the swelling," Fiona said. "But you should really get yourself to the hospital. And drink more milk, too. Your bones are very brittle. I'll see myself out, but expect to get a call from us tomorrow concerning our agreement."

Yuri groaned something unintelligible. Pain. So many people handled it poorly.

"If we still have a deal," Fiona said, "moan three times with your eyes open."

Yuri moaned three times and managed to keep his eyes open the whole time.

"No need to shake on it, then," Fiona said.

8

Every spy knows that tactical success one day may mean tactical failure the next. Assuming your enemy hasn't learned as much from his losses as you have from your victories would be a fatal mistake.

Likewise, brawn may beat brains once, but eventually an intellectually superior enemy will prevail, which is why we needed to be both strong and smart when dealing with Big Lumpy and Yuri Drubich if we wanted to keep Henry Grayson alive, wherever he might be. And then there was the issue of keeping Sugar alive, too, a proposition I hadn't counted on.

The first key was to find Henry, which is why that afternoon, after Fiona told me of her wrist-breaking-ear-clubbing high tea, I had her pick up Brent so that he could meet Sam and me at his father's house. We needed some idea, some path, to where Henry might be hiding. I had a good idea that he was nearby, maybe even tracking his son, as I simply could not believe, even with the two million dollars in life insurance money, that he would let Brent do battle with his demons. Never mind that Henry hadn't bothered to pay Brent's tuition.

The Grayson family home was in Miami Shores Village, an outcropping of suburbia bordered by Biscayne Boulevard and I-95 that nevertheless managed to look like small-town America. Less than fifteen thousand people called Miami Shores home and it seemed as though there was a church, a park and a café for each of them. The village was only twenty minutes from both downtown Miami and Fort Lauderdale, but seemed much closer to Pleasantville.

The house itself was a one-story ranch-style home on Ninety-ninth Street. Judging by the concrete-block stucco design, it had been built in the late 1940s or early 1950s, which was when Miami Shores was first developed. It was repainted recently, so in the sunlight it gleamed a brilliant white. That and the new slate on the roof indicated to me that Henry Grayson had kept the house in good order up to some recent point. The overgrown grass and shrubs told another story.

We parked across the street and walked to the house. Fiona and Brent waited for us on the front porch and I could already tell, just from Fiona's posture, that she was not in the best mood. Maybe having her pick up the kid was a mistake after her experience with Yuri Drubich.

"Nice neighborhood," Sam said. "Except for that high-pitched squealing sound. Do you hear that?"

"They call those birds," I said.

"Annoying," he said. "And it smells funny out here, too."

"That's called fresh air," I said. "That sweet scent is what's known as flowers."

"For my money, Mikey, I prefer air with a bit more bite to it."

I looked down the block and noticed that two rather conspicuous-looking SUVs were now parked on either side of the street. Since no harried parents came tumbling out of them, followed by sugar-filled children, I had the sense that maybe they weren't locals. Well, that and the tinted front windows, which don't have much of a functional purpose for people not in the violence or protection business.

"Looks like we have company," I said.

"Not exactly trying to hide," Sam said. "Maybe more of Big Lumpy's people?"

"Maybe," I said. "Let's see." I stopped in the middle of the street and waved at both cars.

"Michael," Fiona called from the porch, "what are you doing?"

"There are some bad guys parked down the street," I said. "I'm letting them know that I see them and wish them well."

Fiona stomped across the front lawn and into the street, saw where I was looking and then mumbled something under her breath and began rummaging in her purse. She mumbled something again, this time with a bit more vehemence, so I said, "What was that?"

Fiona looked up and her expression was . . . well, she seemed a touch on the angry side. Her face was a handsome shade of red. "I said, 'We should just shoot them.' Maybe you've heard me say that before?"

"We're in the middle of a residential street, Fiona."

"Maybe you haven't noticed, Michael, but I have an open wound on my head."

"I noticed."

"And I turned my ankle—did you see that?"

I looked down. She was wearing, as usual, a nice pair of heels. "It does look a bit swollen."

"While you and Sam were having beers with an evil scientist, I was in a fight for my life. So you'll excuse me for not having much patience," she said.

"Fi," Sam said, "maybe you should just wait in the house. Let the physically fit handle this."

"Where are you going to be, then, Sam?" Fi said and she headed off down the street.

"Uh, Fi," I said.

"I'm in no mood for this," Fiona shouted. She reached into her purse and pulled out a gun, not her Sig, I noticed, and then remembered what she'd told me. Nice that she already had a replacement. I didn't anticipate her pulling another gun from her purse, too. She had both of her arms outstretched as she walked, which made for a rather striking image.

"You want me to run after her?" Sam asked.

"No," I said. "She might kill you."

"Is everything all right?" Brent asked. He'd moved to the middle of his lawn but couldn't see the action.

"It sure is," I said. "Just stay where you are."

Fiona stood directly in between both SUVs, but was far enough away that I couldn't hear her voice. By the way she waved her guns, however, I had the impression that she was stating her points emphatically. After another thirty seconds of this, both SUVs pulled away at a normal rate of speed. Even used their blinkers at the corner.

Fiona stuffed both of her guns back into her purse and walked back toward the house.

"What was that?" I asked.

"Some gentlemen who believe Henry Grayson owes them money," she said.

"Bookies?"

"Loan sharks," she said.

Not good. "What did you tell them?" I said.

"To get in line."

"How much is he on the hook for?" Sam asked.

"They didn't say," Fiona said, "but enough that the kind gentlemen apparently have spotters somewhere on the street to let them know when someone shows up unannounced."

"Great," I said.

"But I convinced them to leave the house alone," she said.

"Permanently?" Sam asked.

"I told them I worked for Yuri Drubich," she said, "and that if they valued their lives and the lives of their children they'd consider the debt a loss on this year's earnings. Now, can we get on this? I have a late-evening appointment at a day spa to get rid of the ugly gash I have in my head. I'd like not to miss it."

Fi brushed past us then, grabbed the house keys from Brent's hands as he stood patiently on the porch and calmly let herself into the house.

"She seem a little agitated?" Sam asked.

If you want to get to know someone, look at their bookshelves. If they have row after row of self-help books, you can assume with absolute clarity that they are insane, since clearly if self-help worked, they wouldn't need dozens of books on the topic. If they have books primarily suggested by Glenn Beck, you can be fairly certain that if they're not home it's because they're busy looking for the black helicopters or checking on the birth records of every elected government official and thus won't be back to bother you anytime soon. If they don't have bookshelves, that's a sign, too. Never trust someone who doesn't read.

In Henry Grayson's case, the bookshelves in his home office were filled with two kinds of books: ones on betting strategy—this included a fascinating work called *Killing the Book*, which, the cover blurb said, was written by "an ex–Mafia bookie" who "knew where the numbers and bodies were buried"—and then books on how to disappear.

The first books were easy enough to understand—he was a compulsive gambler who must have always been looking to end the losses. The second books, of course, spoke to his current predicament and they weren't the kinds of books one generally found on the shelves at Barnes & Noble: *Hiding from the Government: A Guide to Living Off the Grid*; *Faking Your Death for Profit*; *The Minutemen Survival Handbook* and about fifty others of a similar ilk. None of these books were actual bound books; rather, they were bulky photocopied messes held together with paper clips or velo binding or gold brads.

Henry Grayson had spent a good deal of time scouring the dark corners of the Internet for source materials, which I admired—at least he wanted to get educated before he flew off—but the majority of books like these were written by crazy people for crazier people. The keys to disappearing were (1) don't leave evidence sitting around and (2) stop creating new evidence—two things Henry Grayson had notably not done.

His office was decorated in modern-day-man-cave-meets-aging-geek: built-in bookshelves, two flat-screen plasma televisions (which went well with the plasmas in the living room, kitchen, master bedroom, guest room and the one in the garage, which seemed an odd place to keep an expensive television), a small desk decorated with old *Star Wars* action figures (including at least half a dozen different Boba Fetts), framed comic books and photos of Henry's deceased wife and of Brent.

It was also surprisingly clean compared to the rest of the house, which was bachelor-dirty: old sports magazines on every available surface, dust bunnies under all of the furniture (which Brent assured me were there long before his father disappeared) and DVDs scattered throughout.

The desk itself, with its carefully laid-out calendar in the center, the action figures along the rim, and the phone placed at a perfect diagonal to everything else, made me think of a catalog. There was a stack of papers inside a wicker mail organizer that by themselves weren't noteworthy—a flyer for a notary conference next January in Palm Desert, California, the receipt for a small donation to hurricane relief in Haiti and a Post-it reminding him to pay Brent's tuition and housing bills—but together they painted an odd picture. Why keep those things?

There was something off about the office but I couldn't exactly place what it was. The books might have given me an initial clue as to who he was, but the rest of the office told me something different. A *Star Wars*–obsessed notary who kept only one room in his entire home clean? And who needs two plasma TVs in one small room?

I went back to the bookcase and examined his reading again, my eyes landing on a book called *Building Bunkers, Safe Houses and Underground Domestic Dwellings* by a writer calling himself "John Q. Keep Me Out of the Public." Cute. I pulled it out and flipped through the pages once, stopping to ponder the entirely inaccurate information about planting trip wires before I headed to the living room.

Fiona and Brent sat on the sofa going through stacks of old bills and bank statements. Sam was in the kitchen tinkering with a desktop computer that looked to be at least fifteen years old, which made it the perfect age for Sam's computer skills.

"Would you like some light reading?" I said to Fiona. I handed her the book but she just set it on the coffee table. She'd calmed down some. Or at least enough to patiently go through stacks of unopened mail Brent had found in his father's bedroom, in the trash can and overflowing out of the mailbox.

"Sorry," she said. "I'm engrossed in the correspondence from the homeowners' association." She showed me a stack of yellow papers, all of which bore the telltale sign of an angry group of residents: a propensity to overuse capital letters.

"What seems to be the problem?"

"Uncut grass," she said. "One letter says that every blade of grass over three inches in height is subject to a fine. Really, Michael, who chooses to live among these people? Why not just move into a gulag?"

"Anything we can use?" I asked Fiona.

"He let his beer-of-the-month-club membership slide," she said quietly and then tilted her head in Brent's direction. He was looking at an invoice with more attention than I'd been aware he could muster.

"It was a gift from my mother," Brent said. He handed me the invoice. His membership had lapsed three months ago. "He always made sure it was paid. Always. Each month, it came with a greeting card from my mother, or not my mother, but my mother's name. It was a gift. He didn't even drink that much."

"It's okay," I said. "I'm sure if he pays his bill, they'll start it back up."

"That's not the point, Michael," Fiona said. I knew she was right, but I was just hoping to reel things in, if possible. I'd forgotten, again, that I was essentially dealing with a child.

I handed the invoice back to Brent. "It's silly, really," Brent said. "It's not like they got along when she was alive."

"It's hard to tell with parents," I said. "I thought my mom and dad hated each other, and, maybe after a while, they did. But what I think of as the worst years of my life, my mother tends to remember differently. Maybe it's the same with your father, Brent."

"He once told me that he gambled because it was the closest thing to feeling normal that he had," Brent said. "Does that make any sense?"

I told him it did. One thing I'd learned all of these years, and why I've struggled so long to get my name back and clear my burn notice, was that I never felt more like who I was supposed to be than when I was a spy. It was the most natural state of calm and being I'd ever possessed. And then one day it was gone. Helping people like Brent salved the wound some, but nothing was the same.

Sam came into the living room and plopped down in a caramel-colored recliner that was positioned about four feet from one of the ubiquitous flat-screen televisions. He attempted to turn on the television using one of the four remotes that were tucked in the recliner's pocket, but none of them worked.

"Life was easier when there were only thirteen channels," Sam said. "I'm telling you, if Reagan were still in office, there would be one remote control in every house and it would operate every television in the universe."

"I'm guessing you didn't find anything," I said.

"He had software on that computer from the nineties," Sam said. "And judging from the amount of music he downloaded from Napster in 1999, I'm going to say he's lucky he didn't get thrown into record-industry prison."

"That was my mom's computer," Brent said. "He didn't want to change anything on it."

"Your mom," I said, "how did she die?"

"Car accident," Brent said. "Dad fell asleep at the wheel. They were driving home from the Keys. They'd gone down there for their anniversary and left me with my nana." The way Brent recited the information was robotic. He'd given the answer so many times in his life that it was now just a series of simple, declarative facts. He'd boiled down the worst part of his life into three mundane sentences.

"Jesus," Fiona said. "How old were you?"

"Nine," Brent said.

The problem in dealing with teenagers is that they sometimes leave out salient bits of personal information.

"Let me ask you something," I said. "Do you know if your dad gambled when your mom was alive?"

"No, no, never," he said. "He was a completely different person."

"Grief will do that," I said.

"No, I mean he was actually a different person," Brent said. "He got thrown out of the car in the accident and his brain, it was like it got rewired. He was in the hospital for three months and when he got out, he had a different personality pretty much. I mean, you know, he was a notary. And now he's like this . . . dirtbag."

Traumatic brain injuries resulting in changes in personality aren't uncommon. In Henry's case, married with the inadvertent death of his wife, it was pretty much textbook. That he was ready and able to risk everything on the outcome of a sporting match spoke to a larger mental instability, certainly, but in light of everything else I'd learned about Henry subsequent to his disappearance, there was a strong sense of paranoia at work here, too, and a certain fatalistic streak. He'd left his son to fend for himself, but also left him with a fortune in life insurance. Nothing *about* Henry made sense, because nothing *in* Henry made sense. I had a sinking feeling that when we found Henry, he wasn't going to be in a good mental state.

"When did your dad start collecting plasma TVs?" Sam asked.

"That was a recent obsession," Brent said. "For a long time he was just really into *Star Wars*."

"How recent?" I asked.

"He started stockpiling them a few months before he skipped town," Brent said.

"Any idea why?"

"He watched a lot of sports," Brent said. He then shrugged for maybe the thousandth time in the last two days. I was empathetic toward Brent for the odd life he'd been forced into, but I wondered if his shoulders ached from the amount of shrugging he did. "He's a hoarder when he puts his mind to something."

I was pretty sure that wasn't it. Ten plasma televisions was obsessive even for an obsessive. There had to be something else.

"Your father's gambling," I said. "He ever think about turning the tables?"

"What do you mean?" Brent said.

"Going into business," I said. "Starting his own sportsbook." I remembered what Sam had said about his insurance coverage: You don't hoard plasma televisions and then remember to add them to your home insurance. It spoke to a stability that seemed curious in light of everything else.

"I don't think so," Brent said.

"Your pop hoard any of those beers of the month I heard you mention?" Sam asked.

"Probably," he said.

"You mind if I find out?"

Brent shrugged, which was all the permission Sam

needed to pop out of the recliner and head to the kitchen. He came back a few minutes later with cold beers for all of us, even Brent.

"I'm not twenty-one," Brent said.

"It's all right, kid," Sam said. "Your uncle Sammy is."

I sat there in the comfortable living room of Brent Grayson's childhood home and pondered what it must have been like to grow up within these four walls. They weren't so different from the walls I'd grown up around and crazy parents are crazy parents. The difference is that I had Nate and Brent had to be with his father on his own. I coped by becoming a spy. Brent coped by becoming the kind of nineteen-year-old who was smart enough to dupe a man like Yuri Drubich.

I had no idea where Henry Grayson was. I thought I could take Big Lumpy at his word, but in light of the men on the street that Fi had dispatched, it seemed Henry had more people after him than could reasonably be accounted for, and that was a problem.

I took a sip of my beer. It was ice-cold. The logo on the side of the bottle showed a cresting wave and so for a moment I imagined what life would be like if I were one of those people who actually was able to spend the majority of their Miami time beachside covered in suntan lotion versus constantly running into and out of trouble, mine and other people's, in well-ventilated homes, hotels and secure government locations.

And then it occurred to me: I was drinking an ice-cold beer in an air-conditioned home. A home that had been unoccupied for at least two months.

I grabbed the stack of mail from the coffee table and began sifting through the envelopes until I found what I was looking for: the electric bill. It had a credit balance of three thousand dollars. Why would a person disappear but keep his electricity on? Actually pay for it for months in advance?

I picked up the book on underground dwellings. If you want to find out what pages of a book have been read the most, you can do a simple fingerprint test using a variety of chemicals, but in a bind you can just use iodine and an oven. After the iodine is heated, the prints will be revealed, but only for a short period of time—just a matter of minutes. More effective is a brushing of silver nitrate followed by some good old-fashioned ultraviolet light, better known as black light to anyone who happens to watch too much television.

Or, if you simply don't have the time to do a fingerprint test, you can figure it out the old-fashioned way: Look for the dog-eared corners, which, in this case, led me to page sixty-seven, a chapter titled "How to Build False Walls, Floors and Crawl Spaces."

"Your dad do any redecorating, Brent?" I asked.

"His bedroom and his office used to be one big room," Brent said.

"When was that?" I asked.

"A couple of months ago."

"The bookshelves," I said. "Those new?"

"Yeah," Brent said. "He used to just stack his books up all around the house, but then he got those built-in shelves. He was pretty proud of them."

"I'm sure he was," I said. "Brent, would you mind getting me another beer?"

Brent, not surprisingly, shrugged and then headed off to the kitchen. I handed Fiona the open book and pointed at the photo of a small room built behind bookcases on page sixty-eight. Fiona made a grunting noise, as if viewing the page actually pained her—it had been a long day already for her, clearly—and then handed the book to Sam, who looked at the page with a slight air of bewilderment. "What am I looking at here?" he said.

"Henry's in the house," I said quietly.

"What's our move?" Sam said.

"You and I are going to stay here," I said. "Fi, I want you to take Brent back to my mother's. Make sure no one tails you out of the neighborhood."

"You're aware that I've done this before?" Fiona said.

No one likes to be ordered around. Fiona likes it even less. "Yes, I know," I said.

"Thank you," she said. "And can I pick up your cleaning?"

Brent walked back into the living room, saving me from my own likely response. "Brent," I said, "Fiona is going to take you back to my mother's while we finish up here."

"Can't we just go back to my dorm?" Brent said.

"Your dorm isn't safe," I said. "I don't think your vampire friend King Thomas will actually bite anyone if they come looking for you."

"Your mom has a shotgun," Brent said, but not in a positive way.

"I know," I said. "But she knows how to use it."

"I've got class at nine a.m. tomorrow," he said. "I really can't miss again."

"Uncle Sammy will write you a note that says hired killers are looking for you," Sam said.

"My professor said if I miss one more class I'll get an F," he said.

"Then tomorrow we'll go to school," I said.

"We?" Fiona said.

"You," I said.

"Me?" Fiona said.

"We'll figure it out," I said.

After Fiona and Brent left, Sam and I stood in Henry's office and examined his workmanship.

"Nice shelves," Sam said. "Oak?"

"I believe it is," I said.

"Be impossible to rip those out," he said.

"It would," I said. We examined the shelves closely and my assessment was correct: They'd been bolted into the wall and reinforced with steel cross-supports. The door that had been created by the shelf opened out, which meant that it locked from the inside, just as the handy guidebook had suggested.

We stepped out of the office and walked down the hall to the bedroom and examined the wall that Henry had erected. It was just plain old drywall. Wallpapered drywall, but drywall nonetheless.

Drywall comes in a standard size. Half an inch thick and four feet wide. You don't need to be a spy to know this. You only need to spend half of your childhood kicking and punching walls out of frustration to learn specifically what home improvement stores keep in stock. You can get thicker drywall for soundproofing, or for fire retardation, but if you just want to build a wall and you have limited resources and ability, a nice ten-foot length of drywall can be turned into a very flimsy wall in a day.

You don't need a battering ram to break down a wall made only of gypsum, which this one was. You just need a good pair of shoes and a strong side-leg kick to the weakest seam—which would be the first panel on a three-panel wall.

Neither Sam nor I was wearing particularly good shoes for the deed, so we went back to the office. I knocked on the wall.

"Henry," I said, "my name is Michael Westen. I'm helping your son, Brent, out. I know you've heard us in here for the last hour, so you know it's safe. I'd like to talk to you. I mean you no harm."

When no answer came, I said, "Henry, either you come out or I'm leaving here with all of your Boba Fett dolls."

That did the trick.

I heard three different sliding locks being moved, and then, oddly, both televisions in the office turned on and shortly thereafter I heard noise coming from the living room and from down the hall as well. The bookshelf made a creaking sound and then it popped open to reveal a small, well-appointed room with a single bed, a dresser, a recliner, a television and several framed family photos on the wall. Standing in the middle of the room was a man wearing white boxer shorts and a tank top that barely covered his potbelly. His hair was messed up and he had at least a three-day growth of beard, but otherwise he looked just like the photos of Henry Grayson that could be found around the house.

Really, if you didn't know any better, you'd have thought Henry had just woken from a Sunday nap. Sure, he was a bit unkempt, and there was the fact that he was inside a hidden compartment inside his house, but he looked otherwise very normal if you were able to discount the fact that he was holding what looked like an ignition switch for a bomb in his hand. I now had a pretty good idea why he had so many plasma televisions in his house, too.

"I will blow up this entire house if you touch my son," Henry Grayson said, "or any of my toys."

"Your son isn't here, Henry," I said. "I just sent him somewhere safe. It's okay."

"Who are you?" he said to Sam.

"I'm Sam," he said.

"Sam," he said. "That's a friendly name."

"I'm a friendly guy," Sam said.

"If you touch my toys," Henry said to me, "I will blow up the entire house and Sam."

"Actually," I said, "you'd probably kill everyone in about a two-block radius."

This gave Henry some pause. "Two blocks?"

"You have the televisions rigged?" I asked.

"Maybe," he said.

"I'm going to guess that you've rigged a heating line to them. Would that be accurate?"

"Maybe," he said.

"Pump a little heat into each television and the xenon, neon and helium in the plasma cells will act like hundreds of tiny bombs. How hot does it need to be? Three hundred degrees for, what, ten seconds? That sound about right?" I stood back and examined his bookshelves again for a moment until I found the right book: *Your House Is Your Kingdom: How to Stop Radical Islam and Communism at Your Door, Literally.* I pulled it off the shelf and handed it to him. "You find that recipe in here?"

"It's in a couple books," he said. "All from very reputable sources in the counterterrorism community."

"See, the problem is, Henry, you can't just turn off three hundred degrees of heat. You didn't figure in cool-down time, did you? And that ignition, where'd you get that? A fireworks store? You're more likely to explode yourself than the televisions, but say you're lucky. Say everything works perfectly. Odds are still fair that you broil alive and so do a bunch of innocent people you don't owe money to."

"Who are you with?"

"I'm with your son," I said. "You've left him in a very tight spot, Henry."

"I mean, who are you with? What agency?"

"I'm not with any agency," I said.

"You haven't been watching me?"

"No," I said.

"Because many people are watching me," he said.

At that moment, I realized how very lucky we were that Brent was gone. Because his father had gone mad. Plain and simple. My second-worst fear had been realized, at least as it related to Henry.

"My name is Michael Westen," I said. "And he is

Sam Axe. Your son, Brent, has been staying with me since you disappeared. He sent us to help you. Do you want help?"

"Can I Google you?"

"You can," I said. "If you hand me that ignition switch I'll let you do whatever you want to do."

When you're negotiating with a crazy person, the best thing to do is let them feel like they are in charge of the situation, while still maintaining the position of mental and physical power. In a hostage negotiation, this is usually done by accepting whatever condition the hostage taker wants.

They want a plane that will fly them to Beirut? Roll a private jet onto the street in front of them.

They want eighty million dollars? Make an electronic deposit in their foreign bank account.

They want to talk to their dead mother? Find a Ouija board.

None of it matters in the long run because what you have that the hostage taker doesn't is, invariably, overwhelming firepower and operational intelligence. They know this, too, but usually are under the impression that the human life that waits in the balance is too much to risk.

"How do I know I can trust you? That you're not with . . . *them*?" Henry asked.

"For one," Sam said, "we don't have any black helicopters."

Henry nodded. "What about the fluoride? Are you doing anything with the fluoride in the water?"

"Nope," Sam said. "Not us. We're promoting tooth decay and other freedoms."

Henry looked at me and I could tell he was waging a war of many voices in his head. Sam's probably wasn't helping.

"You'll just have to take my word for it, Henry," I said.

I decided I'd wait five more seconds and if Henry didn't hand me the ignition, I'd punch him in the face and take it. It wasn't personal. I just didn't want to die.

Apparently, Sam felt the same way, since I only made it to three in my head before Sam punched Henry flush on the chin, knocking him out cold. I reached down and picked up the ignition.

"Sorry, Mikey," Sam said. "He was sweating an awful lot and I didn't want him to short out the system and cook us."

"It's all right," I said. "I was about to do it, too."

Henry opened his eyes, but they clearly weren't focusing yet. "Mom?" he said.

"Oh, Mikey," Sam said, "this isn't good."

9

Weapons of mass destruction aren't all that difficult to build. If you really want to kill hundreds of people at a time, all you need to do is go to the grocery store and purchase a few different cleaning agents, a box of nails, an artificial fire log, a few pressure cookers and, if you really want to cause problems, put all of those items into a car loaded with containers of hydrochloric acid. And then if you really want to make an impression, park the car next to a convention center hosting a gun and ammo show, and when it blows up, well, you'll also have people against the Second Amendment up in arms, too, since in this case unchambered ammo would kill an awful lot of innocent bystanders.

To cause a horrible, tragic and ultimately doomed catastrophe, follow the steps found in most "how-to" books produced by those concerned citizens who think every helicopter is black and every government worker is secretly a member of the Trilateral Commission. Getting advice on how to kill from the paranoid and delusional is never a wise decision, a point I didn't try to elucidate to Henry after we'd convinced him we were the good guys, since I wasn't sure just yet where he fell along the continuum between paranoid and delusional. It was hard enough to convince him that no one was going to touch his dolls—which he preferred to call his "men."

I carefully explained to Henry that the setup he'd rigged with his plasma televisions hooked to the house's gas line was likely to trigger an underground explosion that would crater around his home. He seemed oddly elated, which I found disturbing.

I couldn't exactly pinpoint the level of his loss of sanity—at some points he seemed fine, and at others he seemed . . . lost. It was evident that he'd had some kind of break from reality. Nevertheless, I wanted him to know that he could have taken out a lot of innocent people.

"Really?" he said. "That big?"

"That's why I had to hit you," Sam said.

"I'm a pacifist," Henry said, just like his son.

"Do you hate your neighbors, Henry?" I asked.

"Oh, no, no, they're all very nice."

"Then why would you want them dead?"

"Oh, oh, I wouldn't," he said, serious now. "I just think it's very interesting how these sorts of chain reactions occur. One person with a desire to keep his house protected could, with a push of a button, take out a city block. It's chaotic, isn't it?"

Henry and Sam and I were sitting in his bedroom, the only room in the house that didn't have a window easily accessible to the outside world, as it looked out to the side yard, and even then the window was largely blocked by an armoire that Henry had moved almost directly in front of it. Not exactly design 101. But then

Henry was probably more concerned about the black helicopters than the editorial staff of *Architectural Design*.

"No," I said, "it's not chaotic, actually. It's dangerous, Henry. Can you appreciate that?"

"You can't appreciate the synchronicity?"

"No."

"Well, it's a theoretical synchronicity that I find fascinating," he said. "Now, where's my son? Have you told me where my son is? You did, didn't you? You said he's working for a Russian syndicate?"

I had, in brushstrokes, explained the situation to Henry, but this time I went into a bit more detail, including that Brent had tried to pay off Henry's debts, that he'd duped Yuri Drubich and that Henry's notary office had been destroyed. The problem was that everything I said essentially fed directly into Henry's current delusions. I needed to see how he handled the information in order to gauge a bit more accurately where he fell on the scale of things.

"You see," Henry said, "this is the upside of everything that has happened with my son. Look at how industrious he's become in my absence. I couldn't be more proud of him. He could very well have fallen into the clutches of the fluoride people, but he didn't. Did you know that we've all been poisoned for almost fifty years? It's true. It's a systematic poisoning of the American people so that we are dulled to our wit's end when the New World Order takes over."

I decided to change the subject before I was unable to stop myself from shaking him. I've never been particularly good at dealing with crazy people. Henry was relatively harmless—once you took the explosives out of his hands—but that didn't mean I had any real idea how to deal with him.

"How do you get in and out of the house?" I asked.

"Oh, it's very simple," he said. "I only leave in the middle of the night. The satellites can't track me. I'm invisible at night."

"Literally invisible?" Sam said.

"Is there any other kind of invisible?" Henry asked.

"No," Sam said, "I guess there isn't."

The nice thing about the people looking for Henry was that they weren't professionals, which meant their dedication was likely far from monastic. They were bookies, so they tended to keep daylight hours and they weren't very sophisticated. They survived on intimidation, but they didn't like to actually work. It's why they didn't have real jobs. They probably didn't have night-vision goggles, either, so he probably was, literally, invisible.

"Henry," I said, "why don't you lie down in your own bed for once? Sam and I will keep the house guarded while you nap."

Henry looked around his room as if he hadn't seen it before. "This is my room?"

"Yes," I said.

"And you'll be just outside the door?"

"Yes."

"Should we cover the windows with tinfoil?"

"I don't think we need to do that," I said.

"I brought an extra force field with me today," Sam said.

"Oh, okay," Henry said. "I guess I could take a nap.

I haven't been sleeping very much. I'd feel more comfortable if you both stayed with me until I fell asleep. It's usually right before REM when the transmissions begin."

"No problem," Sam said. "We'll be right here to intercept them."

Within five minutes of getting underneath his covers, Henry Grayson was snoring, so Sam and I crept back into the living room.

"I've decided Henry Grayson is crazy," Sam said.

"Yeah, he might be," I said.

"He did build himself his own secret hideaway," Sam said. "Can't say the man isn't industrious. What are we going to do with him?"

"He needs to be hospitalized," I said. "Possibly forever."

"Not even loan sharks are going to try to take a pound of flesh from a crazy guy, right?"

"I doubt it," I said. "I have a feeling Big Lumpy might be sensitive to it, if we can get Drubich to pay him."

"But that doesn't get rid of Drubich," Sam said.

"I know," I said. "And Fiona snapping his wrist probably didn't put him in a charitable mood."

"She was a little cranky today," Sam said.

"Forced captivity does that to her."

"And then there's Sugar," Sam said.

"I want to thank you for that," I said.

"Boy Scout oath forced me into this situation, Mikey. Mentally awake and all that."

"I don't think you're living up to the spirit of the oath in agreeing to help Sugar with anything."

"Maybe not," Sam said.

"We need to get Henry out of this house," I said. "And into a safe facility. And I'm not talking about my mother's garage."

"I've got a buddy does a little work with unstable types for the VA," Sam said.

"What kind of work?"

"Well, it's not really the VA as it's legally consti-tuted," Sam said. "More like she helps with secret pris-ons and that sort of thing. But her business card says VA on it."

"She owe you any favors?"

"Mikey, everyone owes me a favor."

"Henry needs help," I said. "Not confinement."

"You mind if the help is mobile?"

"Mobile?" I said.

"Let me talk to my buddy," Sam said.

A thought occurred to me. "Your friend," I said. "She be willing to sign an official death certificate?"

"Mikey," Sam said, "that's a federal crime."

"I know," I said. "But so is being a Russian national with a rocket launcher on American soil. They call that terrorism now. We have a witness who had a psychotic break after a horrific terrorist attack on his business and now fears for his very life."

"Henry's not exactly a viable witness, Mikey."

"When has that ever mattered in matters of national security?"

Sam pondered this for a moment. "That's asking my buddy to extend herself pretty far."

"You're a persuasive guy," I said.

"I do have my charms," Sam said.

"First thing," I said, "is we need to get Henry out of this house and into some kind of care. And maybe keep him away from anything explosive. He had this place wired pretty well."

"What do we tell Brent?"

"Nothing," I said. "Not until we know he's safe from all of this. He gets compromised and he'll spill everything."

Sam agreed. He took out his cell phone and made a call. "Marci? Marci, this Sam Axe. Sweetheart, I have a small favor I need to ask. . . . No, no, not that again. Unless you want to do that again. I'm not opposed to that, just let me adjust my insurance coverage again. . . . Now that—*that's* not even legal on a Sunday in Florida, sweetheart. . . ."

A high-pitched squeal erupted from Sam's phone—loud enough that Sam had to pull the phone away from his ear—which was my cue to move to another part of the house while he convinced his buddy to acquiesce to his demands. I didn't want to ruin my dinner.

Two hours later, a yellow Econoline van pulled up in front of Henry's house. According to the sign on the side of it, the van belonged to ALL-AMERICAN INSULATION & AIR-CONDITIONING REPAIR. According to the bulletproof tires, I had a sneaking suspicion that the van actually belonged to Sam's friend Marci and her cohorts. It's not every air-conditioning service that can afford Teflon-honeycombed antigun, antiexplosion, extreme-terrain experimental tires that I'd only previously seen in Iraq.

From the living room window I could see the van's passenger door open and a woman of no less than six full feet of height step out. She wore a tan jumpsuit with a utility belt and held a clipboard, the universal uniform of anyone who wants to look nonthreatening. Though I had a slight twinge of fear that Henry might think it was also the universal uniform of the New World Order. Fortunately, I could still hear Henry snoring away. Well, snoring and intermittently shouting in his sleep.

Sam came up behind me and looked out the living room window. "That's my girl," Sam said.

"That's a woman," I said.

"You don't need to tell me that," Sam said.

"She's a doctor?"

"Among other things."

"What other things?"

"Geneva Convention prevents me from saying," Sam said. He stepped away to open the front door and in walked Marci. She greeted Sam with a hug that practically lifted him off his feet and then she gave him a firm slap on his backside. It was . . . awkward. But Sam seemed to like it.

"What do we have here?" she asked. She walked into the living room, regarded me with nary a mention, and then sat down in the recliner and stared directly at her clipboard, as if she didn't want to take in too much information other than what she was asking for. That or plausible deniability was big in her world.

"Big favor, Marci," Sam said. "We've got a subject in the bedroom that we need to get off the grid."

"Enemy?"

"No," Sam said.

Marci wrote something on her clipboard. "Client?"

"Not in the traditional sense," Sam said. He looked over my way. "Maybe you noticed another person in the room?"

"I don't see anyone," she said.

"Well, the person you don't see, he's a friend of mine named Michael," Sam said. "We sort of—how should I say this—help people occasionally."

"I've never heard of Michael Westen," she said, which was interesting since Sam hadn't said my full name.

"Right, great," Sam said. "At any rate, the subject in the bedroom is, uh, emotionally unstable. We're helping his son with some business regarding, uh, well, a gentleman named Big Lumpy and another gentleman named Yuri Drubich and, uh, we need our emotionally unstable client to get the help he needs in a secure facility and, uh, well, here we are."

Marci looked up. "Did you say Big Lumpy?"

"I did," Sam said.

"This house," Marci said. "I expect that it will be cleaned after I leave?"

"Of course," Sam said.

"No fingerprints, no hair, nothing?"

"Pro job all the way," Sam said. "I'll burn it down if you want me to."

"And Yuri Drubich, correct?"

"Correct," Sam said.

"I'll get back to you on the burning. Where's the asset?"

"Back bedroom," Sam said.

"You mind if I drug him? We're going to pile him in an insulation roll and people, especially crazy people, tend to get claustrophobic when wrapped in insulation."

"Be my guest," Sam said.

Marci finally turned my way. "Like your work," she said.

"I haven't done any in a while," I said.

"Belgrade in 2001," she said.

"Ah, yeah, that was fun," I said.

"You single?"

"Uh," I said. "Not really. Yes, in a way. It's complicated."

"Always is."

"My ex-girlfriend is violent."

"She get mean and beat you up?"

"It's happened," I said.

"I knew you looked like a good time." She stood up, walked toward me and then stopped a few feet away so she could look me up and down. I actually misjudged Marci's height when she got out of the van, because now that she was standing directly in front of me and the distance between us seemed to be closing incrementally with every breath, I thought she was probably closer to six foot three. Tall enough to cast a shadow on me, at any rate.

"Maybe some other time," I said.

"You'll be in a military prison some other time," she said.

"Maybe," I said. I tried to catch Sam's eye, but he was busy staring at the floor. I couldn't tell if he was jealous or, like Marci, wanted plausible deniability should Fiona learn about any of this. "Listen. I might need another small favor down the line with the asset."

"Yeah?"

"Any way we might be able to get him declared dead?"

"Why?"

"Insurance," I said, "against getting killed."

"We can make him go away for a long time, but I thought he had a kid."

"He does," I said. "It's insurance against him dying, too."

Marci finally looked around the living room. She picked up a photo of Henry and Brent from the fireplace mantel. "Cute kid."

"He's older now," I said.

"He know his father is crazy?"

"That's why we're working for him, Marci."

"I like the way you say my name," she said. "You like Italian food?"

"I'm more a Persian food guy," I said.

"I like Persian food," she said.

"I know a great little place in Fort Lauderdale," I said. "Outdoor seating. Breeze from the ocean in your hair. Palm trees swaying in the wind. It's like being on the Mediterranean."

Marci licked her lips, which made me feel like I was watching a nature documentary. She might have been six foot four.

"Did you just ask me out on a date?" she said.

"I think you just made me ask you out on a date," I said.

This got Marci to smile. Thank God. And then she made that same high-pitched squeal I'd heard earlier through Sam's phone. "You live through this," she said, "I'll consider all of your propositions." She pulled a walkie-talkie from her utility belt. "Come on in," she said into it. "Bring the barbital and the insulation roll."

10

Getting ambushed isn't any fun. One moment you're happily going about your normal life, worrying about taxes and cancer and what to eat next. The next moment someone has shot you in the face and you're dead. That's the second-best-case scenario, really. What you don't want is to be ambushed, captured and then tortured to death. All things being equal, a bullet to the brain is a far more humane way to die.

There exists, of course, a third possible result of an ambush, the first-best-case scenario, as it were: You're taken by surprise but not injured beyond repair—physically or emotionally. The problem with this angle is that if someone didn't want to hurt you physically or emotionally they wouldn't ambush you in the first place.

Which is why I was somewhat surprised when Big Lumpy appeared at my loft later that evening. There was a knock on the door and when I looked out the window I saw Big Lumpy's Escalade idling across the street, the glow from the nightclub on the street turning the bright white paint yellow, then pink, then blue.

I didn't bother to look through the peephole to see

if Big Lumpy was alone. If he had guts enough to show up at my door unannounced, he probably wasn't here to kill me.

Plus, if you want to kill someone without ever touching them, the best way is to wait for them to stare at you through a peephole. A peephole is structurally the weakest portion of a door. It's just a hole, bored through wood, with glass on either end. So if you want to stab someone in the brain, wait until you see light being interrupted on the other end of the hole and then shove a long-bladed—preferably serrated—knife through the hole with as much force as possible. A serrated knife will do far more damage, so it really is the weapon of choice.

Or just shoot a single bullet through the hole. That will also do the trick. If you're any good, you won't even leave a fingerprint.

Even still, you can't be too careful these days, so I got my shotgun from under the sink, racked it and opened the door.

"Can I help you with something?" I said.

"Is this a bad time?" Big Lumpy said. He was still wearing that absurd white outfit, but now had a portable oxygen tank with him, too, as well as a slim laptop.

"I'm a formal guy," I said. "You should have called first. I would have taken out the nice linens and china."

"I would have, but you're not listed. I looked all through the Yellow Pages under 'burned spies' and the only name that came up was a Jesse Something-or-Other."

"Yeah," I said. "Call him next time." I stepped around

Big Lumpy and swept my shotgun over the courtyard where I park my car. It was empty and the gate was closed. "Where's your manservant?"

"In the car," he said. "Where is yours?"

"I gave him the night off," I said. "He had a near-death experience this afternoon."

I put my shotgun down to my side and invited Big Lumpy inside my loft. He stepped in, pulling his oxygen tank behind him, and then stopped to survey his surroundings.

"Spartan," he said.

"I didn't intend to stay long," I said.

"How long ago was that?"

"Longer than I thought." I said.

"Longer than you deserved?"

"Depends on who you ask." This answer seemed to satisfy Big Lumpy. He walked over to my kitchen counter and set his computer down and took a seat. "Make yourself at home," I said to his back. I put my shotgun on my bed and went into the kitchen and stood across the counter from Big Lumpy and waited for him to say whatever he wanted to say.

"I don't suppose the boy is here?"

"No," I said.

"Good. Wouldn't want him seeing me and being unimpressed."

"You ever meet his father?"

"Once. He wasn't aware of the fact that he was meeting me, however. I used a proxy. Better to convince him to pay. I watched from a distance. I'm a bit of a voyeur in that way."

"He's crazy," I said.

"I don't doubt that," he said. "I put the fear of God into mortal men."

"No," I said, "I mean he's nuts. Clinically."

"You found him?"

"I've found evidence of him," I said. I didn't know what Big Lumpy was doing at my place, but the fact that he was there at all told me something was niggling at him, so I decided to take a few chances, see where they led. "And the evidence indicates to me that he's had a break from reality. If he's alive, he might be too far gone to matter."

"This is my problem how?"

"I don't think he knew what he was doing when he was betting with you," I said. "Did you know he accidentally killed his wife?"

"I was his bookie, not his therapist," Big Lumpy said.

I told him the story Brent had told me that afternoon, including the part about his personality changing. I even told him about the conspiracy books I found in Henry's house, figuring the more evidence for madness I could provide, the more likely Big Lumpy might feel . . . something. I wasn't sure what he was made of exactly, but I knew that his impending death had to have some effect on him, even if he didn't want to admit it.

"Terrible story," Big Lumpy said when I was done. "Maybe Lifetime will make it into a movie that the whole family can enjoy."

"Are you really that dead inside?" I asked.

"Do you think I'm stupid, Michael?"

"No." And I didn't.

"Then why are you trying to squeeze empathy out of me?"

"I'm just trying to see if you're a human being."

"There's no empathy in my business," he said.

"Or mine," I said.

"That's not true," he said. "Look at you now. Helping the helpless. Friend to the great unwashed masses who embark on stupid criminal pursuits. You're like Robin Hood in Armani."

"This isn't my business," I said. "This is my life. I've been forced to separate the two. You might look into it."

This got Big Lumpy to smile. "You're an odd man," he said.

"I've had an odd life," I said.

"I know," he said. He opened up his computer then and swung it my way. "I've been reading your file."

"I don't need to look at that," I said. "I have my own copy."

Big Lumpy nodded once and then made a few clicks on his keyboard. "Have you seen mine?"

On his screen was a series of documents that were largely redacted. "Impressive," I said. "You've been a real black mark."

Another smile. He still hadn't told me what exactly he was doing at my house and I wasn't going to ask. He seemed to be enjoying this cat-and-mouse game, showing me that he was in as deep as I was with the government, letting me know that the stakes of Henry's life were small comparatively. I just didn't know why yet.

"I spent some time looking at the InterMacron Web site," Big Lumpy said. "Impressive."

"I thought so."

"How old is he?"

"Nineteen."

"Only child?"

"Only child."

"And his father, you say he's crazy. His mother is dead. Grandparents?"

"I don't know. Probably dead," I said. "I think he has an aunt somewhere."

"Texas," Big Lumpy said.

"Right," I said. "I forgot you'd threatened her life."

"I only provided intel. I made no actual threats of my own. Outsourcing, Michael—you should look into it."

"Next career change I might," I said.

"I spent some time quizzing Sugar on his friend's life today, too. Just to make sure no one was lying to me about things. I'd hate to think I was dealing with a nineteen-year-old savant only to learn that I was dealing with some intricate multinational plot."

"That happened before?"

"More than once," he said. "It helped that I was the nineteen-year-old." He made a few clicks on his computer again and up popped a photo of Sugar strapped to a table and covered in electrodes. "I figured it would be easiest just to polygraph your friend Sugar versus figuring out all of his slang. Did you know his legal name is actually Sugar?"

"No."

"It came up as a lie, but he swore it was true. It made for a good control question."

"So?"

"So it seems everyone is being honest. A true revelation."

"You came here just to tell me that?"

"I came here to make a deal."

"We already made a deal."

"No, you won a bet."

"You don't have anything I want," I said.

"This isn't about us. It's about the boy. Brent." Big Lumpy's oxygen machine made a beeping noise. He looked down at it and swore under his breath, then reached down and came back up with a power cord. "Would you mind plugging this in for me? My man-servant apparently didn't juice it up enough before I left and so now I have only fifteen minutes of oxygen left and then you'll have to give me mouth-to-mouth."

I wanted to avoid that as much as possible, so I came around the counter and took his cord. It was too short to reach anything nearby, so I went upstairs and came back down with an extension cord and then plugged everything in.

"Thank you," he said.

"You weren't on the machine earlier," I said.

"Days are better for me. I can sometimes go a full hour without the machine, but nights seem to be worse. Soon days will be worse, too, and then I'll be dead. No odds on that one, I'm afraid."

"What do you want with Brent?" I asked.

"His mind." Big Lumpy clicked back to the Inter-Macron site and began going through each page. "His ideas? These foolish ones he came up with? This sham? This is terrible science, but it is brilliant propaganda. And surprisingly accurate to what I suspect is actually being worked on. That is a rare talent. To be a fool. To be a genius. And to be able to synthesize all of that into a believable package. Does he have any idea what he's capable of?"

"He's just a kid," I said.

"So was I. I took down Las Vegas when I was his age."

"Everyone does that now," I said.

"But I was the first. He could do the same thing with just a slight bit of training. You say he goes to the University of Miami?"

"Yes."

Big Lumpy *tsk*ed. "Talent like this should be at a real school."

"I mentioned his father is crazy, right? Degenerate gambler, too."

Big Lumpy waved all that away. "Michael," he said, "are you happy with your life?"

"Sometimes."

"I love my life, apart from the dying aspect, but that's true of all humans. We have superpowers, you and I, Michael, and we've both used those powers for evil."

"Speak for yourself," I said.

"I am," he said. "You could have joined some anti-violence movement, but you chose the armed forces and chose to go around the world shooting heads of state. I have no problem with that, I honestly do not, but without a sanction you're a criminal, as you are now in the eyes of the law, I assure you. I can show you that file, too, if you like."

"No, thanks," I said. Big Lumpy had me confused

now. I wasn't sure what he wanted or if anything he said was worth listening to. But the strange thing was, despite my best instincts, I found myself liking him. He was smart—there was no question about that—but he was also conflicted and lost in his own identity, so I was intrigued by whatever it was he was about to propose. "So, what, you're going to adopt Brent?"

"No," he said. "But I could help him. Do you read, Michael? I mean other than books on counterinsurgency and the like?"

"I've been known to curl up with an operations manual for small submersibles."

"I'm thinking Dickens. *Great Expectations.*"

"I'm familiar with it," I said. "I take it you don't see yourself as Pip."

"I don't have much time left, Michael. Maybe I can do a little good. Maybe I can send Brent in a direction in life that would use his talents. Talents that have not been cultivated, as far as I can tell."

"He did dupe Yuri Drubich," I said.

"He could dupe our own government with this site," he said.

"He's not as impressive in real life," I said. "He says 'like' a lot. And takes Ambien recreationally. And counts Sugar among his friends."

"He doesn't need friends," Big Lumpy said. "He needs someone to lead him. Like you did. And like I did. Or he needs someone to at least provide him the path to a better life. I could be that person."

"You didn't sound like that kind of person this afternoon."

"It was something you said, actually, if you must

know. You called me a sideshow. At the time, it just made me angry. But then I got home, thought about torturing Sugar, but instead just polygraphed him for what I needed to know. And you know what, Michael? I felt . . . gratified."

"So you had an epiphany," I said. "You could change your mind tomorrow."

"Do you want to know how long I have to live?"

"I'd say three months," I said.

"Could be less, really. My number of epiphanies is limited. I'd like to spend my last days happy, if you can believe it. Maybe I'll travel. Maybe I'll buy a spot on a Russian spaceship. Or maybe I'll just keep running numbers and sending my minions to beat the shit out of people until I take my very last breath. Before today, those seemed to be my best choices. But then I had this . . . *epiphany*, as you call it. I call it a moment of reckoning. A moment of understanding my place on this planet."

This all sounded too good to be true. "I don't believe that I can totally trust you," I said.

"You shouldn't," he said. "You'd be foolish to." There was another beeping sound, this time from Big Lumpy's iPhone. "Do you have anything to eat? I have to eat something every hour or else my medication will make me sick. Isn't that funny? My medication will make me sick."

"It's ironic," I said.

I opened up my fridge and took out two yogurts, blueberry for me and strawberry for Big Lumpy. He regarded the yogurt like it was poison, then exhaled in resignation, asked me for a spoon and started eating.

When he was finished, I offered him a glass of water or some orange juice, but he declined both. I didn't bother offering him a beer.

"Big Lumpy," I said. "You like that name?"

"Not particularly."

"What do your friends call you?"

"I don't have friends."

"What about family?"

"My brother, Jeff, calls me Buddy," he said, "but I hate that, too. But then I haven't spoken to him in a decade. So he probably just calls me 'asshole' now."

It was weird to think of someone like Big Lumpy having a brother. Or parents. People like him just seem to exist outside of the normal world sometimes. "Anyone ever call you Mark anymore?"

"No," he said, "no one calls me Mark anymore. Not in a million years."

I've never trusted adults with nicknames. If you want to hold on to some childish thing, make it that you look both ways before crossing or that you are slavishly dedicated to making others share. But letting yourself be called something like Big Lumpy suggests a larger emotional problem. Which it was clear Big Lumpy had. Here he was nevertheless, as raw and vulnerable as a newborn. I could step on his oxygen line and he'd be dead. Or I could just shoot him. Or break his neck. He'd come unarmed and alone into an enemy war zone.

He was acting like a person with nothing to lose, which I suppose was true.

"So, Mark," I said, "tell me what you want to do."

Big Lumpy made a few clicks on his computer again.

"Yuri Drubich, you recognize, is not a positive part of international relations. He deals with terrorists. As much as I don't care for working for our government, that has more to do with pay rates and backstabbing than some jihad madness, as I'm sure you can appreciate."

"I can."

"So you didn't really blow up a preschool in Panama?"

"No," I said.

"Good to know," he said. "I'd like to represent your interests to Yuri. Tell him I'm the man behind the plan and that I have all of the actual information, but that it will cost him. What sounds like a good round number?"

"Four million?"

"That's not a round number. Six has more curves."

"So he pays. You give him the information and then when he finds out it's bunk, what then?"

"You get him for purchasing government secrets with the intent of distribution to terrorists."

"But this isn't a government secret," I said.

"Not yet," he said. "But when I share Brent's ideas with a few associates of mine in the NSA, it certainly will be. His broad ideas for transference are nothing short of profound. Just because they are theoretical doesn't mean they aren't inherently plausible."

Or valuable. I wasn't sure what angle Big Lumpy was working. Part of me wanted to believe that there was this new soft core of altruism inside the artist formerly known as Mark McGregor. And part of me knew that I was dealing with a man who played incredible odds in every part of his life. What was the bet here? And who got the payoff? At the worst, this was a suicide mission on Big Lumpy's part. At the best, it was a path toward freedom for Brent, if indeed that was what Brent wanted. What nineteen-year-old knows what he wants, after all?

"And who gets the money?"

"I do," he said. "And then I leave it to Brent, with a few provisos."

"If I say no, what then?"

Big Lumpy spun his computer back toward me. On the screen was a satellite image of a house. I didn't recognize it, so I pulled the image back until I began to see recognizable landmarks: the Stratosphere Casino, the Luxor Pyramid, the stretch of cars along the Las Vegas Strip. The house didn't look familiar because I'd never actually been to Nate's place in Las Vegas.

"Your brother Nate still owes me money, but I've taken that as a loss," Big Lumpy said. "No use crossing state lines just for a few hundred dollars. Killing someone, that's a reason to travel. Do you know what he used as his call-in code? Goldfinger007. Funny, isn't it?"

"Hysterical."

"I'm a reasonable man now, Michael," Big Lumpy said. "And I'm a serious man. I trust that we have a partnership?"

"I can't tell you what Brent will decide," I said. "You're basically asking him to sit beside you and learn how to be an evil genius. Kids today, they have their own ambitions."

"He'll have choices. Good or bad genius is still genius. He can be good if he wants, too. You must know that eventually someone will come along to try to corrupt him, if he's not dead before then."

Big Lumpy had a very good point. A man like Yuri Drubich, even if he was arrested and imprisoned by the American government, would still be able to come at a person. He'd keep coming for as long as it took. It was a compelling argument.

"I'll talk to him," I said. "What about Sugar?"

"He's an exceptionally annoying person."

"I shot him once," I said.

"You should have finished the job." Big Lumpy got up from his seat and began to make his way to the front door, then realized he was still plugged in and waited for me to unhook him from the extension cord. He was an odd combination of extreme smarts and confounding helplessness. He was strong of mind but incredibly weak of body, so he was smart enough to threaten Nate's life, smart enough to know that I was powerless to stop anything from happening to Nate three thousand miles away and blacklisted from conventional air travel, but too weak to do anything himself. Like take a breath, for instance. Or kill Nate.

It's hard to kill someone once they've stopped being an object and started being a person, which is likely what Nate now was to Big Lumpy. But he wouldn't be the one killing him. He'd just hire that out. If nothing else, I'd come to know that Big Lumpy was a man who covered all of his possible angles. I could muscle him if need be, but I wouldn't outthink him.

I helped him to the door. When I opened it, his assistant was waiting on the landing with Sugar. Or someone who I presumed was Sugar. It was hard to be definitive since he had a canvas bag over his head and his torso was wrapped in what looked to be the plastic wrap commonly used by movers.

"He's unhurt, at least physically," Big Lumpy said. "And there's nothing there emotionally to tarnish, so I suspect he's fine."

"Nice of you to wrap him up for me," I said. I watched as Big Lumpy was helped down the stairs by his manservant—I really needed to get one of those—and was struck by how difficult it was going to be to explain all of this to Sam and Fiona, when Big Lumpy stopped at the bottom of the stairs and looked back up at me.

"Thank you," he said.

"For what?" I said.

"Trusting me. No one trusts me."

"I'm not sure that I do. You did threaten to kill my brother after all."

"It's just part of the odds. You know that."

"I suppose I do. I just don't want to take a bad beat like Henry Grayson."

"You won't," he said. "We'll speak tomorrow and in a few days all of this will be over and I'll be dead or dying and your friend Brent will have a new life. Isn't that nice?"

Big Lumpy didn't wait for my reply. He and his assistant walked through the courtyard and out into the street, climbed into the white Escalade and were gone. I pulled the canvas bag off of Sugar's head and saw that they'd also duct-taped his mouth and stuffed his ears with cotton. That they hadn't just cut out his tongue was probably only due to Big Lumpy's new world-

view. I ripped the duct tape off of Sugar's mouth and
he immediately began apologizing, making threats and
essentially babbling incoherently, so I put the tape back
over his mouth, but pulled the cotton out of his ears.

"Sugar," I said, "I want you to listen to me. You
ever tell anyone who I am, where I live or even the
color of my eyes again, and I'll kill you myself. We
clear?"

Sugar nodded his head. It was about all he could
do, since he was still wrapped in plastic.

"All right," I said. "Come on in and I'll make you
some yogurt."

11

The first kamikazes, the first fighters willing to commit suicide in order to defeat their opponents, are generally thought to have been the Jewish Sicarii and the Islamic Assassins. Unlike modern-day suicide bombers, the Sicarii and the Assassins weren't required to die in order to do their jobs, but if that was what happened, so be it. Undertaking a suicide mission requires a different psychological makeup than merely putting yourself in a position where you might die as a result of your actions.

With someone like Big Lumpy, however, where his death was already foretold, taking a risk like presenting himself to Yuri Drubich in order to defraud him was an entirely different beast. He could die in the process, but maybe it would be a less painful way to go than via whatever was eating him from the inside out. No matter how this all played out, Big Lumpy was a dead man. And in the end, if he went for it, Brent's father's debts would be gone, he'd be able to get the help he needed, and Brent would have choices about how to use his talents. Or at least he'd have the financial security to make choices. I couldn't imagine

what Big Lumpy's provisos would be, as he said, but
they'd hardly be enforceable with violence after he
was dead.

"What sort of person goes by Big Lumpy?" my
mother asked.

It was the next morning and I'd just finished ex-
plaining to Brent (and a befuddled Sugar ... and my
chain-smoking mother) the deal Big Lumpy was offering him, right down to the potential for millions of dollars. We were sitting at the same kitchen table where
I'd had eight thousand conversations with my own
mother and father about how crime doesn't pay. The
same table where Fiona and Sam—who were on their
way over to take Brent to school—and I had planned
more than one enterprise that might normally be considered criminal if we weren't such good law-abiding
citizens ... or, well, at least Sam and I were, in any
case.

I hadn't mentioned to my mother that Nate was being threatened in all of this, figuring that all things
being equal, she really didn't need to know that Nate
was also into a psychopath—or a former psychopath,
as it were—for some marginal sum of money. Parents
really don't need to know everything about their children.

"It's a nickname," I said. "Because of his huge brain."

"What about you, Sugar?" my mother asked. "Why
do people call you that?"

"I'm sweet, Mrs. Westen," he said.

"Isn't that nice," she said. She reached across the
table and squeezed his hand. "Brent tells me you used
to live under Michael's place. Isn't that a coincidence?"

"It's a small world," he said.

"So you're the drug dealer, then, that he had to shoot?"

"Yeah," he said. "You know. We all got checkered pasts, right, Mike?"

"You don't have a checkered past," I said. "You have a checkered present. You really do need to consider another line of work, Sugar. Eventually someone is going to have better aim and will get you in the head."

"I was thinking maybe I'd go back to school. Hit up twelfth grade again at night school and then just bounce once I get my paper. You know, but I gotta get mine until then. I'm going to get up out of that game when I can, Mike, on the real. Soon as I get a new ride."

"I'm sorry," my mother said, "but I have no idea what you just said. Could you interpret into English for me, Michael?"

The thing about my mother was that she could *be* lost and adrift and then she could just *seem* to be lost and adrift. It was a good defense mechanism and a good way of putting people like Sugar in their place. She would have made a good preschool teacher or Cossack.

"He's going to quit dealing drugs just as soon as he gets his high school diploma and a new car," I said, "but not in that order, I suspect."

"And do you also call yourself Sugar because you sell cocaine?" she asked.

"Allegedly," he said.

My mother turned to Brent. "If you're smart," she

said, "you'll get him out of your life as soon as possible."

Brent shrugged. If he could figure out a way to convey the word "like" by using a repetitive body action, he'd have the basis of his entire emotional range covered.

"Anyway," I said to my mother, "Big Lumpy is a genius. Geniuses get to call themselves whatever they want. Though my understanding is that he doesn't actually care for the name, if it makes you feel any better, Ma."

"He might be all smart and stuff," Sugar said, "but he's mean."

"He let you live," I said. "He didn't need to do that."

"Whatever," he said. "He wrapped me in plastic wrap like I was a sandwich or some shit. That's messed up, yo."

Through all of this Brent was strangely silent. "So," I said, "what do you think, Brent?"

"Why does he want to do this?" he asked.

"Honestly? I think he sees himself in you."

"I've never met him," Brent said.

"I don't mean it literally," I said. "But in your work. The Web site. The guts it took to stand up to him and to screw Yuri Drubich over. He thinks you're smart, Brent. I think you're smart, too. But I'm not offering you an opportunity to do . . . well, whatever he wants you to do."

"What do you think that will be?"

"My guess is that he wants you to go down a better road than he went on," I said. "At least eventually. My sense is that he thinks he can train you a bit. And then send you to work for people who could use you for the good of our country. What you did to Yuri, what you came up with, InterMacron, that technology you just made up out of the ether? He thinks it could work, Brent. That's the biggest thing. He thinks your theories are sound."

"I was just doing what I could to help my dad," he said. "I did what anyone would do."

I looked across the table at my mother. She was sitting beside Brent attempting to be as motherly as possible, which wasn't easy, since she was always better at being vaguely distant and demanding, and I could tell she wanted to say something. She kept opening her mouth and then closing it, like a fish.

"Go ahead, Ma," I said, "say what you're going to say."

"Well, Michael," she said, "I think Brent makes a very good point. Doing whatever he could do to take care of his parent. That's a very kind, very wise, very sweet thing for a boy of just nineteen to do."

"Yeah," I said. "Princely."

"At least he didn't run off and become some . . . whatever you are."

"A spy," I said.

"Which is badass," Sugar said.

"Totally," Brent said.

Not the response my mother was looking for. "Anyway, Michael, I just think that maybe Brent needs a good, solid family surrounding him. What kind of life is he going to have doing whatever this Big Lucy wants him to do?"

"Lumpy," I said. "Big Lumpy. And the truth is, Ma, that Brent can make his own choices of what he does. You want to work for the government, Brent?"

He shrugged. Of course. "I dunno. That sounds pretty cool."

"Would he get to carry?" Sugar asked.

"Probably not," I said.

"Whatever, bro," Sugar said to Brent. "I could get you a piece."

"He would need to get certain criminal elements away from him," I said.

"What about my dad?" Brent asked.

I hadn't told him yet about finding Henry. I wasn't sure what might happen next, but I knew that if Yuri or perhaps Big Lumpy could use Henry as collateral, they would. It was best that Brent still be kept in the dark about his father's whereabouts and mental condition, but I didn't want him to be in constant fear about his possible death. I had to make a choice.

"He's safe," I said.

"You found him?" he said. "Where is he? Why didn't you tell me?"

"I couldn't," I said. "And I can't tell you where he is now, but understand that he's in a place where no one can get to him."

"When did you find him?"

"Yesterday," I said.

"What?" Brent pushed back from the table and then stood up abruptly. "What? Why didn't you tell me? I'm not a little kid, you know. I'm a full-grown man, you know. I'm, like, almost twenty."

"Brent," I said, "please sit down."

"No," he said. "No. I mean, like, I'm valuable and you're just, like, pulling my strings and I'm not down with that."

He stalked across the kitchen and into the living room and then back into the kitchen. His face was puffy and red and I realized he was near tears.

I don't do well with tears. Especially not on men. Or boys. Or women. Crying animals aren't my area of expertise, either.

"Uh, Ma," I said, as quietly as possible, since I figured she might have more experience with this than I did.

"He's right, Michael," she said. "Nineteen is a full-grown man. I've heard that before."

"Not helping," I said.

Brent did another tour of the house, mumbling under his breath and stomping the entire time, before basically throwing himself down onto the sofa in the living room. "I need to go to school," he said finally, as if we'd not spent the better part of an hour talking about the rest of his life. "I'll be late if we don't leave in, like, fifteen minutes."

"Sam will take you as soon as he gets here," I said.

"What about Fiona?" he said.

"That's my boy," Sugar said.

"Shut up, Sugar," I said . . . at precisely the same moment my mother said it, too. There are things we agree on without condition.

"I'm just saying," Sugar said, "Sam's gonna stick out on campus like a narc. But Fiona, she can rock that grad student game. Put some horn-rimmed glasses on her, she'd make that shit work like 24-7."

For once in Sugar's life, he made a convincing argument. I didn't think Fiona would go for the horn-rimmed glasses if she didn't have to, but I suspected she would like the idea of being mistaken for being twenty-two. Fortunately, I didn't have to wait long to find out, as she and Sam rang my mother's doorbell just a few minutes later.

Sam looked like he hadn't yet slept, his hair freshly slicked down with water and yesterday's hair gel, his Tommy Bahama shirt open too far down his chest, not because of any fashion sense but because he'd just put it on in the car. Fiona, however, was radiant as ever in a white sundress accented by black sunglasses and a turquoise handbag. She looked like Jackie O, if Jackie O were still alive and packing a nine in her purse. Not exactly dressed for school, but I'm sure she'd make do.

"How's your head?" I asked.

"Better," Fiona said. "Nothing a hot stone massage and an evening spent reading *US Magazine* and cleaning my knife collection couldn't soothe."

"My head is killing me," Sam said. "What's that bright orb in the eastern sky?"

"They call that the sun," I said.

"What's it doing over there on that side of the heavenly firmament?"

"That's where it starts every day," I said.

"So every morning at eight thirty, I can expect to see this same phenomenon?"

"Pretty much," I said.

"Reason enough to sleep in or drink early," Sam said.

Brent popped up from the couch, grabbed his satchel and announced, "I'm going to be late. Can we go?"

"Fiona," I said, "I need you to take Brent to school."

"I already refused to do that yesterday," she said. "Besides, Sam was looking forward to meeting some coeds."

"I need Sam with me today," I said. "We're going to have some Yuri business and he can't see you again, at least not until his wrist heals. What we don't need is another combustible situation before we have Brent safely taken care of."

Fiona pursed her lips and exhaled hard through her nose. It was actually sort of cute when it didn't portend violence. "What classes do you have today, Brent?"

"Um, history, which is totally lame. And then I've got a game design class, which is badass, you know. And then I've got a three-hour seminar on women's studies."

"Lovely," Fiona said.

"I assume Western civ and women's studies are held in big lecture halls?" I said.

"Yeah. Like two hundred people are in those classes. But game design is just twelve of us, so it would be weird if Fiona was with me, but also sort of cool."

"Tell it," Sugar said. He was still in the kitchen, wisely keeping his distance from Sam, but he couldn't stop being Sugar, no matter where he was.

"Oh," Fiona said, "you're still alive?"

"I'm cold-kicking it live, doll," Sugar said and then he began reciting lyrics to some rap song.

"Don't speak to me," Fiona said to Sugar, which got

him to stop speaking/rapping immediately. "So I'm to wait outside this other classroom? Is that the idea?"

"Yes," I said. "If someone is coming for him, I suspect they'd come for him there."

"Then why are we even going to school?" Fiona asked.

"Because I'll fail if I miss any more classes," Brent said.

"This is ludicrous, Michael. You realize that?" Fiona said.

Sometimes the most important thing in the world is to let a person think that what they care about most is, in fact, extremely vital to their long-term well-being. Having something he could control, like when and if he attended class, was giving Brent a locus of normalcy. And if that was what he needed, that was what we'd have to give him, dangerous or not.

"We're living in odd times," I said. "You have a gun with you?"

"One in my purse, a dozen in my car. I'm supposed to sell a few this afternoon. I guess I'll cancel that."

"Please," I said. "And keep in touch during the day. Let me know if there are any problems."

"Yes, sir," Fiona said. "Come on, Brent. Let's go get you some book learning. And maybe, if you're nice, I'll let you pretend to be my boyfriend so that we can help you pick out a suitably slutty young woman for you to make mistakes with once you're incredibly wealthy in a few days."

"That sounds cool," Brent said.

I walked Fi and Brent outside to Fi's car, made sure

he was buckled in safely and then pulled Fi aside ever so briefly. "Try not kill anyone today," I said to her.

"What if I have to?"

"Try to just injure them," I said. "Guns on college campuses are sort of frowned upon."

"Hmm, yes, I seem to remember your government killing a bunch of kids on a college campus."

"I'm thinking more of crazed gunmen in towers and in crowded classrooms, really," I said.

"Ah, yes, your Second Amendment's downside," she said.

"Just be careful," I said.

"I will be," she said and then got in her car and was gone. When I turned around, Sam was standing on the front porch watching me. He had my cell phone in his hand.

"It's always sad when they leave the nest," he said. "You've got a call."

"Who is it?"

"He called himself Big Lumpy's Manservant Monty."

I took the phone from Sam. "This is Michael."

"I am sorry to bother you," Big Lumpy's Manservant Monty said. "But Mr. McGregor asked me to phone in the event of any problems and address myself as Manservant Monty."

"Mr. McGregor? That's . . ."

"Big Lumpy, yes," he said.

"Okay," I said.

"Yes, sorry to say, he's expired."

"Pardon me?"

"He's expired. In bed."

"You're telling me he's dead?"

"He met his transition, yes."

"That's not good," I said.

"On the contrary, it was very peaceful. He was very ill, as I'm sure you know, so this is a relief. He was very happy last night, you should know. As happy as I've seen him in years. He worked well into the early morning on your proposal, so I have it here for you. He instructed me that should there be any problems, as I noted before, all contracts remain enforced, so your brother, Nate, is still at risk here, so you should know."

"What about Brent?"

"Yes, he has been provided for provided he does as Mr. McGregor wishes."

"Which is?"

"Mr. Grayson will be delivered a copy of Mr. McGregor's conditions."

"When?"

"He left your mother's home approximately five minutes ago—would that be correct?"

I looked over my shoulder and down the street. Nothing stirred. There were no men with cameras hidden in the bushes. Which meant I probably didn't realize Sugar was bugged. If I had to guess, it would be his earrings. It's where I would have put a bug.

"Correct," I said.

"A messenger will be arriving shortly. Within the next ten minutes if you'd like to remain outside. Please do not kill him. He is literally the messenger and not an emissary of any kind. Mr. McGregor specifically wanted you to know this."

"Great," I said. "This information he left. It's about the wind technology, is that correct?"

"That's my understanding, yes. He was very thorough, you should know. He worked on it until he passed. It will certainly be enough to force Mr. Drubich into complicity provided it is brought to him by a believable source."

"Big Lumpy was to serve that purpose," I said.

"Yes, sir, I understand that," Monty said. "I'm afraid, as I said before, that he's expired and thus will not be able to play that role."

"Henry Grayson," I said.

"Yes?"

"Any information I should know regarding him?"

"Yes, well, I might add that Mr. McGregor was disappointed in you in that regard, but understood your position."

"What position was that?"

"The position you took in lying to him about his whereabouts. Nevertheless, Mr. Grayson is still missing. Mr. McGregor would like you to know you won that bet."

I'd had a feeling I hadn't fooled him. But what I had done was convince him that Henry was crazy. If that hadn't been the case, he wouldn't have let me parade that lie in front of him. Even in death, he was exerting control.

"Do you have a body?" I said.

"The body has been removed," he said.

"By whom?"

"The coroner. That's who usually does that sort of thing, correct?"

"I just didn't know if maybe Big Lumpy's body was privy to government secrecy or anything. You'll excuse me for presuming he was important."

"He was important," he said. I thought I caught a waver in Monty the Manservant's voice, which made me feel bad. Big Lumpy was, after all, his friend. Or his employer. Or his . . . something. It really wasn't all that defined what their relationship was and wasn't made easier by the fact that they both wore those absurd white outfits, like they were about to star in a Wham! video.

Apologizing would show weakness, so I just pressed on. "Do you happen to have a death certificate?"

"One has not been issued yet. You'll need to wait two days. The state of Florida is filled with dead people this time of year."

"Then I need proof of death in some other fashion," I said. "Otherwise I have no reason to believe you, apart from your very fine diction and that nice car you drive."

"Would you like to come over and sniff his room?"

"That was a joke, Monty?"

"That was a joke, Mr. Westen. But I'm sure you can call the coroner's office and they will confirm receipt of his body."

"Is there going to be a funeral?"

"He was a man just like any other," he said. "He has his wishes and they are that he will be buried in Massachusetts. If you'd like, I can see if we can get you a special pass to leave Miami to attend."

Smart. But I wondered how smart.

"Monty," I said. "That's your real name? Because I've never known an Asian person named Monty."

"No, not really."

"What's your real name?"

"Steven."

"Steven," I said, "why don't you go on home? Get on with your life. You don't work for Big Lumpy anymore. He's dead. So you can stop with the formality of things. No one is going to hurt you, okay? You can just head on back to whatever life you thought you wanted to lead. I'm sure you've been provided for, right?"

There was silence on the other end of the line.

"Really," I said. "Feel free. I'll come and pick up the documentation you have for me and then fly free."

Silence.

"Or do what you want. It's your choice. You just don't need to wait around for your orders anymore."

"Mr. Westen," he replied, "do you think everyone is you?"

"You've been briefed, apparently."

"Apparently," he said. "The messenger who arrives will have your information as well. When the money is made available to you from Mr. Drubich, you will contact me and your brother will be safe and all will be fine in the world."

"And who is going to let the government know that Yuri has top-secret documents?"

"Do you think I am really a manservant?"

"I guess I did," I said. "But I'm going to guess now that you're some kind of super assassin and also some kind of genius—would that be correct?"

"I think Mr. McGregor overestimated you," he said.

"Wouldn't be the first," I said. "Are you the eyelid guy or was that someone else, just so I know who I'm actually dealing with here."

"My contact information will be enclosed with the documents you will be receiving. Call me when you are ready to transfer the money."

"And what do I call you? Monty? Steven? Agent Zero?"

"Agent Zero sounds fine," he said and hung up.

I scrolled through the phone to see if the call had come from any specific number, but it came up blocked, naturally. I'd need to confirm that Big Lumpy was dead, but my sense was that he wouldn't go to such lengths just to complicate things.

"That didn't sound like a great conversation," Sam said.

"Big Lumpy is dead," I said.

"I got that," Sam said. I filled him in on the rest of the information Monty/Steven/Agent Zero gave me and let him digest it all. "Anything else?" he asked finally.

"I think Sugar is bugged," I said.

"We need to give him a full pelvic?"

"I hope not," I said. "I'm going to guess it's either in his earrings or his watch."

"His watch is the size of a hubcap," Sam said.

"That's where we'll look first, then. Save the pelvic for later, in case he resists."

Sam nodded. It was nice outside. A pleasant breeze. The palm trees were free of rats. The sky wasn't smoggy. I couldn't smell my mother's cigarette smoke. I could probably get into my car and drive to the Keys and come back in a week and all of these problems would be gone, one way or the other.

"This might be a good time for me to say, again, that I apologize for getting us into this mess," Sam said.

"How much do you know about wind technology?" I asked.

"I once had to go out to the Marine base in Twentynine Palms, outside Palm Springs and I saw that big wind farm they've got out there. Sort of creeped me out. Windmills look dangerous."

"Apart from that?"

"Apart from that, not much."

"Well," I said, "when the messenger arrives with the information Big Lumpy came up with for us to deliver to Yuri Drubich, I suggest you spend some time getting acclimated to the nuances of all things involving wind technology."

"So . . ."

"Yes," I said. "You're now Big Lumpy. You have any all-white outfits?"

"Not since *Miami Vice*," he said.

The front door opened and Sugar stepped out. "Your moms wanted me to come out and check on you," he said. When I didn't respond, because I knew he was lying, he said, "All right, man, you know, she's relentless with the judgments. I've had a bad week, bro, and she's all up on me for my life choices, so I had to bug out."

I said nothing.

"And so, yeah, I was thinking, maybe I'd bounce, if that's cool?"

"You planning on taking the bus?" Sam said. That he'd spoken at all was a surprise.

"Naw, man, I was hoping you could set me up with a ride and a safe place for a few days, till this Russian madness ends."

"Sugar," I said, "the moment you leave this house, you're a dead man. Do you realize that?"

"Your mom hates me," he said.

"You're easy to hate," Sam said. "Give me your watch."

"What?" he said.

"Your watch," Sam said. "Give it to me."

"Look, I'll hook you up with those Dolphin tickets—you just gotta give me some time."

"Sugar," I said, "give Sam your watch before he takes it with your arm still attached."

"If I give him my watch," Sugar said to me, "will you get me out of here?"

"Sugar," I said, "I have a feeling Big Lumpy bugged you. The easiest place to look is your watch. After that, we start going through your internal organs. So please, with cherries on top, give Sam your watch."

Sugar unclasped his watch and handed it to Sam. "Be careful," he said. "It's a Rolex."

"Aren't you a little young to have a Rolex?" Sam asked.

"I got big money," he said.

Sam handed me the watch so I could look at it. It said ROLEX on the face and it was covered with diamonds . . . except that the diamonds were obviously cubic zirconium, since the only person who could afford the size and sum of encrusted diamonds on Sugar's watch was the Sultan of Brunei. Even he would think it was gaudy.

I turned the watch over. It said MADE IN CHINA right there on the plate.

"Where'd you get this?" I asked.

"You know. I got people who find me deals."

"They got you a great deal on this one, then," I said and handed it back to Sam, who set it on the ground and stomped on it until it broke apart. The "diamonds" crumbled like . . . well, like the glass they turned out to be.

"What are you doing?" Sugar fairly shrieked.

"It's a fake, Sugar," I said. "It was made in China."

"What about the diamonds?" he said.

"Those were made in a window store," I said. I reached down and pulled out the parts and found the bug immediately—Big Lumpy hadn't bothered to put a small, top-level bug into the watch, opting instead for one about the size of a nickel.

"This come with your phone?" I asked.

"Aw, man, c'mon," Sugar said. "You think I knew they'd bugged me?"

"During your traumatic time of capture," Sam said, "were you ever without your lovely Rolex?"

"That weird little dude? Monty? He asked me if he could shine it for me. Right before we came to your place, Mike. I was like, damn, you know?"

"This was before they wrapped you in plastic and stuffed your ears with cotton and taped up your mouth?" I said.

"Yeah," he said.

"And you found nothing suspicious about the fact that they returned your watch to you all shined up and sparkling like it was the day you paid all eleven dollars for it?" Sam asked.

"Man, I was out of my mind. You know? I just, you know, like reacted to freedom and wasn't thinking about it. I'm not a pro at being kidnapped like you guys are. Maybe I had that Frankfurt Syndrome or some shit."

"I think you mean Stockholm," I said.

"Frankfurt, Stockholm, Fort Lauderdale, my shit was scared, yo."

It was hard to stay mad at Sugar. He was like a dog that pees on the floor every time the doorbell rings. Not much you can do but shake your head and drag it outside and tie it up when people come to visit—the difference being that you couldn't just leave Sugar chained up outside for the rest of the day. At least not legally.

I examined the bug for a moment. It was a government-issue high-density bug—the kind they hand out like M&Ms to spies around the world—which lent credence to both Big Lumpy's bona fides and Monty's . . . or Steve's . . . or Agent Zero's. Whoever he was. I looked for a fingerprint on the bug but found nothing. He'd be too good for that.

"Sam," I said, "you think you could find out who Big Lumpy's manservant Monty actually is?"

"You don't trust him?"

"No," I said, "I actually do trust him. But I want to know who our new business partner is before we send you into combat with Yuri."

"I'll make some calls," he said.

"I need to know if he's someone who can be reasoned with or someone I might need to shoot first, like

Sugar, but I have a feeling you're going to have a bit of homework when the deliveryman shows up."

"I was afraid you were going to say that," Sam said.

"You're the only person here who resembles the words 'Big Lumpy,'" I said.

"I can tell you right now," Sugar said, "that Monty fool has his swerve down. He made my watch look tight even if he did bug it. But if you want to put a cap in his ass, I'm with that."

"No one is putting a cap in anyone's ass," I said. "Least of all you."

"Just saying, Mike, I'm riding with you, I'm riding with you to the end, player."

"Do you practice these lines?" Sam said to Sugar. "Or do they just roll out of your mouth as natural as the day you were born?"

"You know," Sugar said, "when you got game, you got game."

A black van with the logo FOUR POINTS DELIVERY SERVICE pulled up in front of my mother's house then. The delivery guy got out and saw us standing there. "This the Westen Spy House?" he asked.

"Yes," I said. Good old dead Big Lumpy. He had a sense of humor, at least.

"Cool. One of you want to help me with the boxes?"

"*Boxes?*" I said.

"Yeah, I got two file boxes full of stuff, plus a couple envelopes and a laptop computer."

"Have at it, Sugar," Sam said.

Sugar, to his credit, didn't respond in any negative way to Sam, and instead went to the curb to help the deliveryman. The delivery guy opened up the back of the van, and Sugar stepped in and came back out with two white boxes stuffed with information.

"Where you want this stuff?" he asked when he got up to the porch.

"Put it in the kitchen," I said, "and tell my mother not to touch it."

"Man, I'm not telling her anything. I don't need her yelling at me like I'm her kid."

The deliveryman walked up behind Sugar with the envelopes and the laptop. "You need to sign for all of this," he said. He handed me the envelopes—one marked with my name, one marked with Brent's—and handed Sam the laptop. He went back to his truck and came back with a clipboard and showed me where to sign. "Okay, thanks."

"Can I ask you a question?" I said.

"Sure," he said. "Is it about the creepy dude?"

"The creepy dude?" I said.

"The little Asian dude," he said. "If he's your cousin or something, I apologize. He just gave me the creeps."

"It actually is about him," I said. "Where did you pick this information up?"

"That's part of the creepy bit," he said. "I picked it up about a block away from here."

"From here?" I said.

"Yeah. Parking lot of that church down the street? You know it?"

"Yes," I said.

"Weird since he could have just dropped it off himself, right?"

"Right," I said. And then a thought occurred to me. "When did they place the delivery order?"

He flipped through the pages on the clipboard. "Uh, let's see. Looks like the order came in two days ago."

"Are you sure?" I asked.

"Yep. Prepaid delivery authorized on Saturday."

Saturday. I hadn't even met Big Lumpy yet on Saturday. "What time?"

"Uh, let's see. Did it online at eight in the morning. Early risers, I guess."

And with precognitive abilities. Sam and I met with Big Lumpy on Sunday at noon. Which either meant Big Lumpy had the world's best Ouija board or was well aware of Brent's situation—and his connection to me—long before we ever met. I had a suspicion that either Brent's home phone was bugged—likely, really— and that more than likely Big Lumpy had been tracking Brent for a very long time. It made sense if Henry Grayson was in as deep as he appeared to be. I could see Big Lumpy wanting to have a pawn to play with for his money, only to discover something far more interesting and then, as was his wont, taking a few bets on how things might turn out. All an elaborate game for his enjoyment and, perhaps, a little deathbed edification.

"Thanks," I said. "That's helpful."

"No problem," he said, but then he didn't go anywhere. "Information, you know, it's the currency of the future, but you can't pay your rent with it, if you get my meaning."

I did.

"Sam," I said, "tip the man."

"You should wear more comfortable shoes," Sam said. "Trust me. You'll be having back problems soon enough if you're not careful. You need to start lifting from your legs and then carrying all boxes in what we in the ergonomic profession call the strike zone. So, middle of your thigh to the middle of your chest." Sam patted the delivery guy on the shoulder in such a way that he actually managed to get him turned around back toward his van. "No need to thank me now. Your sciatica can send me a thank-you note from the old folks' home."

We watched the van drive off in silence, both of us contemplating the news we'd learned.

I looked at Sam and tried to imagine him all in white and filled with two file boxes and a laptop computer's worth of information. He apparently was having the same revelation, since he now looked even more sickened than usual by the early hour.

"Better go inside and ask my mother if you can borrow her reading glasses," I said to Sam.

"You ever learn that Evelyn Wood Speed Reading technique?" he asked.

"No," I said, "I always preferred to actually read."

"They say if you learn something in an altered state, you'll recall it better in an altered state. So I'm thinking maybe a mimosa is the call here."

"I'm going to say no," I said.

"You sure you don't think Sugar could pull off being Big Lumpy?" he said.

"No."

"So Big Lumpy knew we were coming," Sam said.

"Seems like it."

"I wonder how much more he knew."

"I'm going to guess quite a bit," I said. I told him I

thought Brent's place was probably bugged and my ideas about Big Lumpy's initial reasoning.

"Makes sense," Sam said. "You really think he's dead?"

"I'll call the coroner to find out," I said, "but I'm going to guess that he killed himself."

"Why?"

"Because it would be more entertaining for him to watch this from some spectral plane than to actually be in it. And because he was already dead, for the most part. Last night he told me he had three months, but I wouldn't have placed money on that being true. The man could hardly function. He didn't even torture Sugar."

My mom stepped outside then and slammed the door behind her. "He's an idiot," she said.

"I know," I said.

"Are you going to stow him in my garage while you go out saving the world?"

"Not this time," I said.

"Good," she said, "because he's not safe here."

"I understand," I said.

"It's bad enough that he's an idiot," she said, "but his self-tanning lotion is giving me a migraine. Someone should tell him that the color orange does not occur in nature."

"I'll mention it to him," Sam said. He put an arm around my mother. She had a soft spot for Sam, probably because Sam had an ability to make anyone like him, and probably because she knew he'd kept me alive on more than one occasion. "Why don't we go inside and you can help me learn all about the fascinating world of wind, and if Sugar does anything to annoy you, I'll put him in a sleeper lock. How does that sound?"

Before she could answer, Sam had her turned around and was walking her back into the house. The man could defuse a nuclear bomb with a drink in one hand.

I'd planned on leaving Sugar behind, but circumstances had changed. I hadn't expected Big Lumpy to die. I hadn't expected to be the unwitting dupe in some larger game—a position I was absolutely not comfortable with, but which I'd need to react to with suitable force and control. And I hadn't expected the need to get Sam trained in the fine art of wind technology, the burgeoning echo system of black market bandwidths and, of course, make sure it was all plausible enough to get Yuri to bite on it, so that the rest of the plan could go forward. Getting a man who shot rockets into businesses off the street was a good thing, but the more tangible issue was that otherwise he would kill Brent the first chance he got. And Fiona's death was a real possibility, too. Yuri Drubich probably considered Fiona's breaking his wrist as bad form. What I did know, however, was that Yuri wanted to see Brent and Henry, wanted to make them pay for his inconvenience. They probably knew what Brent looked like by now, but they probably had no idea what Henry looked like. They knew enough to blow up his office, but not enough to destroy his home, which told me they were still grasping at straws.

So I needed to find someone who could plausibly pass for Brent's father.

I needed someone who would do exactly what I said and wouldn't ask too many questions.

I needed someone who might know how to manage a few million dollars discreetly . . . and who wouldn't mind working with Sugar, if need be.

That decreased the pool by a legion.

I opened up the envelope Big Lumpy had left for Brent and read the terms and conditions of his inheritance, such as it was. A good lawyer would help, but the closest thing I had to that was another man good at moving papers around. And, as it happened, the perfect person for the job at hand, too.

"Barry," I said into my cell phone when my favorite money launderer answered, "I need you."

12

When you occupy a defensive position, it's important to find good cover. If good cover isn't available, a spy will try to conceal himself as best as possible. This can mean that he hides behind a bush or a mustache, in a burned-out car or on a crowded bus. Concealment provides time to reorganize and recalibrate an attack and, if done correctly, might also allow a spy to do a little . . . spying. Because there's nothing a spy appreciates more than the opportunity to view and analyze his own information—which is why Sugar and I were sitting on the patio of Odessa sipping tea while we waited for Barry to show up.

None of Yuri's people knew about me, as far as I could tell, and Sugar had escaped out the back door of Henry's office before he could be spotted. And since Sugar's car wasn't registered in his name, whoever Yuri thought he was intimidating by destroying the car wasn't actually Sugar.

If we were going to exchange information and money, I'd want to do it in public, but I'd want to do it in a place where Yuri felt comfortable, so I figured visiting his place of business was a nice way of getting the lay of the land.

Plus, I'd placed bugs inside the main shop beneath several of the shelves holding tea and accoutrements while we waited to be seated.

"You really think this is a good idea?" Sugar said.

"Well," I said, "if anyone here suspected we were anything but tea enthusiasts, they would have poisoned us already."

"I do feel itchy," Sugar said.

"That's probably an allergic reaction to being wrapped in plastic."

"Man, I wasn't made for this spy game," he said.

"Which is why you shouldn't say things like 'I wasn't made for this spy game' in public. It tends to be a red flag."

"You just want me to sit here and shut up?"

"Yes," I said. "Sip your tea. You may find you enjoy it."

"It tastes like dirt, you want my opinion," Sugar said.

"That's one thing I don't want."

We'd been there for only fifteen minutes and thus far I hadn't seen a man with a broken wrist or a woman with balance issues who was also bleeding from the ears, so maybe they were both taking a personal day. Our waitress was a young Cuban woman—maybe nineteen or twenty—who didn't seem to possess any outward signs that she was a Castro supporter here to overthrow the American government, nor did she seem all that interested in bringing us hot water in a timely manner. In fact, the entire tearoom seemed to be filled with people mostly interested in doing their jobs at the rate tea steeps. Which was fine. They didn't even bother to attempt to peek at the folder filled with documents that I brought with me. I was just another business-man on a business lunch with his drug dealer.

But across the street from the tea shop was another story. Though the information we'd received said that Yuri's business was registered here—which it was—I could tell now that it was both an issue of keeping up appearances and total convenience.

On the southeastern corner, there was a seven-story condo complex that looked to be made entirely of metal and glass, which made me first think that the air-conditioning bills would be enough to drive any man into an illegal trade, but then when I saw the name of the complex—the Rai Gardens—a familiar tingling sensation began working up my spine.

On the northeastern corner was a five-story office complex that flew the flags of several different coun-tries, including, right in my line of site, the flag of Mol-dova, a former Soviet state located between Romania and Ukraine. I called Sam.

"How good is your Russian?" I said.

"I've had to replace all verb conjugations with in-formation about bandwidth, I'm afraid. Why?"

"Because I'm sitting here at Odessa looking at a condo complex called the Rai Gardens."

"Doesn't *rai* mean 'heaven' or 'paradise' or some-thing like that in Russian?"

"See," I said, "you've retained just enough informa-tion to be useful."

"I'm trying my best," he said.

"I need you to do me a small favor," I said. "Find out where our Ukrainian friend's wife is from."

"Why?"

"Because I want to make sure a hunch I'm having is correct," I said. "The Moldovan Consulate is about fifty yards from the teahouse. I'm going to guess that our Ukrainian friend married a woman from across the border."

"And that he keeps a place inside the Rai Gardens?"

"I wouldn't be surprised if he owns the Rai Gardens," I said. "Fiona said she got knocked out and he was there in a matter of minutes. It makes sense that he'd live close enough to asylum and his business interests. It's too coincidental not to be true."

"Just as soon as I finish digesting some very interesting information about the wind turbines in Dubai, I'll be on it. But listen, Mikey, this information Big Lumpy gave us? It's a lot more comprehensive than whatever Brent knows."

"What do you mean?" I asked.

"This laptop, it's loaded with video of test sites. We've got formulas here that mean nothing to me but must mean something to someone. I mean, when he said that he'd make the information government secrets, I really think he meant it. He has a whole Power-Point presentation on here that I'd say he didn't just whip up overnight before he died."

"You know his connections," I said.

"But what if he's trying to screw us? What if we give this information to Yuri and it really is the kind of thing that will give him a leg up, give terrorists a leg up, too?"

I thought about it for a moment. "I don't know, Sam," I said. "He was NSA. I don't see him doing that. He said it would bring Yuri down, and I want to believe him."

"I don't know, Mikey," he said.

"Look," I said, "he won't have the chance to get anywhere with it. We give him the information and twenty-four hours later, he's in a prison somewhere. It's a chance we need to take."

"We're putting our faith in a whole slew of untrustworthy people. He's got three zip drives full of information we're supposed to hand to Yuri. I can't make sense of anything on them."

"Sam," I said, "I've got a good feeling Big Lumpy was preparing for this moment for a very long time. He knew way too much about everything way ahead of time."

"But why would he care about screwing Yuri Drubich?"

"I don't think he did," I said. "I think he wanted to help Brent."

"He's got a funny way of being nice," Sam said.

"Speaking of which," I said, "anything yet on Monty?"

"No," Sam said. "Big Lumpy kept a tight organization. You want me to poke some lowlifes, I can do that, but it may raise suspicion."

"No," I said. "I'm meeting with a lowlife shortly. Maybe he'll have something we can use."

I hung up and took another sip of tea. I could tell Sugar wanted to say something, anything, because staying quiet to him was like swallowing castor oil was for other people. But before he could say anything, I gave him an order. "I want you to count how many Denalis drive down the street and park either over there by the condo or over there by that embassy-looking building. If they have tinted windows, count them twice."

"Why twice?"

"Because no one with tinted windows drives alone," I said.

"Do I win some kind of prize at the end?"

"If everything works out the way I think," I said, "you're going to get to keep on living and selling drugs to college freshmen."

This got Sugar's interest. "Cool," he said. He turned his chair so that he was facing the street more directly and then took off his sunglasses, since apparently he has a hard time concentrating with sunglasses on. "You think I could get another one of these teas? I sort of like the buzz it's giving me."

I opted not to tell Sugar he was drinking the Russian equivalent to chamomile and went ahead and poured him some of my zavarka, the strong, sometimes pungent tea favored by Russian diplomats the world over. He took a sip and I watched as he tried to keep from coughing it all back up. To his credit, he remained strong and kept drinking from his cup as he counted cars.

A few minutes later, what I hoped was a rented purple Ford Focus pulled into the parking lot and out stepped Barry, right on time and dressed just as I'd ordered: a blue polo shirt tucked into a pair of tan slacks. He wore a pair of hideously ugly brown Crocs on his feet, which was counter to my order that he be wearing loafers, but it was suitable enough. He had also shaved, as instructed, and wore a pair of sunglasses that made him look like someone's father—a pair of barely tinted aviators—and had managed to comb his spiked hair into something vaguely resembling a normal hairstyle.

Combine all of this together, along with Barry's usual countenance, and it made for the perfect package of world-weary middle-class angst. Wonderful.

I waved at Barry and he just sighed and made his way across the parking lot toward the tearoom.

"Who's the square?" Sugar asked.

"Barry," I said.

"Bad Check Barry? The money launderer?"

"Same guy."

In fact, Barry was far more than a money launderer these days. He'd diversified his talents to the point that he was practically a one-stop shop for all your illegal paperwork needs. Like an Office Depot, but with the ability to get you a fake passport and safe passage to Ecuador at a moment's notice.

He wasn't a lawyer, but he'd be able to help me with the conditions of Brent's new wealth that Big Lumpy had set forth and with the lengths (or depths) we'd need to go to in order to secure Brent the opportunity to find that wealth.

But he didn't know all of that when he sat down at the table with Sugar and me.

"You look good," I said.

"I feel like one of those tourists serial killers keep an eye out for, since they know no one will miss them. I had to go into Walmart to get all of this stuff. Do you know how degrading that was for me, Michael? What if someone I know spotted me?"

"You'd be forced to vote Republican from here on out," I said.

Barry handed me a receipt for $127.98. "You don't need to pay me back for the sunglasses," he said. "I like the way they look on my face. Might be good for business meetings with people not quite as fashion forward as you and your Scooby Gang. Plus it makes me look a little more authoritarian."

"That's why cops wear them," I said.

"These pants are some kind of polyester blend," Barry said. "I'm sweating in places I didn't know I had places."

"I appreciate you coming in costume," I said. "I'm going to make it worth your while."

"You working with some fetish gang or something?"

"Not quite," I said.

"Not even close, bro," Sugar said, which made Barry do the one thing he hadn't done yet: acknowledge that someone else was sitting at the table with me. One thing most criminals have in common is the ability to completely ignore people they have absolutely no interest in. It makes it less likely those people will be able to positively identify them later or, worse, testify against them.

"Who are you?" Barry said to Sugar.

"Sugar."

"I thought the Spice Girls broke up," Barry said and then he turned back to me. "Who is this person to my left?"

"He's a drug dealer. He used to live downstairs from me."

"Oh," Barry said. "The guy you shot?"

"Same guy," I said again.

"Why does everyone know that?" Sugar asked.

"It's a funny story," Barry said. "I didn't even hear it from Michael. Shot him through the wall, right?"

"Right," I said.

"Classic," Barry said. "You doing some kind of 'Up with People' thing with him now?"

"We've done some work together in the past," I said.

"I'm pretty much on the team," Sugar said.

"No, you're not," I said. "He's currently part of the reason we need you."

"My lucky day," Barry said.

"I already know you," Sugar said. "You're Bad Check Barry. See, I know all the gangsters up in this piece."

Barry stared at Sugar for a long time without speaking. Normally, Barry is the kind of guy who likes to chat a bit, but I could tell he felt uneasy about Sugar. Finally, he turned to me and said, "I'm going to pretend he's not here. Is that okay?"

"That's fine," I said. "Sugar, go back to counting Denalis."

"I've already got five," Sugar said.

"Good. Stop if you get to twenty." I waved the waitress over—since we were now the only people on the patio she actually managed to get to our table in a reasonable amount of time—and ordered another samovar of tea for Barry. I needed him alert, so I poured him a healthy-sized serving. He took a sip, grimaced and tried to act cool.

"What do you call that flavor?" he asked. "Communism?"

"Gorbachev's favorite tea," I said. "Served it to Reagan and then they talked about movies with chimps."

"I thought I recognized it," Barry said. "It's strong. Tastes a little bit like something the Russians would pour in your eyes to make you talk. They ever do that sort of stuff?"

"They were known for their persuasive interrogation techniques," I said.

Barry took another sip and then looked around the place. "It's nice here. The kind of place I could bring a date later on. You ever bring Fiona here?"

"She came on her own recently and now she's not welcome back," I said.

"That happen a lot?"

"Yes," I said. I reached into my pocket and pulled out the envelope Big Lumpy had delivered to my mother's house that outlined the terms by which he'd leave Brent enough money to live on for a very long time. "I want you to read this, tell me if you think what's outlined here is possible."

"Legally possible?"

"Possible possible."

"And then you'll tell me why I'm dressed like this?"

"I will," I said, "but those shoes were your choice."

"I take my foot care seriously," he said. "These I can just throw away later and I won't feel like I've wasted your money after bad podiatry."

He unfolded the letter and began to read. It wouldn't take him long, since Big Lumpy had outlined Brent's life into ten easy-to-digest points, perhaps because he wasn't confident Brent had much in the way of reading comprehension skills:

1. In order for you to collect on the terms of my will, which, by the time you receive this, will already be in active probate, I ask first that Michael Westen make it clear to you that I was aware your father was not dead and that I chose, nevertheless, to go forward with this agreement. Surprisingly, Mr. Westen has your best interests at heart.

2. You shall receive the proceeds of the sale of your "technology," minus the existing debts of Henry Grayson and Nate Westen (as have been outlined under separate cover), the small sum that will be needed to show that the transaction was made with my estate (no more than $1 million) to ensure prosecution of purchaser of "technology," any middleman fees incurred by Mr. Westen and any property costs associated with fires, explosions or burials incurred by Mr. Westen, in monthly allotments until the age of 25. However, this money must go toward living expenses, schooling and research only. No gambling.

3. You shall attend MIT. You need only to apply. The rest has been taken care of.

4. You shall work for the United States Government until age 25. I would prefer that you not become a spy, but rather a scientist. If you must, a position at the NSA would be acceptable. The position in the United States government is also already taken care of.

5. You must provide your father with whatever medical or mental care he needs; however, you are to provide him with no money. You may pay his bills for the rest of his life if you choose, but he should not be in a position to actually spend money (apart from small items like groceries, toothpaste, etc.). If at any time your father has an outstanding debt to what would normally be considered an "underworld figure" your financial support will be removed, even if you are beyond the age-25 threshold. (Though I am dead, trust me that your accounts will be debited from the sum you've received thus far.)

6. After age 35, if you choose to embark on a life of crime, you are not allowed to go by any demeaning nicknames.

7. The money derived from the sale of your "technology" will be deposited into a foreign bank account, as the money will technically be from an enemy combatant. Either my associates will be able to facilitate this or certainly Mr. Westen will know some people of ill means who will be able to provide cover in this regard. I would recommend Iceland rather than a traditional island or an Eastern European haven.

8. Keep friends close. My associates are prepared to offer educational packages to at least one current friend that is not Sugar.

9. See that my grave is kept clean. As you will be in Massachusetts attending college, I expect that you will visit my grave in Cambridge at least twice a year with proper cleaning supplies.

10. In the event you are unable to secure funding for your "technology" or are otherwise damaged in the pursuit of said deal, all of the above is still valid, including your education and position in the United States government provided Nate Westen's debt is paid in full. No further financial benefit shall be made from this estate.

Barry took off his glasses and rubbed at his eyes. "Who is this from?" he asked.

"You ever hear of someone named Big Lumpy?"

Barry made a slicing motion over his face. "The eyelid guy?"

"That's him."

"He's dead?"

"Yep," I said. "Coroner confirmed it."

"That doesn't mean anything," Barry said. "You should ask to see a body. And even then, you never know. Voodoo and all that. Did you know Miami is considered one of the most haunted cities in the United States? So, who knows. I could be dead and you could be talking to my ghost."

"Barry," I said, "calm down."

"He's a bad guy, Michael," Barry said. "I made a New Year's resolution to spend less time with bad guys."

"You're a bad guy," I said.

"I mean people who are evil," Barry said. "I'm just a criminal. You drop your wallet, I'm giving it back to you. You need a fake passport to get out of the country, I'm your man, because I believe in a world without borders."

"That's why?"

"In a perfect utopian world, yes," he said.

"You'd need to find a new line of work," I said. "In any case, Big Lumpy just had a good press agent. He kidnapped Sugar and didn't even torture him."

"You have a weird idea of what torture is, bro," Sugar said. "And that Denali parking across the street? That's number twenty."

I pulled out my wallet and handed Sugar a fifty. "You see that building over there with the flags?"

"Yeah?" Sugar said.

"I want you to walk over there and hand the security guard at the front desk this fifty-dollar bill and ask him how often Yuri Drubich visits the building."

"What if he won't tell me?"

"He will," I said. "If he says he can't tell you, that's all the answer we need."

Barry and I watched Sugar walk through the tea shop and then out into the street, where he was nearly hit from both sides.

"He's not a smart person," Barry said.

"He has his uses," I said.

"Did you say Yuri Drubich?"

"Did I?" I said.

"Did you?"

"I don't think I did," I said. I needed to keep Barry rooted in time and space before I brought the Yuri element into play.

"I thought you told Sugar to go ask about Yuri Drubich, and, as policy, I don't do business with ex-KGB. They aren't very responsible people and they tend to act violently, like they still think they're a superpower. I'm not down for that business. Russian Mafia?

Not so bad. They've got a code, at least. So they wear leather trench coats and quote *Scarface*, fine. But they're predictable. Move a little H. Do a little human trafficking, whatever. But these ex–KGB guys all think the Cold War is still going on and that the Soviets are winning. I can't deal with that arrogance. You don't see the English coming here and trying to refight the Revolutionary War. They understand, and look at us now. Kissing cousins." He paused, took a breath and then leaned toward me. "Anyway, my point is some evil never dies," Barry said. "I saw a movie about that. Be that Big Lumpy or Yuri Drubich."

"If Big Lumpy's ghost comes back and wants to hurt you, I'll be there to stop it."

"Oh, you're a ghostbuster now?"

"He's dead," I said. "And even if he wasn't, he would be soon." I explained to Barry the condition Big Lumpy was in when last I'd seen him. And then I decided it was best to tell him the rest of the story, from the Web site to Brent's deal with Yuri Drubich, to Big Lumpy's role in this and, finally, that Henry Grayson was now in a safe location. The more I told him, the more pale he became.

"You know what would be nice?" Barry said. "If one day you just called me and said you needed to launder some money."

"It's a more complex world than it was when you first started in business," I said. "You should be happy you haven't been left behind."

"I guess so," he said. He examined the letter again. "Well, this Iceland thing is a pretty good idea. After their banks collapsed in 2008, they've been hungry for

American dollars, so they relaxed a lot of their regulations. You ever seen one of their bills? The krona? It's got one of the ugliest men in a wig on it I've ever seen. It's like a drag show you can buy food with."

"That's not helpful in the least," I said.

"It's still a good place to stash money," Barry said, "as long as you don't mind a low interest rate. The American dollar to the krona is almost as bad as the euro to the krona, which makes it not a great place to invest, but a good place to stash."

"So you can take care of that?" I said.

"Sugar could do it."

"What else?" I said.

"How much does Henry Grayson owe?"

I pulled out a handy Excel spreadsheet Big Lumpy had been kind enough to provide me—which also included Nate's debts—and gave it to Barry. He examined it for a few minutes. "This guy should not bet," Barry said. "He shouldn't be allowed to make any decisions whatsoever, really."

"Hence the conditions," I said.

"It says here he's already paid off a couple hundred thousand and he still owes, what, another four hundred thousand?"

"And that's not with any further vig," I said. "Big Lumpy cut off the vig at his death."

"That's proper," Barry said. "Can't take it with you, I've always been told. It says here Nate owes . . . two hundred dollars?"

"Correct," I said. "A purely symbolic gesture by Big Lumpy."

"You sure he's dead?"

"Sure."

"Well, everything he lays out here, I can get it all set up for the kid. Big Lumpy's got some guy who's still breathing who's taking care of it from his end?"

"You know an Asian guy named Monty?" I said.

"Wears white all the time?" Barry said.

"Yes," I said. "Where do you know him from?"

"Couple years back he was in a hot stone massage class with me at the junior college. We bump into each other periodically on the circuit."

"The circuit?"

"You know, galas on the Fish that are just veiled pyramid schemes, casino yachts run by Cubans in the Biscayne, parties with Jay-Z, that sort of thing. He's an ex-something-supersecret."

"Yeah," I said, "that's what I got from talking to him." I thought for a moment. "You took a class in hot stone massage?"

"It's a fascinating art, Michael," he said. "You learn all about pressure points that can be manipulated for the release of tension. It can be a very useful technique for a single man."

"Or someone who needs to torture people periodically," I said.

"No, there's an oath you take that you'll never use the art for ill. A whole creed you have to say before class. Something about using might for right. I remember that part."

"He's Big Lumpy's guy Friday," I said. "What's his reputation?"

"You work for Big Lumpy, perception is that you're

best of the best, but that could mean best at breaking arms or puncturing lungs or whatever."

"I'm asking if he's someone to worry about."

Barry thought for a moment. "Worry? No. At heart he's a gentle soul. He liked to paint these very small poems onto his hot stones. Said they gave the stones emotional power, too."

"You think you can work with him?"

"I can work with anyone," Barry said, "provided their money is green."

"You'll be compensated." Across the street, Sugar was already dodging oncoming traffic again as he made his way back to Odessa. Maybe, I thought, remembering my impressions of Big Lumpy, some kids never did get the "look both ways" thing down pat. "I need you to be Henry Grayson," I said.

"Doesn't Yuri want to kill him?"

"Yes," I said. "But he also wants to kill Fiona, so you'd be in good company."

"You're not making this sound any more appealing," Barry said. "Besides, I'm not old enough to have a nineteen-year-old kid."

"No?"

"No," he said. He didn't sound all that convincing.

"How old are you, Barry?"

"That's confidential information," he said. "You can't ask me that."

"I'm going to guess forty-three," I said. "Normal person, by the time they're forty-three, they've got a kid."

"I'm not a normal person and I'm not forty-three," he said. "Do I look forty-three?"

"Right now you look about fifty," I said. "The Crocs aren't doing you any favors."

"These pants make me look fat," Barry said.

"Pleats do that," I said.

"What would I need to do?"

"You'd need to come with me and Sam and Brent to meet with Yuri. While you're there, you're going to apologize for doing some untoward things and then we'll all go home."

"That's it?"

"That's it," I said. "Essentially."

"What does 'essentially' mean?"

"Won't know until it happens," I said. I poured Barry another cup of tea and pushed it toward him. "Put some honey in it. It will calm you down."

Barry took a sip and grimaced. "The honey only makes the bitter things stick together," he said. "So this Brent. What's he like?"

"Shrugs a lot. Says 'like' every other word."

"Is he worth all of this trouble?"

"He's a smart kid. Big Lumpy thought he was the real deal, obviously. He's had a bad life," I said. "I think everyone deserves a chance for a better one. Maybe this will give him that."

"In the end, it's just money."

"You saying money can't buy happiness?"

"Personally," Barry said, "I derive great pleasure from money, but you know how kids are today."

"I guess you'd know better than me, being closer in age to most children," I said.

Barry didn't respond to that. "And I'm to portray his father?"

"Yes."

"Will I get a script?"

"Do you need a script?"

"I did a bit of theater in high school," Barry said. "Thurber and the like. So I at least need to know my motivation."

"Not to die," I said.

"That's easy enough," Barry said.

Sugar finally navigated his way across the street, the parking lot and the tea shop and found his seat back at the table. He still had the fifty-dollar bill in his hand, along with a flyer for some event.

"Bro," he said, "you won't believe what I found out."

"That this isn't a pedestrian state?" I said.

"Our boy is gonna be all up in some black-tie shit tonight."

Sugar handed me the flyer. Across the top it said THE CONSULATE OF MOLDOVA SALUTES ITS PHILANTHROPIST OF THE YEAR. In the center of the flyer was a huge photo of Yuri Drubich, his lovely wife and three lovely children. There was even a dog in the photo. Some kind of spaniel with a very pink tongue. It was suitable for framing or turning into a Christmas card. At the bottom of the flyer it said that the evening's black-tie celebration would begin at eight p.m. and that Drubich would be honored for his "tireless efforts in expanding technology to the children of Moldova." To reserve a table of five was a mere $10,000, though ten people got you a discounted rate of just $15,000. Checks payable to the Drubich Trust for Electronic Education.

I showed the flyer to Barry. "You have a cheap tuxedo?" I asked.

"If I wear black tie, I go all-out," he said. "I prefer Armani."

"We'll get you a nice rental," I said.

"Nothing with ruffles," he said. "My senior prom I went ruffles and I've regretted it ever since."

"Do you have any bad checks you'd like to pass?"

"Cashier's or certified?"

"Let's go cashier's. More cachet. Make it from Inter-Macron Industries."

"You'll need to give me some time," he said.

"How long?"

Barry looked at his watch. "Best guy in town is just down the street," he said. "Factor in schmoozing and gossip, I can be back in fifteen minutes."

"Go," I said.

"How much you want the check for?"

I took a sip of tea and looked out at the street. The number of consulates in the same building as the Moldovan Consulate would make things difficult security-wise, I suspected. Bringing guns inside would be nearly impossible, yet I knew for certain that Yuri's security detail would be fully loaded, which presented some problems. If we met privately with Yuri and his men were forced to kill us, it would be easy to cover up under the guise of an attack on the Moldovan Consulate by a burned spy, an ex–Navy SEAL and an Irish terrorist; Brent and Barry would be more difficult to explain, but they were also two people not many other people would miss, just as Barry feared. Plus, I'd need to find a place to stash Sugar where he couldn't hurt himself or others.

This would take some planning, but I had some ideas.

"Make the check for a hundred thousand," I said. "That should be enough money to ensure the opportunity to make a toast at this event, don't you think?"

"Why not make it a million?" Barry said.

"Yeah, boy," Sugar said, apparently feeling that he was allowed to speak again. "Go big or stay home. That's how I roll."

I hated to agree with Sugar. But even a clock is right twice a day. "Do it," I said and Barry was up and gone.

It was just after noon, which meant I had a little less than eight hours to make it all airtight. I texted Fiona with some of the new details and then called Sam.

"Thank you for calling InterMacron," Sam said.

"We've had a slight change of plans," I said.

"Don't tell me I learned all of this for nothing," he said.

"No," I said, "you'll need it." I told Sam about the event honoring Drubich that evening and about the generous donation I thought InterMacron should make in his honor. "How do you feel about doing a little public speaking tonight?"

"As long as they have an open bar," Sam said, "I'm prepared to speak at length on any number of subjects."

13

College boys, Fiona thought, were the worst of their species. Aesthetically, there was very little wrong with a twenty-one-year-old male at the peak of his conditioning, his body healthy and able to withstand punishment. Fiona was happy to admit that. And she couldn't resist staring at a few of the particularly lovely specimens as she walked with Brent across the campus of the University of Miami. In fact, if college boys could just learn to keep their mouths closed and their bodies toned, they'd be perfect chew toys for a woman like herself. Fun, disposable, not terribly annoying.

But when they opened their mouths . . .

It was as if they forgot they had mothers, or sisters, or even beloved pets, since surely they didn't treat their dogs as poorly as they treated women. What base form of human, other than boys in college, thinks it's appropriate to walk up to a woman and ask her if they could "get with that"? Or ask if she was "down for it" or if she'd be interested in "getting your drink on with me at the frat house" as if any of those invitations weren't little more than veiled requests for sex?

It was just before noon and Fiona was escorting

Brent to lunch before she'd be forced to sit through yet another class. She'd spent the previous two hours and thirty minutes in a lecture hall listening to some crusty professor in a tweed jacket telling complete and utter lies about history, to the point that she'd finally raised her hand to ask a question, but fortunately for the old cud behind the lectern, he didn't bother to look up from the text he was reading. Fiona would have let him know, in exacting detail, how American education was apparently predicated on misperception.

It was more than she could take, really, listening to the professor butchering the past. He'd gone on some long-winded jag about how the British had attempted to oppress their colonists living in America and that's what started the Revolutionary War, a war that was scantily discussed in the history books Fiona recalled, though her memory was very precise on the minimal material she was taught about the issues related to that particular war: the colonists were a wanton band of separatists, an issue she was well versed in, but unlike the Irish, they didn't have the advantage of being right.

It was just madness, though it did help her to understand Michael a bit more (and, to a lesser extent, Sam), who wore their patriotism like both a badge and a shield. A false history can do that to you.

And if suffering through the indignity of that experience wasn't bad enough, the boy sitting beside her for those one hundred and fifty minutes of revisionist drivel kept "accidentally" brushing his hand along her thigh. She'd intentionally sat in the back of the lecture hall, a few rows behind Brent, so that she could keep the entire room in her vision at all times. It was set up with stadium seating, but the two doors into the hall were at the bottom of the room, on either side of the lectern stage, so from her vantage point in the back Fiona would be able to take out anyone who might wish to do Brent harm long before he or she laid eyes on him.

So Fiona found a seat next to a boy in a light blue Oxford shirt, with combed and parted Republican hair and a fair complexion. The kind of boy she presumed called women "ma'am" and men "sir" and probably grew up in a city like Savannah, Georgia, and was filled with Southern courtesy and wouldn't try to look into her purse and thus wouldn't have questions about why she was on campus with a chrome-plated Glock.

She sat down beside him and he smiled at her wanly—the kind of smile she'd expected him to give her. A gentle declaration that she was, indeed, the most beautiful woman he'd ever seen, but also that she was so far out of his league that he'd just let her know, by showing his perfectly white teeth, that he'd be no bother to her at all.

For the first ten or fifteen minutes of the dreadful lecture, the boy beside her bounced his left hand off his knee as if to a beat in his head. It was annoying, but far less annoying than listening to Sam chew, for instance. And then Fiona felt a slight . . . nudge . . . on the middle of her right thigh. She looked down and saw that the boy's pinkie was touching her; she scooted over a bit.

"Pardon me," the boy said quietly and without even turning to look at Fiona.

"No problem," Fiona said.

Then, five minutes later, he did it again and Fiona scooted again.

"I'm sorry," the boy said. This time he turned to look at Fiona and flashed a more active smile. He got his eyes involved. "Listening to him drone on makes me jumpy."

"No problem," Fiona said, because she truly empathized with the boy.

"I haven't seen you in here before," he said.

"I'm just sitting in," she said.

"Cool," he said.

Thirty minutes later, Fiona felt a bit more pressure on her leg and looked down to see that the boy was essentially resting his pinkie and his ring finger on her thigh.

"You have really soft legs," he said. "I thought I was touching my chinos."

Fiona leaned toward the boy and the boy leaned toward her, taking up most of the middle distance with what Fiona now discerned was far too much cologne. Polo or something else meant to make nineteen-year-old girls swoon in their Dress Barn rompers.

"If you touch my leg again," Fiona said, "I'm going to dislocate your fingers."

"Dislocate," he said and gave her that smile again. "I like that word. I'm sorry. I'll move them myself if you like. You don't need to *dislocate* them."

Fiona got the sense the boy didn't know what "dislocate" meant, since he was still trying to flirt with her. Another failure of American education. She'd be happy to show him the word's precise meaning.

A few minutes later, Fiona felt a tapping on her

knee—this time it was clear that it was intentional. Fiona decided to give the boy the benefit of the doubt that he wanted something from her and thus was tapping her with a purpose. Maybe he needed a pen? Some paper? A punch to the neck?

"Yes?" Fiona said.

"You smell really great," he said.

"It's called sweat."

"Then your sweat smells like lavender and freshly cooked beignets."

Some people, really, didn't deserve the gift of speech.

"I am trying to concentrate, if you don't mind," Fiona said, because she just didn't want to create a scene in the lecture hall. She might overreact and cause a compound fracture and no one wanted to see that. Plus, she didn't want to be splashed with blood.

"Would you like to get a beer sometime?"

Did no one have common decency anymore?

The boy had left his index finger on her knee, so Fiona reached down and very casually sprained it by shoving her thumb in between the last joint and the fingertip. The boy let out a little yelp and then immediately shoved his finger into his mouth and scurried out of the classroom. The professor still never looked up.

The rest of the class went well enough, provided Fiona kept focused on any potential assassins and not anything having to do with whatever manifest destiny was, since the professor had managed to jump a hundred years to discuss some other trivial American policy and how it was originally tied to these violent separatists, though he didn't use those words. The fool.

Now, as she and Brent went in search of what he

deemed "the best rice bowls, like, ever" for lunch, Fiona kept being accosted by young men with flyers promoting different off-campus events, all of which boiled down to wonderful opportunities to get drugged and raped in the comfort of a beer-soaked fraternity house.

"Do you ever go to these parties?" Fiona asked. She handed Brent a flyer for a Sigma Upsilon party called the Pimp and Ho Ball. "No," he said. "They don't invite guys."

Well, that made sense. Little else about the day had. While she'd sat in the classroom, Michael had texted her about Big Lumpy's death and the potential for bugs in Brent's room and possibly even in his computers—he and Sam were dismantling the ones left at Madeline's—and informed her that she should avoid going to his dorm room at any cost, not that that was something high on her list of desires, anyway. And he also told her about the conditions of Brent's inheritance, which could be both dangerous and ludicrous. Michael didn't want her to tell Brent about Big Lumpy's death or his conditions until they were away from the school, since they didn't know who might be listening in. Any college kid could be one of Yuri's people for all any of them knew and Fiona should treat any and all of the university's thirty thousand students as suspects.

Great.

And then he'd texted her again just a few minutes ago to tell her that they had a black-tie event to attend that evening and to find Brent appropriate clothing for it, as if she was his accommodating yet exceptionally hot aunt or, well, whatever. It was just another piece of an increasingly odd puzzle. Her main goal now was to keep Brent safe, but unfortunately that didn't extend to his food choices, apparently.

Brent finally found the haute cuisine he was looking for—it wasn't much more than a trolley with a man cooking rice in a wok over a Bunsen burner—in front of the Otto G. Richter Library and now that he had his food, it was like the kid turned on for the first time all day. He was making observations about the people walking by, asking Fiona what she thought about the history class ("Egregious," was Fiona's reply).

"Can I ask you a question?" Brent said. They were sitting across from each other at a small café table that overlooked a fountain surrounded by grass.

"That depends," Fiona said. "Is it going to be some sort of disgusting come-on?"

"No," Brent said. "I don't think of you that way."

"Why not?" Fiona wasn't aghast. At least not entirely.

"You're more, like, I don't know, motherly, I guess."

The rules for what constituted justifiable homicide were nebulous, but Fiona surmised that any man telling a woman she was motherly counted. "Go ahead," she said.

"So, like, what would you do? Big Lumpy wants me to, like, be his stepson or something. Wants to get me into MIT and to work with the government and all that stuff, but I'm, like, not even sure what I'm going to have for dinner."

Fiona wasn't exactly equipped to deliver life advice. Her mantra all these long years usually boiled down to a simple "Why don't we just shoot them?" which, when truly examined, didn't seem like sound advice to give to a young, impressionable boy like Brent.

So Fiona asked Brent the one question she thought was banal enough not to drive him toward a full-time life of crime. "What do you want to be when you grow up?"

"I am grown-up," Brent said.

"You're nineteen. That's like being grown-up without any of the side benefits, like money or class or a plan. No offense, of course."

Brent didn't seem offended. It actually seemed to make him rather contemplative. He shoveled his mouth full of teriyaki chicken and rice and chewed with real determination, as if obliterating his rice would somehow bring about a universal truth or two.

"I guess I want to do stuff with computers," he said, "but also something where I can get girls. Most computer guys? They don't get many girls and I don't want to be like that. I mean, I like role-playing games and stuff, but I'd rather have a real girl than, like, a really intimate relationship with an elf or an orc or some fey creature or something."

"I don't blame you," Fiona said.

"Like, you and Michael? You're pretty much a couple, right?"

"Sometimes."

"But, like, okay, I mean, not to be gross, but, like, you guys have hit it, right?"

Fiona couldn't decide if she wanted to be offended, which made her realize that she probably shouldn't be. Brent meant no actual harm. He just didn't know how to speak like a human being. "Yes," she said, "we have had sexual relations in the past."

"And that's not because, like, he can analyze stuff, right? It's because, like, he can see stuff and then, like, beat ass and stuff, right?"

"Among other things, but yes, I suppose that's part of the allure."

"Well, I want that, then," he said.

"If you take Big Lumpy's offer—whatever it is—you understand that the life you have now will no longer be the life you have, right?"

Brent shrugged. "My dad? Michael said he's somewhere safe, but, like, I'm not stupid. I know my dad is nuts. He's, like, clinical probably. I want to help him, but I also don't want him to ruin my life. Do you know what I mean?"

Fiona knew exactly what he meant. He might love his father, but there was going to be a divide between them now larger than the one that already existed. Distance is always best when dealing with family members of dubious mental standing, Fiona had found. The Atlantic worked well in that regard, at least for her. "I understand," she said.

"I don't really have any other family here. And I'm apparently, like, good at something I didn't know I was good at. I'm like Batman, but without the car or the freaky little friend. I could be down with that."

"I guess," Fiona said, "you have to decide, then, what you use your intelligence for. If he is going to somehow provide you an opportunity to change your life, it will be your choice how to spend the time."

"Or, like, he could cut off my eyelids."

What was it with everyone being afraid of getting their eyelids cut off by Big Lumpy? Even if Fiona told Brent that Big Lumpy was dead, she was sure he'd still fear this fate.

"Have you ever seen anyone who's had their eyelids cut off?" she asked.

"No."

"That's because it probably never happens. You'd remember seeing something like that. It's a good threat, though, because it's pretty hard to imagine it not being horrifying."

"I guess I hadn't thought of that," he said.

"You do also have to think about your father," she said. "I know what Michael told you and I know what you just told me, but the fact is, Brent, that you're going to need help to care for him. And this business with the Russians might go away soon or it might linger. So you have to consider how best to help your father live a safe life, too. Nothing is permanent but family."

Tears began to well up in Brent's eyes, which was about the last thing Fiona needed to see. She'd much rather a man leer at her than cry on her, which was a personality glitch that she wasn't proud of, but, well, there you go. No one's perfect.

Brent sniffled once and Fiona thought, Okay, he's got control of himself now . . . and then he broke into full-fledged shuddering sobs, and it occurred to Fiona for the first time during all of this that no nineteen-year-old should be faced with these kinds of problems, that the weight of what Brent was going through would be enough to drive anyone to the brink, much less a boy. What the hell were they doing at school? Trying to keep his life as normal as possible, but it was time to admit that nothing would ever be normal again for Brent Grayson.

She reached across the table and took Brent's hand in hers. "It's going to be okay," she said.

"How?" he asked.

"Michael is going to fix it—you'll see," she said and for one of the first times in her life, Fiona realized how much she hoped that was true. That he'd be able to just fix it all and make everything right.

Brent blew his nose and then looked at his watch. "I'm going to be late for class."

"Let's not go," Fiona said.

"I have to," he said. "I'll fail."

"Have you ever failed a class in your entire life?"

"I've never gotten anything lower than a B."

"Then you're due an F," Fiona said. "It will add character to you and women love character."

"They do?"

"What could be more attractive than a computer genius who failed a computer class? You'll be the bad boy."

"I will?"

"You will," she said. "Trust me. I've been with a lot of bad boys and failing was like second nature to them. It suggests a certain unpredictability that women admire."

"Like Sam?"

Boys. Always with the wrong role models. "Like Sam," Fiona said.

"I suppose I could do the wrong thing for the first time. Do you think we could get ice cream?"

"It's not the first time," Fiona said. "Getting involved with Yuri Drubich was a pretty big mistake."

"But it's going to turn out okay and I'm going to be rich."

"Is that what you want? To be rich?" Fiona couldn't believe the words coming from her mouth. Maybe it was a self-fulfilling prophecy. Someone tells you you're motherly and next thing you know, you're dispensing hard-won life advice. Fiona frankly wished she could get back to advocating bullets and bombs, but the situation wasn't quite right, not with the kid crying into his rice bowl and all that.

"What do you mean?"

"I mean, when you get the conditions from Big Lumpy, you're going to meet them just so that you can have money?"

"I don't know," he said. He shrugged, because that's what he did in the absence of anything else he could possibly do. "I guess I need to know where my father is going to be. I mean, like, really. I know Michael and you and everyone are trying to protect me, and that's totally cool, but I'm a grown man and I need to know the truth."

Fiona didn't think Brent was actually a grown man, but she understood his need for transparency and his need to manifest his own destiny, such as it was, so she decided to break the news to him and deal with whatever ramifications might come from Michael down the line. She was a grown woman. She didn't need to ask for permission, after all.

But then her phone rang. "Living still?" Michael asked.

"We're just about to leave campus for an adventure," Fiona said.

"What kind of adventure?"

"Brent has never failed a class. Today seemed like the day to teach him how much fun that is. He's expressed an interest in getting ice cream."

"How's his mental state?"

"Michael," she said, "you need to tell him everything."

"I know," Michael said. "Do you think you can get him to agree to Big Lumpy's provisos?"

"I don't know if he wants to," Fiona said.

"He doesn't have to," I said. "But I'm going to need him tonight. If we're going to bring down Yuri Drubich and we're going to ensure that Brent and his father are safe, he's going to have to grow up fast."

Across the table from her, Brent sat and quietly picked at his food. What had she been like at nineteen? Different, of course, but she'd grown up in a world where there was always something larger at stake. Independence. Freedom. Even if she didn't believe in what everyone was fighting for, it had been a part of her life then and thus at nineteen she'd felt like she was a woman, though if photos were any clue, some of her fashion choices were utterly deplorable. Madonna made every young woman dress like an idiot, she supposed, at one point or another over the course of the last twenty-five years and she, sadly, had been no different. But Brent had real issues. Concrete ones—the death of his mother, his father's descent into guilt and eventual madness, and then all of this. He may have had the outward shine of someone holding on to whatever youthful things he could clench, but the truth, she imagined, was far different.

"I think he already has," Fiona said. "You need to explain to him all of the conditions. And Michael? Tell him what you would do."

"What I would do doesn't matter."

"It does to him," she said.

"Okay," Michael said. "Put him on the phone."

Fiona watched as Brent listened to Michael. He asked a few questions, but mostly he was quiet, until he finally said, "MIT sounds cool. And working for the government could be cool, too. But I don't want the money. All I want for sure is for my father to be cared for. Is there a way to do that?"

Fiona didn't know what Michael said right then, but she was sure that he would say that there was no problem getting that taken care of, even if it would prove to be the biggest problem he'd ever faced.

14

Check fraud used to be the most popular form of financial malfeasance for low-level crooks with high-level ambitions. The easiest way to perpetuate this crime involved rental properties. A person would put on a nice outfit, rent a Mercedes, maybe even bring along some arm candy with a fake wedding ring to fill out the picture, and then the con man would make deposits on several medium-priced rental properties in a weekend, but only those that were being shown by the owners, not by real estate agents, so that no one would bother to check his credit. This was back when people assumed that if you had a Mercedes you had a good credit score.

It also used to be harder for real people to check someone's credit or even a person's simple identity. It took time and money, not like today where a simple Google search can usually reveal enough about a person for one to decide whether or not he's a dirtbag. A savvy con man would pony up a check for the security deposit and the first month's rent, maybe even a pet deposit, and hand-deliver it to the owner on a Saturday at four p.m. Everyone would shake hands. The owner would run off to his bank and deposit the check, only to learn on Monday that the new renter's mother had died, or his wife had died, or maybe the renter himself had suddenly developed terminal cancer, and thus would ask to get his money back. Normal people have a hard time saying no to death and/or terminal cancer. The owner of the property would promptly write a check to the mournful owner, they'd shake hands and the owner would walk back into his home feeling like he'd done the right thing.

Of course, the con man's check hadn't cleared yet, probably wouldn't clear for five to seven days, since if the con man was really smart, his stolen checks were from out of state, which would cause a longer hold and a longer processing time, all to figure out that the check was a *fugazis* all along. But the empathetic homeowner wouldn't know that for many days.

The con man would take the owner's check directly to the owner's bank, cash it, and be off into the world, thousands of dollars richer.

It was a solid con for a very long time. Until people stopped writing checks. Until people started checking the identities of not just people they were doing business with, but every person they encountered, usually out of simple interest. Meet a person on the street, find them interesting or alluring, and two clicks later you're looking at their vacation photos on Facebook, know where they went to kindergarten, elementary school, high school, junior college, college and whatever other clickable institution of learning one can imagine. In short, an entire involuntary database that can tell you whether or not the person you're interested in is to be trusted with even your phone number.

So the world has become more cautious and, for the most part, no one accepts a check for a large purchase without first getting a DNA swab from the inside of your cheek, at least metaphorically speaking.

Except for charitable organizations. Charitable organizations accept checks every single day because they are created to be generous and forgiving. If you write a bad check to a charity, your karma suffers, but they usually won't have you arrested. It just isn't a charitable thing to do.

And when you show up with a cashier's check for a million dollars, they tend to really turn on their warm and caring side. Or at least that's what I was hoping would happen when I walked into the Moldovan Consulate with that check in my hand. Plus, warm and caring people tend not to blanch when you ask them to take you on a tour of their facility, even if they're preparing for a black-tie gala.

So after Barry came back with the cashier's check for me, I brought Sugar back to my loft and called Sam to let him know that I'd need a chauffeured ride over to the Moldovan Consulate. Preferably a chauffeur with a gun, if need be.

"What kind of car?" Sam asked.

"Big and American," I said. "Something we can all fit in tonight."

"Mikey," Sam said, "you realize that the potential for snafus tonight is high."

"I realize that," I said.

"So, in that light, what are you going to do with Sugar?"

"I thought I'd have him sit in the car with the engine running," I said.

"I like that idea," Sam said. "You're not thinking of arming him, are you?"

I was in my kitchen and Sugar was sitting at my counter watching YouTube videos of people getting smacked in the groin.

"No," I said. I smiled at Sugar and then walked outside to my landing, where I wouldn't have to hear Sugar's cinema verité. "What do you have on Drubich and his ties to Moldova?"

"My sources tell me his mother is actually from there," Sam said, "and that while he is Ukrainian he keeps a vacation home in beautiful Chisinau, where he regularly spends his afternoons reading Tolstoy in Stefan cel Mare Central Park."

"He'll have plenty of time to read at Leavenworth," I said. "Where'd you get this?"

"I called the Moldovan Consulate and asked them how they could be so brash as to honor a dirty Ukrainian," he said. "Except I said it in a really bad Russian accent. They transferred me to a very nice woman in the press office named Reva, who informed me that Mr. Drubich has deep, inalienable ties to the area and that in addition to all the time he's spent sitting in the park reading, he also found time to meet his wife in Moldova, too, when they were both just children, which is why he's so committed to the education of Moldova's young ones."

"What a heartwarming story," I said.

"They didn't mention anything about him earning

most of his money selling technology to terrorists, but I thought that was probably just an oversight."

"Maybe mention that in your speech," I said. "See if he's able to pat himself on the back with his arm in a cast."

It would be harder still in a few days when he was wearing a waist chain, too, if I had any say in things.

An hour later, Sam and I pulled up in front of the consulate building (in a black Navigator Sam assured me was loaned to him by a very close friend who'd parked it in long-term parking at the Miami Airport) and parked in a space that was marked NO PARKING—RESERVED TO-NIGHT ONLY FOR MR. SIGAL. I was fairly certain that Mr. Sigal, whoever he was, wasn't going to show up six hours early for anything, so his parking space seemed safe. If you're important enough to have a one-night-only reserved parking spot, after all, you're probably the kind of person who shows up right when the Chicken Kiev is being served and not a moment sooner.

"Mikey," Sam said, "are you sure you should go in there alone?"

"We can't risk both of us being seen ahead of time," I said. "Besides, I want you listening in on those bugs I placed in Odessa."

"Thus far, it's just been a lot of people remarking on how good the butter cookies are when paired with the Prince Vladimir tea," Sam said. "Unless that's someone speaking in code."

"I don't think so," I said. I got out of the Navigator and examined the street in front of the consulate. Even though it was hours before the event, already a valet service was getting set up at the corner, which meant it was going to be difficult to have a getaway car parked right where we'd need it, so I had to hope a million dollars was enough to get me a reserved space for the evening.

Unlike the consulates you might see in Washington, DC, or even Los Angeles or New York—the kind of big, ornate structures that announced the presence of an entire country, or at least the presence of a few key government and goodwill officials who were, most likely, spies themselves—the building that housed the Moldovan Consulate was more like a building that happened to house several very nice law firms, which in this case were called the Isle of Man, Morocco, Antigua and Moldova. There was a security presence in the outer foyer where three very large men who looked bored and tired and hot sat stuffed behind a sunken circular desk. All three wore black suits with white shirts and blue ties, and gold name badges, though no actual badges. They each had Bluetooth earpieces and matching BlackBerrys strapped to their belts, but no guns. Surrounding the men in the sunken area were a dozen closed-circuit televisions showing alternating shots of all sides of the building, including one that showed Sam sitting in his new Navigator. There were also several laptop computers open on the desk. One was running a program that controlled the closed-circuit cameras: Three of them showed open Facebook pages, two were on ESPN.com and the other one I could see appeared to be running an in-progress game of solitaire.

Behind the men and the security console was a bank of elevators that were guarded by yet another large, bored, tired, and sweaty gentleman. The only difference I could see between this man and the others was that he had a key card around his neck on a chain, which probably meant he had to scan visitors in who wished to go upstairs to the various consulate offices. That he also was holding a clipboard made it all the more clear that he was a man of terrible importance, at least in this ecosystem.

To the left of the security console, there were several tables being set up in front of the grand entrance to a surprisingly ornate ballroom that I could see was filled with people dressing tables and such. A woman with a walkie-talkie in one hand stood in the middle of the ballroom and barked out orders, first in English and then in Russian and then, for good measure, in Spanish. I couldn't make out what she said exactly, but the general thrust was clear from the way the workers suddenly picked up their pace. Somewhere in the building food was being prepared. Prime rib. Something made primarily of garlic. A million-dollar meal, no doubt.

"May I help you?" one of the security guards asked. He had an accent that sounded vaguely British, but not like he grew up in Leeds. His name tag said MR. CHISOLM and beneath that THE ISLE OF MAN. I looked at the other two guards and saw that they were Mr. Plutak and Mr. Reigor, from Moldova and Antigua, respectively. Morocco must have been guarding the elevators.

"Yes," I said. "My name is Dr. Liam Bennington. I'm afraid I don't have an appointment, but I'd like to purchase a table for this evening's benefit."

"All of that is handled by the consulate's press

office," Mr. Chisolm said. He began clicking away at the computer directly to his left, one of the Facebook-enabled ones, but nothing seemed to be happening, perhaps because it was on a page of photos of a young woman. "I'm sorry, sir. Just give me a moment." He kept clicking, but all that was happening, as far as I could see, was that he kept letting everyone on the planet know that he was quite fond of a photo of the young woman standing in front of the Empire State Building. "Bloody hell," he said under his breath.

I pointed at the computer. "Is that your wife?" I asked.

"No," he said. "That's the problem, sir."

"Is it Reva who handles this? If so, I can find my way upstairs while you untangle this."

"Oh, that would be a relief," he said. He scribbled my name on a guest pass. "Just show this at the lift."

I gave Mr. Chisolm a two-fingered salute and headed off to the elevator, where I showed my pass to the guard from Morocco, who barely looked at it before swiping his key card and hitting the UP button.

"Fourth floor?" I said.

"Third," he said. Morocco had no accent at all and his name badge said CAPTAIN TIMMONS on it. I was right. A man of power. And a man without a country, apparently, since his name badge didn't actually say MOROCCO beneath his name. What he was the captain of was anyone's guess. "You are seeing?"

"Reva," I said.

He finally lifted his head up and I saw that he was older than the other guards—where they were in their late twenties or early thirties, he was clearly in his late forties or early fifties. "Reva is the Mary of Moldova. What department?"

"Press office."

"Oh, oh," he said, with a laugh. "That's Ms. Lohr. Ask for her by that name or else you'll be greeted by eleven different women."

"Could be worse," I said.

"Don't I know it," he said. He looked down at my pass. "Dr. Bennington. What are you a doctor of?"

"What hurts?" I said. Another laugh. Just two old friends waiting for an elevator. "I'm a scientist, I'm afraid. I can't get you any medication but I can get you an excellent deal on a Bunsen burner."

Captain Timmons slapped me on the back. "Some days, a Bunsen burner would be just fine, if you know what I mean. Place it over one of the fire detectors and get me off early before all the fuss gets started here."

"I'm afraid I'll be part of that fuss tonight," I said.

"Oh, you're fine," he said. The elevator doors opened then and I stepped in. "It's all those Russians with machine guns that make me nervous."

The doors closed in front of Captain Timmons and for a brief moment I was alone with his final observation. If I were still a spy, a full-time spy, I could have defused this whole situation in a much easier fashion. I would have placed a call to my handler in DC, told him about this poor kid wrapped up in a situation beyond his comprehension, and asked if there wasn't something that could be done. My handler would call his counterparts in Ukraine and Moldova; they'd both probably be ex–KGB agents grown fat and happy on Yuri Drubich's graft, but they would be able to see the value in averting an international situation. They would call Yuri personally and ask him to please stop tormenting a child and his crazy father and Yuri, ever the statesman, would say certainly, I will certainly do that, and it would be over.

But what I also knew was that one day Brent Grayson would die in a terrible, unexplainable car accident. Or one day Brent Grayson would be the victim of an apparently senseless home invasion robbery gone terribly wrong. Or maybe it wouldn't be Brent Grayson at all. Maybe it would be his wife, a woman Brent didn't even know yet, who would be walking down the street on her way to her job, or maybe she'd be walking her dog, or maybe she'd be pushing a stroller with their baby in it, and then suddenly she'd be on the ground, a bullet in her head. And then she'd be a statistic. An unsolved murder.

I never liked bureaucrats anyway.

So instead, I would catch Yuri doing what our own government somehow hadn't managed to do during all the years he'd been in business. I'd set him up for the same kind of bad beat Henry Grayson had taken so many times before: a sure thing, a favorite, that ends up being the worst possible bet. And maybe Yuri would be put away forever. Or maybe he'd have favors to cash in down the line that would set him free, but I'd catch him in such a public forum that it would be impossible for him to ever set foot in America.

And if that didn't work? Well, I'd let Fiona shoot

him. Because if what I was planning didn't work, that might be our only way out, though the idea of going Old West in a foreign consulate didn't excite me.

The elevator doors opened directly into the reception area of the Moldovan Consulate. It was an airy and open space—windows went from floor to ceiling and the view stretched all the way to the water, or it would if the afternoon haze hadn't already begun to roll in—and because Moldova had no natural enemies in the United States, that they knew of, anyway, there was none of the implied military presence (like armed men lingering about doing very little of anything but looking intimidating) that one might find at the Pakistani Embassy.

Instead, there was a reception desk behind which a young woman sat reading a copy of *InStyle*, the distinctive blue, yellow and red flag of her home country emblazoned behind her in an ornate frame. There was also a framed photo of a man in a suit, who I assumed was the last president of the country, though it could have been anyone, really, since their last elections had been plagued by fighting between upstart Communists and the loose group of opposition parties and had failed to yield a new leader. If this had been a few years ago, I would have known the precise reasons behind all of it. I may have even played a role. These are things I used to care deeply about. Things I just can't summon any feeling for anymore.

I told the receptionist that I was there to see Ms. Lohr because I was interested in purchasing a table for the evening. The receptionist said, "Yes?"

And I said, "Yes."

She exhaled through her nose and rolled her eyes

ever so slightly as she stood up, as if this was going to be the annoying and time-consuming task of her day. She led me down a brightly lit hallway, past a small cubicle farm filled with young Moldovans who barely looked up as I walked by. The cubicle farm was surrounded by offices, none of which had open doors, which was either a fantastic metaphor for life in Moldova or, more likely, a statement that the leadership keeps its own hours, which was made clear enough by the computer screens I spied here, too, which were largely on Twitter. I had to hope no one would tweet that a burned spy just walked by.

The receptionist, who walked at a pace that would make a slug frustrated if it were following her, finally brought me into a conference room that featured the same framed Moldovan flag and presidential picture as the reception area, only smaller, and an executive-length conference table that was covered in stacks and stacks of programs bearing Yuri Drubich's face, presumably ready to be taken downstairs, and a water and tea service.

"It will be a moment," the receptionist said and left me alone for another ten minutes until the woman with the walkie-talkie I saw downstairs ordering the troops about stepped into the conference room and essentially fell into one of the chairs. She was dressed in a finely tailored Chanel skirt suit. It was gray and she wore a white shirt beneath it that was open far enough to reveal a demure single-diamond necklace. Her hair was professionally done, but it was obvious by the way her bangs stuck to her forehead that she was having a long, stressful day.

"I'm sorry to have kept you waiting, Dr. Bennington," she said. "The security, they do not bother to find out where in the building anyone is, so we must go running around blindly half of the day when we have guests." Her irritation with the guards seemed outsized and apparently she realized that, too, because she quickly added, "I'm sorry. They do a good job. I am at the end of a rope that was already much frayed and you are not here to listen to me complain about having a good job, yes?"

Reva had only a slight Russian accent but still hung on to some of the charms of her language, ending a sentence that was not a question with a rhetorical question no less.

"Why don't you have a glass of water?" I said. I stood up and poured her a glass and then handed it to her. "Everything feels better once you've had a glass of water. My mother taught me that."

Reva took the glass from me without a word and drank it down and then she smiled, revealing perfectly straight, white teeth. Another sign she hadn't lived in Moldova her entire life. That or her insurance plan at the consulate had a strong dental component. "Your mother is very smart," she said. Her walkie-talkie squawked but instead of answering it, she set it on the table and made a big show of turning it off. "You are a doctor? Is that correct?"

"A scientist," I said. "My company, InterMacron, will be much in the news soon."

"Science I was never good at," she said. "I am a people person, all evidence to the contrary notwithstanding. But I have always been fascinated with people who understand how the smallest things on the planet can open up the biggest secrets."

"Like Mr. Drubich," I said.

"Like Mr. Drubich," she said. "He is a remarkable man. Have you had the chance to meet him?"

"I am hoping to tonight," I said, "but I have admired his work from afar for many years."

"He is most remarkable," she said, "a man of science but also of great faith and erudition."

I pointed at the photo on the cover of the program. "And a family man, too," I said.

"He met his wife in Moldova when they were just children," she said, "and they've been married now thirty years."

"We should all be so lucky," I said.

"Yes, yes," she said. I saw her quickly gaze down at my left hand, and when she looked back up, I was staring directly at her, which made her blush, but I didn't look away.

"I've not been so lucky," I said.

"Your mother must be upset about that," she said.

"Among other things," I said.

This got Reva to laugh again. She was an attractive woman, but she wasn't Fiona. For the purposes of my needs that day, however, she was the most beautiful woman I'd ever seen.

"I'm sorry," Reva said. "You must be a very busy man and here I am going on about silly things."

"Stop apologizing," I said. "You've apologized to me three times and I've only known you five minutes. I'm beginning to think this relationship will be built on regret."

Reva cleared her throat, but that didn't help her blushing. "I'm sor . . ." she began, but caught herself just in time. "You wanted to buy a table?"

"I do," I said.

"For how many?"

I handed her the check. "There will be only five of us, unless you'd like to join our table," I said, "but I think this should cover it."

"Dr. Bennington," she said, "this is a check for a million dollars, yes?"

"Yes, it is," I said. "My company has great faith in Mr. Drubich. We would like, if you do not mind, to present him with a copy of the check this evening."

"A copy?"

"We'll have one made that will be large enough for everyone to see when we present it to him."

"Like," Reva paused, searching for what this was like. "Like, the Publishers Clearing House?"

"Similar," I said, "but Ed McMahon won't be able to make it."

"And you do not know Mr. Drubich?"

"Not personally. But my company and his company are about to embark on a very significant project together. I have sadly been in Zurich tending to business there and haven't been able to meet with him, though my people tell me, as you have, that he is a rare human being. Have you been to Zurich?"

"No," she said.

"We should go," I said. "It would be good for you. You need less stress. Zurich removes the stress from your every pore." Reva seemed flustered by all of this—

that I was hitting on her as if my name were Sam Axe and also that she held a check in her hand for a million dollars—so I reached over and touched her hand. "I would like to keep this secret until tonight, Reva. Do you mind if I call you by your first name, Reva?"

"No," she said. "I mean, yes, call me my first name."

"Reva," I said, "we'd like this to be a surprise for Mr. Drubich."

"Of course, of course," she said. "Is there anything we can do to help facilitate this?"

"It would mean a great deal to me if we could have a table near to Mr. Drubich's. And a reserved parking spot out front. Will there be press at this event?"

"We've invited the local stations and reporters, but I'm afraid what we do here in the consulate is not as exciting as what happens on South Beach."

"A shame," I said. "This would be good for Moldova. Particularly in light of your troubled election situation back home, don't you think?"

Reva considered what I said. "I could make another round of calls, yes?"

"It couldn't hurt," I said. "Get your name in the paper back home, perhaps, too."

"I make my home here now," she said. "Much warmer than Moldova. I've learned that winter isn't something I need, yes?"

"I agree," I said. "And the sun suits your skin. And your eyes."

I let that hang there for a moment.

"I should tell you I'm seeing someone," she said. She fingered the diamond necklace around her neck.

"That's good for him. You must make him very happy. Does he let you speak on the phone?"

"No one tells me what I can do," Reva said.

"I'm happy to hear that. Perhaps then I could call you?" I said. "We could talk about less formal things than money and science."

Reva didn't answer right away. Probably because she actually loved the man who gave her that lovely necklace. And probably because she wasn't used to someone being as direct as I was being. Or maybe she just liked my Hugo Boss suit. "There is nothing wrong with talking, yes?"

"Isn't that what we're doing right now?"

Reva took out a pen and wrote her phone number on the back of her business card. Her official title was director of international media affairs. A good job title. One she would probably lose for all of this.

She excused herself for a moment and came back with a stack of papers for me to fill out. The first was just the names of those who'd be attending the event that evening and the rest were more formal documents, namely those the Treasury Department would want to see when their full investigation began.

"I'm sorry," I said, "but I should have my CFO handle all of this. I am good with science but lousy with tax ID numbers."

"That is not a problem," Reva said. "Bring them back tonight."

"You should deposit the check, however," I said. "That would be an expensive piece of paper to lose track of."

"Oh, we will, certainly," she said. "I will take it to the

bank personally and immediately draw a check for Mr. Drubich's trust."

It was certain, then, that she'd lose her job.

"Reva," I said, "have you ever thought of working somewhere other than the consulate?"

"Are you offering me a position with InterMacron?"

"No, no," I said. "No business and pleasure. But you should see about other opportunities. You're better than this job."

Her hand went up to her throat again, to that necklace, which made me wonder if maybe the man who gave her the diamond also gave her the job.

"Can I tell you a secret?"

"Of course," I said.

She got up then and closed the door to the conference room and then sat back down and scooted her chair closer to mine, so that she was only inches from me.

"I have always wanted to model," she said. "Do you think I could model?"

And suddenly Reva Lohr, the director of international media affairs for a foreign government, was just like every other woman in Miami. Every woman who wasn't Fiona, at least.

"You could be on runways in Milan tomorrow," I said.

"My boyfriend, he says, 'You are professional, why do you want to be a walking doll?' And I say, 'I want to be admired, just like anyone.' And clothes, I could make clothes, too. Be a model who designs. And I would also like to be on a reality show. The one with Mr. Trump. I saw him once at a restaurant here. So smart, that man."

I smiled at Reva. It hurt to do so. It made me wonder how Sam did it on a daily basis just for drinks and chicken wings. I decided to go all in.

"Don is a personal friend. I'll see what I can do." I stood then and so did Reva. "One other thing, if you don't mind," I said. "Would it be possible to get a private room downstairs to prep our surprise prior to the event?"

"Of course," she said. "Yes, yes, of course. We have a salon you could use. Just tell the security guards when you arrive and they will show you to it. And I'd be happy to provide any kind of, how do you say, concierge service you might need."

"I wouldn't think of it," I said. I took Reva's hand in mine and raised it to my lips and kissed it lightly. "It was my pleasure to meet you today. I feel it was fated."

When I made it back to the Navigator a few minutes later with an envelope filled with paperwork that I would need Barry to forge, Sam had an earplug in and was writing notes furiously on a pad.

"You got something on the bug?" I said.

"Yeah, Mikey, it's alive in that place right now," he said. "I now have a complete recipe for what are supposedly the best cream-cheese-and-bacon sandwiches the Red Hat club of Coral Gables has ever had. You fare any better?"

"We'll have our own parking space," I said. "And you're going to get to hand-deliver a huge replica check to Yuri Drubich."

"I may wear Kevlar tonight," he said.

"Might be a good idea."

As we pulled away, I took out my phone and made a call to Monty. "It's set up for tonight," I said.

"Excellent," he said. "And will Mr. Grayson be taking Mr. McGregor up on his offers?"

"Number ten for sure," I said. "The rest, I can't tell you."

There was silence on the line for a moment and then Monty said, "It's a very generous offer. He would be silly not to take it."

"He's not like you and he's not like me," I said. "Though I understand he does appreciate a nice hot stone massage." Not a sound escaped from Monty, so I said, "Do you have an account where Yuri's money can be safely wired?"

"Yes," he said after a while. "You will be doing this or will Barry?"

"Barry," I said.

"Iceland is fine with him?"

"Indeed," I said and he gave me the information.

"This account will be locked by tomorrow at six a.m.," Monty said. "And I will be gone shortly thereafter. I need all of Mr. Grayson's answers well before that time."

"You'll have them," I said.

"And Mr. Westen? Mr. McGregor instructed me that he'd prefer cash for the debts owed by your brother."

"Tell him to call me, then," I said and hung up.

I made one last call, this one to Odessa, which I put on speaker. "Mr. Drubich, please," I said to the woman who answered.

"There is no one by that name here," she said.

"Tell him it's Big Lumpy's people and make it fast, honey," I said. Instead of hanging up on me, the woman put me on hold and for the next few minutes I was serenaded by Neil Diamond welcoming me to America. Just when I was thinking that the irony of his Muzak system would be forever lost on Yuri, he picked up the line.

"You have two minutes," he said, so I did the only reasonable thing and hung up.

"Short conversation," Sam said.

"He'll call me back," I said.

"I thought I was Big Lumpy now," Sam said.

"You are," I said, "physically." Sure enough, my phone began to ring. "I just thought I'd cover the intimidation-by-phone angle, but if it means that much to you, go right ahead."

"Nah, Mikey," he said. "You know I like to hear you outsmart people until they get so frustrated they order out hit squads. It's one of my small pleasures in life these days."

I answered the phone by saying, "I'm sorry. We must have had a bad connection. I couldn't make out what you said before."

"I know your organization," Yuri said. "I know your reputation and it means nothing to me. Do you understand that?"

"That's great," I said. "I have the technology that you want and I have the boy and I have his father. Do you understand that?"

"I want the boy dead," he said.

"Well, then, you're going to be out a bunch of money for nothing, because I won't let you kill him. What I am happy to do, however, is get you some death certificates for both of them if it would help you with your investors. I've got the information you need, all of the specs you've asked for and more. You'll be running bandwidth over the wind in three months. Bedouins will think you're some kind of god. They'll probably erect statues of you all over Chad. But you're not killing a kid. I just won't let that happen. Now he'll apologize, and you'll get to meet his crazy father, too, but I'm not having you chopping off his head just because he's smarter than you. You want to pretend to kill him, I have the ability to make that happen."

Sam looked at me like I was nuts, and on the other end of the line, Yuri Drubich must have thought the same.

"What is the price of the technology?" Yuri said finally.

"Six million, American."

"That is insane without a working model," he said.

"Mr. Drubich, you're a smart person, so I'm going to make this simple for you. If there were a working model, you wouldn't have to pay six million dollars for this information. You'd be able to drive out to some wind farm and see it with your own beady eyes and then the technology would be worthless. You don't trust my information, I say God bless you and have a great day and I'm sorry a nineteen-year-old boy took you to school. You do trust me, we'll make this happen tonight."

"Tonight," he said, "is no good."

"Tonight is all you have," I said. "Tomorrow I could be dead. I'm a sick man. Maybe you heard."

"Maybe you heard that your errand girl broke my wrist," he said. "I spend all morning at hospital and to-night I have . . . it doesn't matter. Tonight is no good."

"Seven thirty at the Moldovan Consulate. The salon beside the ballroom. Wear something nice," I said and then rolled down the window in the Navigator and threw the phone into the street, where it was promptly run over. If Yuri was trying to run a trace so he could activate his hit squad, it would be a bit more difficult with the phone in a million little pieces.

"How you planning on getting those death certificates?" Sam asked.

"I thought we'd call your friend Marci," I said.

"You ready to drive down that road?" Sam asked.

"I think I can handle her," I said.

"What about Fiona?"

"It will just be dinner," I said.

"Mikey, I've had dinner with her. It's a full-contact sport. Tore my meniscus last time."

"I'll brace myself," I said.

Sam shook his head, but made the call. When I heard that high-pitched squeal again, I thought once more about how much easier life was when I was just a spy.

15

You spend your entire life pretending to be someone else and it's sometimes hard to remember exactly who you are. You take on false identities, change your past, your future, your present, and end up telling a series of lies that compound into other lies, until you're defined by your ability to keep all of your fictions straight long enough to get out of whatever horrible situation you're in. It's both a survival technique and the bread and butter of being a covert operative: Being a spy means being a professional liar with a gun, over and over and over again.

So you put on your costumes.

You get your backstory in order.

You examine your exit strategies, you ponder collateral damage and you wonder: If things go wrong, will anyone actually know who I really am? Will anyone pick up my body. It is a life made of repetition, but it is a life that you choose and that chooses you.

And if one day you pick up a telephone in a foreign country hoping to broker a deal and find out you've been burned, that all of your backup is gone, that you're still a spy, because that's who you are, but that you don't have anyone to spy for, and then for the next few years you find out that everything you thought about being a spy might be entirely wrong, that it's all one elaborate game . . . what do you do? What do you do with your skills?

Sometimes you help people with their problems.

Sometimes you unwind the conspiracies surrounding your life, only to find out that the more you unwind, the darker and more complex the forces at work in your life are, that your burn notice isn't just an unkind way of saying you're fired, but a way of saying you now work for a new master altogether.

And then sometimes, well, you find out that you're going to get to put on a tuxedo and play James Bond.

In this case, you and four other people.

And Sugar.

"I don't see why I don't get to rock the penguin," Sugar said. We were all in my loft getting dressed for the evening, and since Sugar would be waiting in the car, Fiona, who was in charge of acquiring the black-tie attire for our job, apparently didn't think he needed to be dressed as nicely as the rest of us, since she provided him with only a chauffeur's hat.

"Because I couldn't find a tuxedo made of nylon," Fiona said. "I didn't want you to be uncomfortable."

"You won't be seen, Sugar," I said. "But if you were to be, if things go so wrong that you need to escape, you don't want to be wearing something easily identifiable. You just want to look like you."

Sugar tried to make sense of that. "So what you're saying is, you want me to look like I'm maybe a guy who stole a Navigator, not a guy taking part in some high-intrigue espionage shit?"

"Yes," I said.

"Cool," Sugar said. "I'm like undercover by being exactly who I am."

"Right," I said.

Sugar gave me a fist bump. "I'm with it."

On the other side of the room, Sam was attempting to tie Brent's bow tie and was failing mightily, so Fiona went over to help. It looked positively domestic . . . apart from the fact that Barry was only a few feet away, busily forging the documents we'd need to give back to my girlfriend Reva.

"How's it coming, Barry?"

"Anytime I get to use information stolen from Halliburton, I view that as a win," he said.

"Are you ready to be Henry?"

Barry looked over at Brent and then back at me. "He's a nice kid, Mike," Barry said. "He told me about his dad. It's a sad story." He lowered his voice. "But he really doesn't want the money?"

"Nope," I said. "Just wants his father's debts paid and he'll take the education. Everything else is off the table for him. So we'll move the money to his account and there it will stay."

"So . . ."

"The government will get the money," I said. "That would be my guess. They'll seize it eventually if this all goes as planned."

"Seems like a waste."

"He made his choice," I said. "He wants to earn it himself. He'll get the chance."

"Just so we're clear," Barry said, "if some of that money were to be diverted to, say, accounts of a third party, would you have any issues?"

"I'd be discreet."

"I'm always discreet."

"And then I'd fortify your home against shoulder-launched rockets," I said. "Get some Cipro, too, in case you accidentally ingest anthrax. You know how the Russians love to poison people."

There was a knock at my front door then. I wasn't expecting anyone, what with Big Lumpy dead, and solicitors generally avoided my neighborhood.

"You expecting someone, Mikey?" Sam said.

"No," I said.

There was another knock, this time harder. I looked out the window and could only see that there were two men dressed all in black on the landing holding something long and white. I couldn't tell what it was from the angle of the window and from the darkness. Usually, ninjas tend to dress just like normal people, but maybe these two didn't get the memo about the modernization. Or maybe they were mimes. Either way, I wasn't going to take any risks.

"Brent," I said, "get upstairs. Fiona, go with him."

I went beneath my sink and pulled out three guns, for me, Sam, and Barry, who handled his gun like it was made of kryptonite and he had recently begun wearing red capes.

"What about me, boss?" Sugar said.

"If they get past us," I said, "I want you to act as a human shield."

There was another pound on the door, and before the

person was even finished knocking, I'd yanked the door open and pushed the muzzle of my gun into the forehead of . . .

"Is that a vampire?" Sam asked.

. . . Brent's Goth pal King Thomas, who, after he realized there was a gun pressed to his head, began screaming, as did his friend, but his friend managed to scream and run at the same time, dropping his end of a very large fake check in his wake.

"Calm down," I said to Thomas. "I'm not going to shoot you."

"Then why do you have a gun pointed at my head?" It was a good question. I put my gun down and picked up the other side of the check so it wouldn't get dirty on the ground.

"I take it Brent asked you to make this?"

Thomas nodded. "Is he okay?"

"He's not here," I said.

"But he said he was going to be here," Thomas said.

I stepped out on the landing and gazed down toward the street. Thomas' friend was nowhere to be found. That or he'd already turned back into a bat. "Thomas," I said, "it's not safe here. Brent will get in contact with you tomorrow. Until then, you don't know where he is and you haven't seen him in days. Do you understand?"

Thomas nodded.

"And tell your friend the same thing, okay?" I took a look at the check. It was very well done. "Nice work here, Thomas," I said. "I appreciate it."

"I could have done more if I had more time," he said. "It folds so that you can put it in a briefcase. That was my idea. I'm good with thinking ahead about how someone might, you know, carry things in such a way as to conceal them."

"I'll remember that."

"Like, I could make smaller checks, too, is all I'm saying," he said.

"I get it. Now go." I went back inside and closed the door. "Was someone going to tell me about this delivery?" I asked.

Brent looked over the railing from upstairs. "Oh, sorry. Barry was like, you know, we need a big check and I was like, I know a guy who is really good with arts and Barry was like, okay, and I was like, okay, and so I called him and . . ."

Fiona covered Brent's mouth with her hand. "Say you're sorry," she said to him and then removed her hand.

"I'm sorry," Brent said.

"The vampire lord almost ate a bullet," I said. "We have to be on our game tonight and that includes you, Brent. Do you understand?"

"I do."

"Okay," I said. "Now get your tie right and let's go. We have ten minutes, people."

Brent didn't shrug, he didn't say anything was like anything else, he just stepped away from the railing and did what he was told.

Fiona came down the stairs a few moments later, just as I was tying my own bow tie. She stood in front of me and straightened my collar, then wiped lint from my shoulders. "You look very handsome," she said quietly. She looked pretty good, too, in a simple black evening gown that was part Audrey Hepburn, but all Fiona.

"Everyone looks good in a tuxedo," I said.

"Take the compliment," she said.

"Thank you, Fiona," I said.

"Things get close in there tonight," she said, her voice still quiet, "you protect Brent first and foremost."

"Fiona," I began, but she put a finger to my mouth.

"I can take care of myself. Sam can take care of Barry."

I didn't say anything. I just nodded once. But when she walked away, I said, "Where do you have a gun hidden in that dress?"

"Be good and maybe I'll show you," she said.

Normally, when shaking down an organized-crime figure, I prefer not to have three crisscrossing searchlights pinpointing my location, but when we were still a mile from the consulate and I could see the sky was lit like the blitz on London, I knew things weren't going to be exactly like my past experiences.

The street in front of the consulate was nearly empty of traffic at this hour, save for the slow trickle of cars pulling into the valet station. It was seven fifteen and the event wasn't to start until eight o'clock, which meant the fashionable and the powerful wouldn't arrive until eight thirty. Sugar drove the Navigator past the valet station and there, directly in front of the consulate, and directly next to Mr. Sigal's empty spot, was a sign that said NO PARKING—RESERVED FOR DR. BENNINGTON. Reva had done well.

There was a short line of people waiting to get into

the consulate, which was surprising this early until I saw the reason why. There was a man standing out front in a yellow PRIVATE EVENT STAFF jacket with a metal-detecting wand in his hand scanning each person as he or she walked in. I watched him go over a few people and noticed he tended to take more time on the women, which wasn't much of a surprise. You make eight bucks an hour, you find your thrills where you can.

"That's a problem," I said.

"Mikey," Sam said, "we get caught bringing guns into that place, it's basically an act of war."

Sam was right, but we weren't going to go into a meeting with Yuri with only our wits and the laptop computer Big Lumpy gave us.

"I'm happy to hide more guns on my body," Fiona said, which made everyone but me turn to look at her in the backseat.

"That would be bad," I said, "since Officer Friendly there seems to prefer the ladies."

"You leave your piece with me, Mike, and then you just give me a sign and I'll blow a hole in the sky," Sugar said. "Word is bond on that."

"Let me take that under consideration," I said.

Getting past a metal detector isn't easy. At an airport, it's nearly impossible because of the kind of metal detectors they use, which are full-body scanners tweaked high enough to pick up a bit of tinfoil stuck to the bottom of your shoe. The wands they use at the airport are also the highest grade possible and can't be purchased commercially, lest a terrorist be able to figure out how to jam their signal.

So if you want to defeat a metal-detecting wand,

you have to hope that the one being used is commercial grade, the kind they hand to guys in yellow jackets outside concerts and sell to private security companies. The kind that are used to provide the idea of security, if not a total assurance of the same.

You can attempt to cloak the metal by surrounding it in gelatin or even slow-drying concrete, neither of which I had in the car. Or you can disrupt the wand's ability to "read" the metal by creating an electromagnetic field around the gun. To do this you need a strong magnet and the ability to conduct electricity around it.

The magnets on your refrigerator will not suffice for this, and if you don't have easy access to a storage container filled with neodymium magnets and a good pair of a safety goggles, you need to improvise.

"We need to rip the speakers out of this car," I said. "And I need everyone's BlackBerrys and iPhones."

Speakers contain both electromagnets and permanent magnets, which essentially cause the speaker to function like a piston by virtue of the constant tug and release of the magnetic field. The sound waves come through a coil, and as the magnets piston away, the air in front of the coil vibrates, creating the sound. The bigger the speaker, the larger the magnets.

Commercial metal detectors generally use VLF technology, which is just a fancy way of saying "very low frequency." The metal detector sends out an electromagnetic wave of its own so that when it hits upon a metal object a current is sent back to the device . . . and that's when the beeping begins. To disrupt the metal detector, the same basic principle is at work, except that the field created by the magnets disperses the reading into unreadable garble, provided the field you've created is strong enough.

Which is where the cell phones came in. We'd attach the magnets using the voice coils from the speakers into the cell phones. A smartphone like a BlackBerry or an iPhone runs a one-gigahertz microprocessor, more than enough to create the disturbance we'd need. If I'd had a blowtorch and time, I could have made sure of this. As it was, I'd just have to hope it would work.

There were twelve speakers in the Navigator, but four were buried inside the dash, which meant we'd need to do complex surgery to remove those, so instead we'd need to get to work on the speakers in the doors, which required only that their screens be popped off and then the magnets could be easily cut from the coils.

It was 7:17. We had thirteen minutes to make this happen. I didn't want to make Brent nervous, but I also knew that we had to get this to happen or we'd be walking into a gunfight with not even a knife in hand, just a laptop computer.

Fortunately, Sam and Fiona knew exactly what I was aiming for and got to work quickly on the speakers. And fortunately Sugar had stolen plenty of stereo systems in his life, too, which came in handy.

And by 7:28, Sam, Fiona and I each had our own electromagnetic field surrounding our guns. Not that we'd want to keep these fields for long, since spending too much time in an increased electromagnetic field can cause nausea, vomiting and fainting. Never mind that it wasn't very fashion forward.

"What do we do if things start beeping?" Brent asked.

"That won't happen," I said.

"But how do you know?" he asked.

"Brent," I said, "I'm a spy."

At this, Brent and Sugar fist-bumped and both let out a yelp.

"I love that shit, dog," Sugar said.

"It is so cool," Brent said. "One day, I'm going to be able to MacGyver stuff like you and be all 'I'm a spy,' and people will be all 'Whoa.' It'll be awesome."

Barry actually groaned, which was my cue to get out of the car. "Keep it running, Sugar," I said.

"On it," he said.

From the street, I could see directly into the consulate, and even from the street, I could see bulky-looking men lingering near the entrance to the ballroom, their eyes darting to every person who walked in. I had an idea they weren't there to watch out for people stealing prime rib.

Sam got out of the Navigator and slung a satchel over his shoulder that contained both the laptop Big Lumpy had prepared for him and our large check. He also put on a pair of eyeglasses.

"Nice touch," I said.

"I thought it would make me look smarter," he said.

"You have everything?"

"What I don't have in here"—Sam pointed at his head—"I've got on the computer. I'm pretty much an expert now, Mikey."

"Where are the death certificates?"

"Right here," Sam said and patted his breast pocket.

"Let's try not to generate any more of them, fake or not," I said.

Barry stood nervously beside Brent, and though they weren't related, they both had the look of people who didn't quite know how they'd found themselves in this situation. Fiona stepped between them. "Let's go, men," she said.

Just as we moved toward the short line of people, Captain Timmons came out the door. "No waiting for Dr. Bennington," he said and gave me a wink. He took the wand from the security guard and started over me with just a cursory wave, and then did the same over Sam, Brent and Barry with not a beep to be found.

When Fiona stepped up, he frowned slightly. "I'm sorry I have to do this, ma'am," he said.

"I'd rather be safe," she said.

He wanded down her back without incident and over her purse, where her gun was, but when he came across her front side, the wand began to squawk.

"Ma'am, do you have something metal there?" Timmons had the wand just over her right breast.

"Brass knuckles," she said.

Captain Timmons gave a great laugh and then stepped aside. "You have a nice evening, Dr. Bennington," he said.

I took Fiona lightly by the arm and walked in beside her. "What do you have there?" I asked without moving my lips.

"Brass knuckles," she said. "If I see that Gina woman again, I intend to punch her in the mouth with them."

"This is for the lipstick?"

"This is for the lipstick."

I led our group to the reception table, where Reva stood with a phalanx of helpers who checked us in. "Ms. Lohr," I said. "A pleasure to see you so soon." I took her hand and kissed it again.

"You, too, Dr. Bennington," she said. "Your salon is just down the hall. Mr. Drubich is waiting inside. He said you are aware of this, yes? Or that, uh, Mr., uh, Lumpy is, yes?"

"Yes," I said. "That's correct. I wanted to meet him before our little surprise. It will be more gratifying if I understand personally how important this is."

"You will be very impressed by him," she said.

"Would you be so kind," Sam said, "as to put this on our table?" He reached into his bag and pulled out the oversized check. "Don't unfold it and ruin the secret."

"Of course, of course," she said. Reva handed the check to one of her lackeys. "Place this on table two, if you please. And perhaps we put a cover over it? Would that be good, Dr. Bennington?"

"Please," I said, "and call me Liam."

Fiona let out the slightest grunt of exasperation behind me. Just loud enough for my pleasure, it seemed.

"I hate to ask," Reva said, "but the paperwork? Do you have it?"

"Absolutely," I said. "Mr. Grayson has it." I turned to Barry but he just stared back at me. "Mr. Grayson, do you have the paperwork?"

Nothing.

"Mr. Grayson?"

Barry actually looked over his shoulder to see who I was speaking to.

"Barry," I said.

"Oh, yes, sorry," he said and pulled the envelope of documents from his pocket and gave it to Reva.

She gave the pages a cursory glance. "They're all here," she said. "Thank you."

"Any problems with the check?" Barry asked.

Reva looked at Barry and then back at me. "Should there be?"

"No," I said. "Mr. Grayson, ever the accountant. He's the man who has assured InterMacron's financial security."

"Oh, thank you," she said. "You gave me a start."

"If you don't mind," I said, "I don't want to keep Mr. Drubich waiting on his big night."

Reva showed us to the other side of the ballroom doors, past two men with earpieces who immediately began speaking in Russian when we passed. "End of the hall and to the right," she said.

I thanked her but opted not to kiss her hand again, lest Fiona decide to try out the brass knuckles early. The hallway was filled with service people moving about in something approaching a frenzy as they neared the doors to a large service kitchen, from which the sounds of shouting chefs, clanging cutlery and the intermittent bleat of music erupted every few seconds. If there was a shooting, it probably wouldn't be noticed until the event was over for the evening.

Particularly since no one seemed to pay any attention to the three men standing in front of the doorway at the end of the hall. All three had shaved heads and wore matching black suits and had Bluetooth devices in their ears, making them look like bouncers at the worst Russian disco ever.

As we walked closer they began to advance toward us. They had the slow gaits of men used to scaring other men. No use learning to move quickly when your victims tended to ball up in the fetal position at the very sight of you.

"I've been waiting for this," Fiona said.

"Easy," I said to Fiona.

"On which one?" she asked.

"All of them," I said. "We don't need to be hiding bodies tonight."

"Tell that to Sam," she said, "in case I forget."

Sam was beside me, but I could tell he was paying more attention to Brent and Barry, which was supposed to be my job.

"Everyone," I said, "remember that we're in charge of this situation. Brent, Barry, whatever I do, you just fall behind and do it, too."

We kept walking, our pace nice and slow, and the men kept advancing until there were only twenty feet between us, which was when we stopped.

"If you come any closer," I said, "my coworker Fiona is going to break one of your noses. You can choose ahead of time which of you would like the honor, or you can just let us keep going down the hall to meet with your boss. The choice is yours."

The three men looked at one another and then back at me without much in the way of comprehension, so I repeated myself, this time in Russian. This got them to laugh, which gave Fiona enough time to put her brass knuckles on and to pick her victim. She opted for the one in the middle. He saw her coming and just kept laughing, because surely the idea was ridiculous, a tiny woman walking up to a hulk of a man with anything approaching malice. He was so tall, anyway, that it would be impossible for Fiona to punch him in the face, a fact he sadly realized too late, when Fiona punched him in the sternum instead, collapsing him to the ground in a heap.

If you feel like you're the physically weaker person in a fight, the sternum is one of the best places to attack. It's difficult to defend, it's easy to break if you know where to punch (just beneath the notch in the clavicle) and no one ever expects to be punched in the chest.

Breaking your sternum is not recommended for those with a low pain tolerance, since it feels like you're having a heart attack and, with all the blood you spit up, gives the impression you might have a collapsed lung, too. Unless you pass out from the pain, in which case those would be the things you'd feel once you woke up in intensive care.

When the other two men tried to advance on Fiona, it was already too late. She punched the one on the right in the center of his thigh, breaking the long bone there with an easy crunch, which is a break that requires surgery to fix. He'd probably have metal pins in his leg for the rest of his life. Maybe even a slight limp. All things he would also learn once he woke up in ICU.

Fiona swung around and caught the man on the left

in the center of his pelvis. Another satisfying crunch. He would find walking difficult for about three to six months. Sex would be painful for about a year, if it ever felt right again.

Unlike his friends, the one with the broken pelvis didn't pass out. Which was too bad, because he would actually remember the pain far more than his friends would.

The door at the end of the hallway opened and Yuri Drubich stepped out, shook his head and said, "Idiots." Two men came out from behind him with guns pulled, but Yuri told them to put them down and drag their comrades out of the hallway before someone stepped on them.

"Which of you is Big Lumpy?" he asked.

"I am the one known as Big Lumpy," Sam said, except he gave himself a strange-sounding voice. Not quite like Big Lumpy's, not quite like Sam's and not quite like any other human's.

Yuri appraised Sam and then shrugged. "And you are the boy?" He pointed at Brent.

"It's okay," I said to Brent.

"I am," he said.

Yuri shrugged again. He and Brent had that in common, apparently. "Come, all of you, my family is here and I am being honored. If I am to have you all killed, I'd like to know sooner than later." He shook his head solemnly and pointed at Fiona with his broken arm. "They weren't going to hurt you, but I understand that the appearances weren't good. You made your point earlier. I deal with you aboveboard."

He disappeared back into the room and the two men

behind him came to gather up Fiona's damage while we waited for the path to clear.

"That was weird," Sam said.

"Not as weird as your voice just was," I said.

"I should just play it straight?"

"That would be my call," I said.

"What did he mean about the killing part?" Barry asked.

"Language barrier," I said. "Nothing to be worried about."

"He's actually very polite," Fiona said. She didn't bother to wait for the last guy to be dragged off and instead stepped over the man with the crushed chest plate and headed down the hall toward the door Yuri left open. The rest of us did the only thing left to do: We followed her.

16

When you're a spy, it's important to believe the worst about everyone. That way, you won't be surprised when they do something awful.

The problem, however, is that you never expect the best, never exactly plan for the contingency of decency in the face of strife.

So when the five of us walked into the salon room Reva had reserved for us to shake Yuri Drubich down in and actually found him sitting there with his family, just as he said, it took all of us by surprise. His wife was there, as were his three young children, two boys of about twelve and ten and a girl no more than five. They were all dressed to the nines and looked . . . happy. Like normal people. Each child had a PSP and was quietly blowing up the world, presumably, but it was hard to tell since they also all had white earbuds in.

"Hello," I said to the wife. "I'm Dr. Bennington."

She smiled but didn't say anything.

"She doesn't speak or understand English," Yuri said. "She grew up in Moldova and never had the need to pick it up."

"And your children?" I asked.

"Kids," he said, "they know a little. What they learn in rap music."

"They are adorable," Fiona said and they really were. "It's a shame you won't be able to play catch with them for, what, three months?" Fiona looked around the room with great exaggeration then. "I don't see your associate Gina."

"You burst her eardrums," Yuri said. "And broke her jaw."

"She shouldn't have used my lipstick," Fiona said.

Yuri didn't respond to this. Instead, he walked up to Brent and stood in front of him without speaking for a long time before finally saying, "You are the one?"

"I am," he said.

He turned to face Barry. "And you," he said, "you are the gambler?"

"I'm getting help for that," Barry said. "And technically I am the loser."

"You took a great deal of my money and delivered me shoddy goods," Yuri said. "Did you think you would not pay a price for this?"

"Technically," Barry said, "you blew up my office and all of my notary equipment."

Barry's motivation of "not to die" seemed to be giving him plenty of hubris in the situation. Either that or he was emboldened by seeing Fiona take out three men with literally one hand.

"I did," Brent said. "And I am sorry. I was trying to do the best for my father, just as your own children probably would for you."

And a boy becomes a man, I thought. I also thought:

This is one of the oddest exchanges of government—
or about-to-be government—secrets I've ever had.

"This Web site, you design it?"

"Yes," he said and then he lied and said, "Mr. Lumpy
and Dr. Bennington provided me with the technical
expertise."

"But it was you who absconded with my money
and attempted to defraud me?"

Brent shot a glance in my direction and I nodded
once.

"Yes," he said.

"And why don't I kill you?" Yuri asked.

"Because," Brent said, "I'm not worth anything to
you dead. I'm still alive, there's always a chance I'll
have something else to sell to you."

"I could use someone like you," Yuri said. "You
have any interest in working for me?"

"He works for me," Sam said.

"Hmmm, yes, the lumpy one," he said. "So you are
the brains, Lumpy, and you are also the muscle? I have
heard all about you. People in Miami, they say your
name like it is a threat."

"I believe you've met my muscle," Sam said. "She
can be very persuasive."

"And which of you did I speak to on the phone?"
he asked.

"That would be me," I said.

"You are smart," he said. "If you weren't, you'd be
dead."

"You found my phone?"

"You have small operation here," he said. "But effective. Lessons to be learned." Yuri looked at his watch. "I have twenty minutes before I need to receive my guests." He sat down at the table where his wife and children were. "Please, have a seat, show me what you have. Convince me Kineoptic Transference is what will make me even richer."

We all sat down as well and Sam set up the laptop in front of Yuri and began running the PowerPoint presentation Big Lumpy had prepared, the whole time providing a running dialogue on the different aspects of Kineoptic Transference, starting and stopping the presentation when Yuri had questions. Yuri would periodically whisper something to his wife in Russian and she would nod, or grimace, and once she said, "Nyet" in a tone that seemed to suggest a level of frustration one reserved for one's children.

When it was over, Yuri crossed his arms over his chest and exhaled slowly. "My question," he said. "This works?"

"Of course," Sam said.

"And you?" Yuri said to me. "You who are a doctor, no?"

"Scientist," I said. "It works. Our government is too beholden to Verizon and AT&T to consider it now. Which makes it gold for you. You take this to Europe, to the Middle East, you'll be a billionaire."

"How much?" Yuri asked.

"I told you," I said. "Six million."

"Crazy," Yuri's wife said. She pushed herself back from the table then. "Six million dollars for wind."

"I guess she does speak English," I said.

"I turn that into six billion," Yuri said.

"You make your own choices," she said. "This woman breaks your wrist and you let her live. These men come here and sell you air and you let them live. This is a disgrace." She clapped her hands in front of her children's faces. "Come," she said. "We have guests to meet." She turned to her husband. "I expect you in ten minutes. My father? My father would kill these men. And this woman, too."

You can spend your entire life in covert operations and never feel as uncomfortable as when you see a couple air their dirty laundry. That Yuri's wife did it in English meant a simple thing: She wanted us to hear it, too.

"If it makes you feel any better," Fiona said, "I'm happy to tell your wife that you put up a valiant fight."

Yuri glared at Fiona but didn't say anything. In fact, he sat there at the table in perfect silence for three full minutes before he finally said, "I send you four million dollars now. If the technology works as you've shown, I send you another two million. If the technology fails, I kill you all. Slowly."

"Agreed," I said.

Sam reached into his bag and pulled out the three zip drives that contained all of the information Big Lumpy had provided and slid them across the table. "You'll find what you're looking for there."

"And I need the death certificates," Yuri said. "My associates at home will want to know that I am not getting soft, even on children and degenerates. A head or a pancreas would be better, but they are both diffi-

cult to get through customs. Official paperwork from
the United States is much easier to believe. I can't be
losing my reputation for violence, can I, Mr. Lumpy?"

"Maybe don't let anyone talk to your wife," Sam
said. He produced the death certificates for Brent and
Henry and handed them to Yuri. He put the certificates and the zip drives into the inside pocket of his
tuxedo jacket, as if they were nothing at all, as if they
did not cost him four million dollars. As if they were
not about to cost him his freedom. "It's why I've stayed
single."

"Hmm, yes," Yuri said, "I'm sure that is the most
compelling reason." He looked at the death certificates
and then at Brent and Barry. "How does it feel to be
dead?" He frowned slightly even though neither of
them responded and it occurred to me that seeing father and son together in such a situation—even if they
weren't really father and son—might be causing this
strange melancholy. Or maybe it was because his wife
was waiting in the hall, waiting to call him a failure
again. "You have an account ready for a transfer?"

"Yes," I said. I slid the computer over to Barry and
he pulled up the banking information.

"You trust him with your banking?" Yuri said.

"Like you said," I said, "we're a small operation."

Yuri shook his head but gave Barry his account information. Two minutes later, four million dollars had
been transferred from an account in Ukraine to the account in Iceland that Big Lumpy—the real Big Lumpy—
had given us.

Yuri Drubich, one of the most dangerous men in the
world, at least by reputation, stood up then. "If you'll

excuse me," he said, "I am to be honored for my phi-
lanthropy. It would be a shame to be late for my own
coronation." He then walked past us all and out of the
salon without another word. He opened the door and
his daughter stood there with one of his beefy-looking
security guards. Yuri put his good hand down and his
young daughter grasped it and off he went to be cele-
brated.

I watched them walk down the long hallway, past
the circus going on between the kitchen and the ballroom, and then heard a roar of clapping as he turned
the corner and disappeared from view. Tonight would
probably be the best night of his life and the very
worst.

I detached my cell phone from the magnet in my
pocket and called Monty. "The money is there," I said.

"I see it," he said.

"Make your deductions and transfer the remaining
amount to this account." I gave him the numbers for
the account Barry had set up for Brent.

"And what is Mr. Grayson's decision regarding his
money?"

"You know," I said, "why don't you ask him?" I
handed the phone to Brent. "It's for you."

I walked out into the hallway and Fiona, Sam and
Barry followed me.

"We should get in there," Sam said, "so I can make
my splash."

"No," I said. "He's got his kids here. We've done all
we need to do with him. He'll be in prison by tomorrow morning."

"Michael," Fiona said, "he's a terrible human being.

Why not have the gratification of him being photographed with a huge check from a company that is going to be found to belong to Big Lumpy? The shame alone will be enough to drive him mad."

"Because," I said, "those kids who sat in there with us thought we were his friends. His daughter doesn't know anything and she'll remember tonight as beautiful. I'm not the person who's going to ruin that. I'm not willing to make that choice just for spite."

Brent came out to the hallway and handed me back the phone. "He wants to talk to you."

"He says he wants the money," Monty said. "And that he accepts all of the conditions."

"Then he wants the money," I said.

"It will be sent within the next twenty minutes," Monty said.

"When are you going to let the government know what Yuri has possession of?"

"How long will it take you to leave the consulate?"

I thought about that little girl holding her father's hand and said, "An hour."

"An hour? Are you dining?"

"We just might be," I said.

"Where is the information?"

"He has the zip drives in his jacket pocket and we're leaving the laptop computer Big Lumpy provided in the salon down the hall from the ballroom."

"Very well. Then I will let Mr. McGregor's contacts know of the information Mr. Drubich has in approximately forty-five minutes. Chew quickly," he said and was gone.

I clicked my phone off. "Let's go," I said.

"But . . . when does the shooting start?" Brent asked.

"It's not always like that," I said.

"I thought there was going to be a bunch of explosions and that maybe someone would die," Brent said. "Isn't that what being a spy is all about?"

"Not if you're any good," I said.

Epilogue

Life, it turns out, is full of repetition whether or not you're a spy. There are some things that happen over and over again irrespective of who anyone thinks you are, really. So I wasn't surprised when, a few weeks after Yuri Drubich was found to have purchased "state secrets" as part of a long-range espionage ring involving a rather charismatic (and dead) former government agent named Mark McGregor, I found myself sitting in the waiting room of my mother's podiatrist's office while she had her corns shaved. My mother had a standing appointment for the second Tuesday of every month with Dr. Klinger, and if I wasn't being held at gunpoint somewhere, or didn't have someone held at gunpoint somewhere, she expected me to take her.

I was surprised, however, when Big Lumpy walked in and sat down beside me, oxygen tank, white-on-white outfit and all. He looked as awful as he had when I'd seen him last. Maybe worse.

"You're not dead," I said.

"Not yet, no," he said.

"Did you follow me here?"

"No," he said, "Dr. Klinger is my podiatrist. The last

time I was here, I saw your mother, so I made the appointment after hers."

I didn't bother to ask him how he knew who my mother was. Clearly, he knew more than the average dead person. "Are you dying?"

"Surely," he said. "And according to the coroner, as you found out, I'm certain, I already am dead."

"Brent has been keeping your grave clean," I said. "He'll be disappointed to know you're not inside it."

"As will many others," he said. "I understand he is already doing very well at MIT."

"He's a smart kid," I said.

"What is he going to do with the money?"

"I suspect he'll give it away. That's what he told me, anyway. His father's care isn't cheap, but other than that, I don't see him blowing it on strippers and blackjack."

"Then he's missing out." Big Lumpy smiled and I could see that his teeth had large gaps in them, a common side effect from intensive and long-ranging cancer therapy.

"Are you going to tell me what you're doing here?" I asked.

"You owe me two hundred dollars, cash, for your brother."

"I thought that was just in the game, Mark," I said, using his real name to let him know I was onto him.

"A debt is a debt," he said, "and I always collect."

"I do want to keep my eyelids," I said. I took out my wallet and pulled out all of the cash inside—it totaled sixty-seven dollars. "I'm going to need to owe you a hundred thirty-three dollars."

He took my money, counted it and then stuffed it into his pocket. "We'll call it even," he said.

"How much time do you really have left?"

"Maybe I live out the year. But probably not."

"So why fake your death?"

"I thought," he said, "that I might live like a normal person for the rest of my days. And no one was going to let me do that as the ruthless Big Lumpy. So I'm back to being Mark McGregor for what I'm calling my coda. You should try it, Michael."

"I'm already who I am," I said.

"Really? Helping the helpless? That's you?"

"It is now," I said.

A nurse came into the waiting room and called Big Lumpy's name, so I helped him out of his chair. "For how long do you intend to do this?" he asked

"As long as it takes," I said. I extended my hand and Big Lumpy shook it weakly. "Enjoy the rest of your life."

"I already have," he said.

My mother came out a few moments later, a shoe in one hand, a cigarette in the other. "The doctor takes a perverse joy in my pain," she said.

"I doubt it, Ma," I said.

"I thought I heard you talking to someone. Was it that strange man in all white?"

"Yes," I said.

"Who was he?"

Who was anyone, I thought. "His name," I said, "was Mark McGregor. He was a bad guy. He was the one who got Brent in trouble with the Russians, in a roundabout way."

"And you just let him go?"

"No," I said. "He's dead."